# NOTHING WITHOUT US

## EDITED BY CAIT GORDON
## AND TALIA C. JOHNSON

Renaissance.
Diverse Canadian Voices

Cover art and design by Nathan Caro Fréchette. Interior design by Nathan Caro Fréchette. Additional editing by April Laramey, Victoria Martin, Myryam Ladouceur, and Evan McKinley.
Legal deposit, Library and Archives Canada, October 2019.

Paperback ISBN: 978-1-987963-66-3
Ebook ISBN: 978-1-987963-67-0

Presses Renaissance Press
pressesrenaissancepress.ca

*To Nathan, for supporting our plan to take over the world.*
*And to our authors—this book would be nothing without you.*

# CONTENT WARNING

The stories in this book aren't always pretty or neatly wrapped with a bow on top. Even when in fantastical settings, the feelings and experiences of the characters can be relatable to many of us.

*Nothing Without Us* is a collection of tales that feature protagonists who identify as disabled, Deaf, neurodiverse, Spoonie, and/or who manage mental illness. Sometimes the content includes themes of self-harm, suicide, facing terminal illness, isolation, the death of a loved one, institutional/medical mistreatment, miscarriage, and the spectrum of ableism (from internalized to externalized narratives). Because our authors are from diverse backgrounds, NWU's content also explores experiences of racism, xenophobia, or phobia against the LGBTQIA2+ community.

We wanted to give you, our readers, a heads-up, so that you can be prepared for what's in the coming pages.

But most of all, we must warn you that the content of this anthology includes a whole lot of awesome.

It does not, however, contain any inspiration porn.

We hope you love these stories as much as we do.

# TABLE OF CONTENTS

# FROM THE EDITORS

In September 2018, we called out to our people:

*Not like your ableist patriarchal publishing monocultures,*
*with standard narratives that narrowly define.*
*Here at the beginnings of our anthology we exist:*
*two mighty women with ideas that cannot be contained.*
*"Keep, traditional publishers and editors, your inspiration porn,*
*your stories that objectify and demean," we cry.*
*"Bring us your fabulous stories,*
*with diverse characters.*
*Bring us your Deaf heroes, your disabled, your neurodiverse,*
*your characters breaking free from the shackles of normativity,*
*those who are not refuse, but fabulous.*
*Send these your homeless stories, tempest-tossed to us.*
*We lift them up and celebrate them at the gate of our anthology.*

And our people responded, blowing our expectations right out
of the stratosphere:

*They brought us their fabulous stories,*
*their diverse characters, breaking free of the shackles of normativity.*
*Free of the tempests of traditional publishers,*
*they have come forth to be lifted up,*
*and celebrated with the unified shout:*
*NOTHING WITHOUT US.*

# FROM THE EDITORS

*Nothing Without Us* is a collection of stories where we who are marginalized now head onto centre stage. We are the heroes and not the sidekicks. The stories are told in our voices, spanning multiple genres, combining realistic and speculative fiction.

From deep in outer space to right here on Planet Earth, our protagonists show us how they perceive the world they are in, and how they dwell within it. These tales aren't always neat and tidy. Some are harsh, others hilarious, but we cannot help but feel they all have an edge, a "cool" factor. They are brilliantly crafted and can be read or listened to again and again.

"Nothing about us without us" is an anthem that tells people not to speak (or set policies) for others without sharing a lived experience. *Nothing Without Us* includes authors who represent the intersections of several marginalized communities. The diversity of our writers spans age, beliefs, race, sexual identities, and gender identities. What links us all together is that we know what it's like to live as people who are also disabled, Deaf, neurodiverse, and/or manage mental illness and/or chronic conditions.

Most or all of the people who touched this book also identify as disabled, Deaf, hard-of-hearing, neurodiverse, autistic, Spoonie, and/or manage mental illness. So, really, practically nothing in this anthology was done without us.

And we wouldn't have had it any other way.

*~ Cait Gordon and Talia C. Johnson*

# FOREWORD:

# ONE OF US! ONE OF US!

## BY DEREK NEWMAN-STILLE

Like many disabled young people, I sought out representation of disability in the fiction I was reading, wanting to see stories that included me. I read as a means to find other spaces of belonging, since I was surrounded by messages in the real world that we disabled people didn't belong. I loved literature and thought I could find myself in the books I enjoyed reading. I sought out stories about *us*, stories that represented our lives. Instead, I found trope after trope that reduced disabled figures to simple one-dimensional and highly-problematic characters: the Tiny Tim, the Inspiring Mentor, the Crazy Woman in the Attic, the Disability that is Really a Superpower, the Person Who Fakes Disability, the Self-Loathing Cripple... the list goes on and on. But these weren't fleshed out characters; they were poorly devised plot devices. Disability was used in these stories as inspiration for abled people, as body horror, as signs of social collapse. We were constantly turned into symbols of something wrong.

I sought out autobiographies by disabled people, hoping that at least there I could find *real* stories about *real* people, but even most of the autobiographies were infused with the same ableism—whether it was an internalized ableism that writers who grew up in an ableist culture imposed on themselves, or whether it was publishers telling them that their actual life story needed to be changed to fit with social assumptions about disability, I still wonder about. It became clear to me that writing about disability had constantly meant writing through ableism, and I wanted something richer, something that disrupted ableism, that came from a disabled perspective, that challenged the social assumptions about disability. I wanted something about us, with us.

As a disabled writer, I had a moment when reading Disabled poet Leah Lakshmi Piepzna-Samarasinha's *Care Work: Dreaming Disability Justice,* where I came across this passage:

> "Disability Justice allowed me to understand that me writing from my sickbed wasn't me being weak or uncool or not a real writer but a time-honoured crip creative practice. And that understanding allowed me to finally write from a disabled space, for and about sick and disabled people, including myself, without feeling like I was writing about boring, private things that no one would understand."

I read it while writing from *my* bed, and I realized I was part of something, part of a tradition of disabled writers who used the accommodations at their disposal to get their voices out into the world. I was again reminded of the child I was, yearning for representation, and, more than that, yearning for disability. I wanted to read disability, to read *works* by disabled people, and to get our voices out into the world to make changes. Because our voices *do* make changes. Our words are transformative. We create new ideas with our words and those ideas spark other changes. The things we write matter.

*Nothing Without Us* not only disrupts tropes of disability, it provides a space for our words to drift on the breeze, pollinating other ideas, sparking change, and inviting others to think and write and spark their own changes. Creating a collection like this is more than sharing entertaining stories (and they are so incredibly entertaining), it is also a call to action, an invitation to write with and through disability and to articulate a disabled form of writing. The stories in this collection challenge ableism while also illustrating how powerful *our* stories are. These stories uplift without needing to be Inspiration Porn, they illustrate Disabled struggles with an ableist world without making us look weak, and they tell our stories without being tokenistic.

I can't describe how refreshing it is as a disabled person to read about fully fleshed out three-dimensional characters. Not only are we pulled out of our trope-ridden literary history, we are given substance. The authors in this collection bring in personal knowledge and experience into the creation of their characters and their characters aren't simplistic. They aren't *just* defined by their disabilities. Instead, their disabilities intermingle with other aspects of their life, whether it is career, class, age, sexuality, gender identity, race, or ethnicity. They are like the rest of the disabled community—*complex*. These stories don't try to reduce our complexity, but instead revel in it, because we *are* complex people and can't be reduced to simple tropes or one dimensionality.

These are stories that satiate more than a craving for disability representation, but a *need* for representation, a desire to feel a sense of belonging, a desire to feel at home with our stories and to create a comfortable space through telling our stories. These stories are fictional, but they tell truths that can't always be expressed in simple "here's how it happened" tales. These stories use abstraction to express our needs, wants, desires, fears, and anxieties. They write our disabled identities into past landscapes, other worlds, and the future in a way that says:

> "We've always been here, we are here now, and we will always be here."

Reading these stories, whether you are Disabled or abled, you are being invited into the tradition of disabled writing, you are having the opportunity to share in what matters to us, and you are getting the chance to become, as the characters in Todd Browning's cult classic film *Freaks* say, "One of us! One of us!"

# THE BELLWOODS GOLEM

## MYRIAD AUGUSTINE

The proper manufacture—no, not manufacture. Perhaps assembly? Still too formal. Birthing? Too sentimental. We shall compromise by calling it "crafting," for it is a craft—not quite an art, not quite a science. Let us begin again.

The proper crafting of a golem, what later amateurs have variously dubbed *homunculi* or *automata galatea* or even the rather imaginative *blue smoke drones*, requires four fundamental components. One might call them elemental, in fact, for each of the elements is at the core of their purpose.

A shell or a skin, which can be given a shape and retain it despite weather or impact; this can be said to be *earth*. The earliest of our work was fashioned in mud or in clay, the most ancient stories speak to this; however, this is not the whole. The earthenware golem, as classic as a design as it is, has mostly fallen out of fashion because practitioners forget that the outer shape must be made firm. The clay must be fired, the mud compressed and dried, or you simply have a mound of dough without a crust, so to speak.

This brings us to the second ingredient—the "blood," or rather, that which mimics *water* and grants us motion. To return again to the golem of clay, the traditional pairing would be a slurry, a semiliquid familiar to all who've witnessed the ceaseless churning of a cement mixer during sidewalk repair. Another common mistake of the novice would be to use water, unmixed, but erosion is a lesson that need only be taught once. The sudden, shattered weight of a golem surging forward on a tide of its own magicked fluids is not a sight easily forgotten.

The third, if we deem the first a skin and the second blood, would be the heart itself, though this is where the metaphor becomes imperfect. Whereas our own hearts are mechanically vital for us to move through life, the nature of a golem's heart is entirely philosophical—its reason to be, to continue, to do anything other than plod aimlessly. This is its *fire*, sometimes a literal ember ensconced in its chest, sometimes the quicksilver spark of a lightning bolt, sometimes things far stranger and unmentionable. It is the most important ingredient, but also paradoxically the only one that can be missed and still permit the golem to rise. What does this say about ourselves, I wonder, if a golem is simply an approximation of G-d's creation? Can our fires be extinguished and our lives still persist? I wish to deny it, but I fear the proof marches past us every rush hour.

Our final element, *air*, is deceptively simple to procure and pass on. This determines our creation's longevity, as ours was defined when our creator breathed life into us. And so we all too often use our breath, but it is a fraction of a fraction and raises a child that will never reach maturity. I will not give examples of alternatives, as there have been great crimes wrought in pursuit of such things, but I will confide that there are very different kinds of breaths in the world. This is evident in the first gasp and cry of a newborn or the rattling exhalation of the dying, and it falls on the practitioner to weigh what such vitality is worth and what each truly costs.

And so we are done. But of course, you protest! This is a shopping list, a recipe, not a story. And I know that you crave stories—this last was not intended as a tale in itself, but rather as context. For the crafting is such a careful thing, not to be delayed or distracted from by mundanities, particularly if the need is great. A secret, though: the need is always great, for those in need. It is a privilege to assume we can do without.

Hadas woke in pain, as was usual, but with a curious lingering of sense echoes—a dream with a little more substance than usual, sticking cobweb-like against them. The feel of mud, the scent of dog shit, the bracing cold of a winter wind.

It was cold enough within the little apartment they shared, their bedroom carved out alongside another from what was once a modest and woefully under-insulated dining room. They lingered as long as they could justify within the nest of their bedsheets, trying to root themselves once more in the space where they spent so much of their time. Why the mud? Why the wind? They hadn't been outside in days. They couldn't remember any dream to deliver such things. They hardly remembered dreams most of the time, though; they drank or smoke until the pain gave way to the exhaustion, then slipped off into an empty rest borne of a heavy hand's worth of antipsychotics.

Finally, they began to stand, always a process, hearing and feeling the pops and cracks and realignments as bones and tendons fought to make a semblance of a moving body. With some motions the pain ebbed, while with others it awoke new sources—the usual shuffle of morning. Today their left leg seemed most afflicted, but that might change by the time Hadas reached their door, or by breakfast. Or it might persist for days, sometimes hours. They reached with a practiced, scooping hand for their glasses in the approximate area they'd been discarded; it was not uncommon for things to migrate during the night, as they turned and contorted and re-contorted, in their attempts to find a comfortable position. They pawed clumsily at the light switch, blinked as the lenses brought the room into focus.

Something shin-height but stocky as a toddler stood next to the bed, eyes shining gold and blinking right back.

Hadas was not one to scream, was not overly fond of horror movies or other things to deliberately court fear, but could objectively (long afterwards) appreciate the clichéd jump and shriek they gave in response. In a second, they were back on the bed, cracking the back of their head off of the hanging lamp and shattering the bulb. *Fantastic*, they thought, putting aside the certainty that some rabid raccoon had cornered them, *now it's dark, the bed's covered in glass, and I'm barefoot, surrounded by it.*

They stayed imperfectly still, as still as one can manage with muscles already strained by the basic task of standing, periodic quivers coursing through them like aftershocks. They heard a rustling, the gentle sound of glass against glass like eggshells. They still weren't sure where the raccoon or whatever it was had gotten to.

Finally, their legs gave out, left side first, bringing them down to the bed in a trembling mass. The earthquake following the aftershocks, a reversal of nature in their weary limbs' collapse. They felt done for the day that had only just started, and still, something was in here with them.

*My phone*, Hadas thought, reaching slowly towards the pillow where it usually fell from their hands as sleep overtook them. Nothing. They reached towards the overcrowded nightstand, upsetting precarious piles of bus transfers and half-finished books. Nothing.

A light flicked on.

The creature—not a raccoon, it was clear now—held Hadas's phone as if it were an infant cradled in its dirt-brown and curiously smooth arms. The senses of their dream came back to them, the smell and feel of dirt. It stood at the edge of the bed, illuminated by the phone's flashlight as if telling ghost stories at camp; the light threw strange shadows up from its hunched shoulders and jutting chin, revealing the lack of mouth or nose, and those gleaming eyes and deep-etched forehead. Hadas couldn't read the characters carved on its face, had lost that particular skill memory at some point in the cycle of psychiatric meds or self-care strategy memorization or sheer mental exhaustion, but they recognized the language from the non-transliterated side of their siddur. Hebrew.

*I have to call my rabbi.*

The creature made a rapid movement, clay fingers flickering into definition from the rounded stubs, then softening away again, holding the phone out for Hadas as it began to ring. It had bypassed the password somehow and, sure enough, Rabbi Andrea Myer's number shone up from the screen.

The rabbi hadn't picked up, and Hadas had found themselves incapable of describing the problem in a voicemail. After a long interval of staring at each other, hunger and a failing phone battery had broken the impasse. Hadas had plugged in their phone, giving the little figure a wide berth as they made their way towards and out the door. The glass from the bulb was nowhere to be found, but as the creature followed them into the kitchen it made a slight crunching noise with every movement.

The next struggle was a usual one—what to eat first. It was a balancing act of need and capacity, knowing their body needed fuel and knowing their stomach was all too willing to bring up bile at the wrong taste or temperature or texture. Oftentimes they made do with tea, trying to make up the calories later in the day with whatever fast and easy thing was least offensive.

As Hadas fell heavily into one of the kitchen chairs, trying to summon up the energy, the creature moved past them, lengthening as it went. Soon it was stretched out, Gumby-like, preposterously thin legs supporting that squat torso and blunt little head. It began to root through the cupboards. First for the kettle and the tea, then toast, then jam. In short order a breakfast was ready, and Hadas was pleasantly surprised to find it was the right one, though they couldn't have said so until someone made it for them.

As they drank and ate, the creature waited, returned to its usual dimensions and giving off a warmth now that dispelled some of the apartment's usual chill.

"Th... thank you?" Hadas offered quietly, feeling ridiculous but also not quite sure what the etiquette was in this situation. It moved closer, bringing its head to Hadas's hand like an eager puppy, and the feel of it was like sunbaked brick.

The next days and weeks were confusing ones. The rabbi never returned Hadas's call, and they were shocked to hear, long after, that she had taken ill; she'd been found wandering, coatless and confused, in the off-leash area of the nearby park. She was taken to the hospital, thankfully, but remained weak, and despite Hadas's strange visitor, they felt it would be inappropriate to burden them with yet another question. They were quite sure of what it was, at least, the answer coming to them rather embarrassingly not from a recollection of their Jewish history, but their geekiness—a golem.

Immediately, they began to scour the internet for resources. Mentions were numerous, but practical information was predictably scarce. They also lost a day falling down the surreal rabbit hole of ever more imaginative golem designs in fantasy art (and a startling few minutes in its natural extension, fantasy art *porn*). Soon Hadas's head was full of information on golems, much of it contradictory, the vast majority of it dreamt up to better package them as cannon fodder for this or that hack and slash adventure. The original stories remained the most useful ones: the rabbis scarcely in control of their creations, making the hard choice between a monster of their own making or that of the pogroms. Hadas's golem wasn't much of a monster, though. When Hadas was too tired to clean, it cleaned. When Hadas curled up in pain, it brought blankets and heating pads. And when Hadas had dropped a mug, clumsy with frustration and a spasm of weakness, the golem spirited the pieces and spill away as if they'd never happened.

The golem had limits, of course. It disappeared when any of their roommates were around, it couldn't make phone calls for appointments or trek outside to get groceries. But what it did for Hadas increased their capacity exponentially; no longer struggling with the same base level of tasks to get out of bed and fed and into the world, Hadas was able to do that little bit more to make their life manageable. They had more patience with bureaucracy, they could get to the post office before a package was returned, they wrote long posts on social media asserting their politics when before their fingers ached to type. They felt alive in a new way, even as they could not quite be sure the golem was.

And at night, as it massaged their shoulders, they spoke to it, unburdening long hours of confidences. They spoke aloud the doubts they had about their worth, about being unproductive, about being too sick to work but not sick enough to deserve to rest. It never responded, of course, it could not. But its warmth, the captive sunshine of its eyes, seemed to offer a response of silent affirmations: *you are worthy, you are not your productivity, your sickness is your own and your needs are valid.* Some nights Hadas would cry as the words left them, resting their forehead against the golem's and feeling the rough outline of the word there, which Wikipedia had reminded them how to read. אמת—*emet.* Truth.

And so, of course, Hadas named it Emmett.

When winter came again, the rabbi recovered. She came to sit in Hadas's much less cluttered kitchen, and they drank tea together as Emmett moved between them, courting rubs of its rough clay head and radiating heat like an oven.

She explained the process, the cost, the fruitless attempts at different sites around the city and the wider world. The limits of her knowledge, her uncertainty that it had even worked until Hadas summoned up the courage to send Rabbi Myer a text so many months after the fact: *do you know anything about golems? sorry to bother you.*

"It never moved before, it never *went* anywhere," Rabbi Myer was now explaining, sweeping her hands expressively and nearly knocking her mug to the floor. She theorized, in her raw New York accent unsoftened by years north of the border, that it was the recipient that made the difference, but she wasn't sure why. All the times before, she'd tried to make it simply for itself, but this time she'd been thinking of Hadas. She'd made Hadas brisket, meant to bring it over when this attempt failed like all the others. It had not.

"I was frustrated," Hadas said quietly. "I had this idea of what my life could be, if my body would just let me do what I need to." Rabbi Myers puffed up immediately, to refute that there was any need, but Hadas held up a hand. "I know I just need to take care of myself, to go at my own speed, but I was still frustrated. That night, I was thinking of everything I could do, if it didn't just hurt to get out of bed, to make breakfast, to walk down the street. And it's not like it doesn't hurt now, it still does, but I can... *breathe* a little. I can save my spoons for when I need them, out there."

The rabbi nodded, her expression a mix of contemplation and compassion. Hadas drank from their mug, then continued, pointedly looking away from Emmett as they did.

"That's why I want to give it to someone else now. So they can have that, for a while."

Ariel woke late, with a panic. They'd meant to wake and survey how much snow had fallen the night before, early enough to post online for help if the walk needed to be cleared. As they hugged themselves against the cold, feeling their muscles curdle the instant they left the warmth of their bed, they looked out reluctantly to the front of the house... which was clear. Not just the front of the house, but the sidewalk down to the bus, ten minutes of walking that for them was normally a slippery and treacherous half hour. *Someone got a bad Airbnb review*, they thought wryly, slipping on a pink robe to head to the bathroom. As they turned they caught sight, with another rising panic, of a small figure in the corner and, on the edge of their bed, a handwritten note.

Ariel struggled with their fear and their robe, uncoordinated in their surprise, and grasped for the note, though they couldn't have said why it seemed important to read it. Perhaps a lack of options if the figure was some loosed animal or burglar in miniature. After a moment, reading and re-reading it in confusion, they lifted their head and spoke.

"Thanks... Emmett?"

The golem nodded and beamed back warmth.

# KNIT ONE, PURL TWO

## CAROLYN CHARRON

Maggie had a man problem, an unexpected one that no amount of knitting therapy was going to help solve: somehow she'd rented her basement to a vampire.

She couldn't decide if she was angrier he was a blood-sucking fiend or that he'd kept it secret. Either way, she had to decide if she was going to evict him before she confronted him.

The yarn on her knitting needles grew tighter. She paused to loosen the tension, then rolled her shoulders to relax them.

She ran a finger down the smooth wood of the needle. She wanted to stab it into the ball of pale blue yarn, but instead, her hands automatically began a new row in the tiny sweater—her fifteenth of the year. She knit them for Mercy Hospital's maternity ward but being charitable was the furthest thing from her mind right then. She barely saw the yarn as she tried to untangle her thoughts.

Annoyed, she shook her head, the white curls bouncing around her bifocals. How had she missed it in all the months Edmund had lived in her basement? He wasn't pretending like Maggie's cosplaying grand-daughter with her pale makeup and plastic fangs. He was real.

Her brand-new wooden knitting needles in her hands had been the proof. She glared at the smooth wood.

Last night, after they'd had sex gently, as her arthritic hips were having a bad day, she'd pulled out her knitting bag to show him her newest purchase, a lovely polished wooden set of needles that didn't hurt her hands the way the metal ones he'd bought for her recent birthday did.

He'd flinched away from them, puzzling her at the time, but in the middle of the night she'd woken up with the sure knowledge of his true nature. Fortunately for Edmund, he'd already gone to his apartment; otherwise, she might have stabbed him. She'd certainly been angry enough. How could he have kept this from her?

She stared at the thin wooden slivers in her hands. They hadn't been her only clue. Another dead give-away, pardon the pun, was the coffin in his living room. Edmund claimed he liked the unusual nature of it as his coffee table/work area. She'd been amused by the idea. She'd even placed a teacup there, not once considering it might be his bed.

There had been other hints—the black-out curtains, the pallor of his skin, and never going out in the sunshine. He'd claimed he had a rare skin condition and had to avoid sunlight.

She felt duped. Truthfully, she was more annoyed by feeling tricked than by missing the clues.

A twinge of pain cramped her fingers, and she shook the pain out. She focused on the yarn for a few rows, the repetition calming her mind. At the suggestion of her doctors, she'd taken up knitting—despite the ridiculous stereotyping—while she recovered from the car accident that had broken her hip. It had been one of the few pleasurable things in her life for a long time.

Until Edmund had moved in.

Vampire or not, Edmund was a lovely man. He was good company, even better than her husband of almost fifty years had been. He always seemed to know when her pain needed quiet and when to end the silence with a dirty joke, making her groan even while she laughed. Bent and frail-appearing, she'd thought he was a decade older, but now she had no idea. Vampires were supposed to be young, powerful. Had he been bitten when he was old?

But oh my, he was handsome with a full head of hair, a fading but still delicious British accent, and a devilish twinkle in his eye. That twinkle had convinced Maggie she should rent him the basement apartment. During their first night together a few months into his tenancy, she knew his frailness was appearances only. It didn't affect his lovemaking in the slightest. She shivered at the thought that she'd slept with such a dangerous creature.

She had to tell him she knew. It was only fair. The yarn flew through her fingers as she imagined how the upcoming conversation would go, but she wasn't truly worried for her safety. He'd shown no violent tendencies, and she *had* taken Taekwondo at the senior's centre before her hip got bad.

She pictured telling the girls at Thursday's knitting circle. They'd be unbelieving but envious, she was sure. One of their group, Harriet, regularly regaled them with tidbits from the vampire and werewolf books she devoured avidly.

Maggie's fingers paused. She glanced down to see she'd dropped a stitch a few rows earlier. She hooked it up and laddered the missing stitch back up through the fabric. She was trying to do the same thing, adding Edmund's true nature into her life, trying to stretch herself around the knowledge without distorting the fabric of her existence.

It annoyed her he'd never told her in all the months since he'd moved in. Although if she were being honest, she had to admit her tenancy agreement hadn't exactly asked for those kinds of details. She made a mental note to alter the tenant application. Just in case she gave him an eviction notice.

She wasn't sure if she wanted to. He was a very nice man other than the bloodsucking thing. Would another tenant bring her tea when she couldn't face walking twenty feet to the kitchen? Would he point out flattering clothing that fit under her back-brace? And where would she find another lover who would be careful of her bad hip?

Her knitting needles flashed faster, and the yarn threatened to tangle again. Maggie pursed her lips in vexation, then huffed out a sigh and laid the small sweater down in her lap.

How long had he been this way, and did he age? She hated not knowing and decided to ask, once he'd admitted what he was. She'd had plenty of practice bringing up difficult questions. Her late husband Charles had been hesitant to have any sort of intimate conversation, so she'd learned to be circumspect with sensitive topics like arranging times and places to have sex without their son knowing what they were discussing. A flickering image of the last time she'd seen her son and granddaughter reawakened the sorrow of the past year, and she pushed the memory of the double funeral away. The past couldn't be changed, but she could do something about her future. She didn't want to lose Edmund too.

It wasn't just the regular sex she liked with Edmund, although she enjoyed it tremendously. It was the companionship. Over the months he'd lived in the basement, they'd become friends, then lovers. Now they spent at least three nights a week together. They'd have dinner, and if her arthritis wasn't unbearable, they'd spend a few minutes in the bedroom as dessert.

Picturing those nights together, Maggie realized he'd never tried to bite her. Was she too old? Did old blood taste stale? Or was it something else? She thought she was still reasonably attractive to the opposite sex. Edmund had slept with her, and George and Harry down the street were always making suggestive comments as she walked past, annoying on a good day and enraging on the days she was hobbled by pain. She'd thrown more than one dirty look their way but hadn't quite gotten to the point of throwing anything else. Yet.

Wrack her brain as she might, she could not see any reason why Edmund was so nice to her if he didn't want a regular blood donor.

There was no option but to ask him straight out.

Maggie threw her knitting into the basket and hitched her way down the hall to her bedroom to hunt down the makeup bag her granddaughter had given her the Christmas before—she pushed the memory away and stared at herself in the mirror. She'd never worn much more than mascara and lipstick, but this was definitely a good occasion to vamp up a little. She snickered at little at the pun.

"Would you like some more wine?" Maggie asked, trying to be coquettish, but not entirely sure she was succeeding. It had been far too long since she'd practiced her feminine wiles.

"Are you trying to intoxicate me? Perhaps take advantage of me?" Edmund smiled suggestively and leaned back on the sofa, his hazel eyes twinkling. He'd mostly lost his unusual London accent but when they were intimate, it reappeared, giving Maggie the shivers. She wondered if the oddness of speech was because of *when* he was raised, rather than where. He sounded nothing like a modern Londoner.

"Maybe. Would you like that?" She licked her lips. The collar on his freshly pressed shirt was open—she loved how he ironed them himself. She could see the pulse beating in his throat. She stared at it, wondering if he'd fed while he'd been out for his daily walk. Wondering if the idea disgusted her or excited her. Her cheeks felt hot.

Edmund eyed her closely. Maggie could tell he suspected something was up. She inched her skirt up her thigh to distract him. Edmund's eyes followed the movement.

"Maggie, you know you don't need to be this way." He touched her hand. His fingers felt cool.

Maggie sat up straighter on the sofa. "Oh, all right then! I'll just ask you. Why didn't you tell me?"

"Tell you what?"

"About your blood lust, of course!"

Edmund's pale cheeks grew even paler. "I beg your pardon?"

"It's no use. I know you're a vampire. You can't hide it from me anymore." She shook her finger at him as if he were a recalcitrant child.

He shook his head, "Margaret..."

"I don't mind. Really. I just wish you'd told me." Maggie peered up at him, through her mascaraed lashes.

"There's nothing to... I don't drink blood, for pity's sake!" His accent was stronger.

"Well, if you're not going to tell me the truth, I'm leaving!" She levered herself up from the sofa, intending to stomp out theatrically. Catching her toe on the carpet, she lurched awkwardly, almost falling over the coffin. Pain flared in her hip.

Edmund steadied her. His touch felt icy now, her whole body was aflame.

"Maggie, please stay." He half-smiled, a crooked little grin he knew full well drove her wild with desire. His thumb stroked over her hand, leaving a trail of cold that felt like a brand.

"No. Not until you tell me the truth." She wanted to stay, the memory of the taste of his lips pulled at her, but she drew away. Despite the throbbing in her hip, she stomped all the way up the uncarpeted stairs. It was a petty thing—she knew the noise echoed dreadfully in the basement—but she was unable to resist.

In the morning Maggie stared at the basement door from the kitchen table but didn't open it—he had to make the first move.

Claiming a headache, she skipped the knitting get-together that afternoon at Gloria's house. Some of those women were pretty good at ferreting out secrets.

All that afternoon, he was very quiet in his basement lair.

Later, as she lay sleepless in her too-large bed, she wondered if maybe she was wrong. Maybe there was another reason he'd flinched from the wooden needles. Could he have a phobia about sharp bits of wood? She snorted with wry laughter and stared at Edmund's empty pillow. It still smelled like his shampoo.

No. She was right about him. She rolled over and willed herself to sleep.

On Friday she skipped the pot-luck lunch at Harriet's apartment. And then Monday's class at the library on internet safety was abandoned to research phobias and vampire lore.

Then another Thursday knitting circle. Harriet called to make sure everything was fine, and Maggie put her off while staring at the closed basement door. Not even a radio broke the wounded silence behind it.

Another week went by. Maggie avoided her friends and speed-knit three baby sweaters—breaking her previous record.

On Wednesday, exactly two weeks later, she woke early from a restless sleep, her hip and shoulder aching from the night's rain and decided she'd had enough. Either he told her the truth, or he would have to move out.

She clumped down the stairs to tell him.

His door was already open, and Edmund sat, a pale shape in the dark, on the sofa. Waiting for her.

"So?" she demanded, "Are you going to admit it?"

"It's not what you think. I don't drink blood."

Maggie felt a quick flash of satisfaction and eased herself onto the sofa beside him, close enough to feel his slight body heat, "Tell me more."

"It's a disease. I...my blood...it's complicated."

Maggie gave him the stern look she'd perfected on her son, folding her arms across her chest.

Sighing, Edmund began talking, his accent thick enough to spoon on bread. "I don't drink it. I give it. I need to bite two or three people each month, or I get old."

Maggie shook her head, "Vampires drink blood. Everyone knows that."

"No, we don't. We make a trade. I take a little in and give a little back. I don't drink any, that is a disgusting idea," he shuddered slightly.

"I don't... I've read..." she sighed.

"There is something in my blood—like a bacteria or virus. I don't entirely know how it works, but the man who turned me was a doctor, and he studied it. I shed the excess into a host, and I stay young."

"You had eternal youth, and you let it slip away? You should be giving your blood more often."

"It feels wrong. And nowadays, it stinks to get close to people. Literally. Have you noticed how much scent people use nowadays? It's horrid up close." Edmund shuddered again.

"Oh, for heaven's sake, you silly man! Did it never occur to you to do a blood-letting?" Maggie rolled her eyes. Grabbing his hand, she dragged him to his feet, "Let's get a knife."

Edmund allowed himself to be led up the stairs to Maggie's kitchen. "Maggie, darling, it's not that simple. There's a kind of enzyme in human blood that mixes with mine and cancels out the virus. Or my blood cancels out the virus from another vampire—I don't know exactly. I just know that I can't simply drain it without accelerating the aging process. I need a host or a fellow vampire."

He waved a hand to his face, pointing out the wrinkles, "I'm sure you wondered why I look old. I tried bloodletting, and age caught up to me."

Maggie's hand touched the knife block on the spotless counter, but she didn't pull one out. "Well, that puts a different twist on things."

"It's better if I simply pass when it's my time."

She spun to face him, "After all these years, you'll throw your life away?" Maggie thought for a moment, "How old are you anyway?"

"I was born in 1719. Geoffrey turned me in 1739." Edmund stared at his shoes, shiny polished Oxfords.

"Just a wee bit older than me then."

Maggie's small attempt at humour didn't lift the shadow from Edmund's eyes. "Geoffrey and I took turns bleeding each other. But when he was staked…" He shuddered slightly.

Maggie blinked, thinking hard. "Medicine has made a lot of advances recently. You've not found any other ways to deal with the excess?"

"No."

"Then bite me. I'll take Geoffrey's place." Her heart thundered so loudly she wondered if he could hear it.

"No!" Edmund shook his head, his grey hair catching the light. He caught her by the shoulders, "You don't know what you're asking. Immortality won't give you your youth back. You'll be healthy but no younger. It won't take away the damage in your back and hip. It might not even take away the pain."

Maggie snorted, "Did I ask for that? I've got my pain meds, and I rather like being this age. Old enough to be as cantankerous as I want and still young enough to enjoy sex." She leered at him. "I get senior discounts and have plenty of free time now that I've retired."

She tilted her head sideways and brushed the white curls away from her neck, shivering a little. "Go on, you know you want to."

"What about your son and granddaughter?"

Maggie looked away, "They won't be a problem." She stared at the photos hanging from the wall in the dining room. She'd avoided looking at the pictures for a few months after the accident, but now she took a long look at their faces, remembering.

Edmund followed her gaze, "So you've been keeping your own secret. It's not just Charles who's gone, is it? It's all of them, your whole family. Was it the same car accident that broke your hip?"

She nodded. Their absence had left a huge hole in her life. Edmund had filled it with his dry wit and knack for knowing exactly what she needed from the day he'd moved in. She couldn't lose him too.

"I'm so sorry." The strange look on his face caught her attention; it looked as if he was holding back tears. "I know what it's like to be alone."

"When did you... lose Geoffrey?" she asked softly.

"A long time ago, just before the first World War." He couldn't meet her eyes.

Maggie cleared her throat, knowing he wanted pity as little as she did. "Let me stay with you. Turn me."

"You're serious." His eyes met hers, wide with surprise and dawning hope.

"Of course I am! I haven't done everything I want to yet. I'd love to do more travelling, and I haven't even come close to finishing all the knitting projects in my bucket list." She tucked a curl behind her ear and winked.

Edmund slanted a look through the kitchen door into the living room where her knitting basket sat on the floor, wooden needles peeking over the rim. "You'll have to get rid of those."

Maggie snorted, "Not on your life. I need some way to keep you in line." She smiled and stroked a finger over the pulse in her neck. "Bite me."

Edmund searched her face for a long moment, then stepped so close she felt his coolness. She shivered and wrapped her arms around his waist, warming him and taking the weight off her bad hip.

Bending his head, he kissed her softly on the lips before he moved his mouth to the vein throbbing in the wrinkled skin of her neck. "As you wish."

# NAMES

## JENNIFER LEE ROSSMAN

A coyote crosses my path, just a few yards away and making eye contact the entire time. I don't usually mind looking animals in the eye, but there's something too human about his beady, yellow eyes. Like he's looking right at my soul.

Granny always told me to turn around when a coyote crosses my path, that it might be a trickster or something worse, but Mama told me to come straight home today and I don't know who to listen to.

So I freeze in place and stare at the patch of blue sky above the coyote's head.

He pauses on the edge of the wagon trail that's the same dusty color as his fur, and I can feel him looking at me. I should meet his gaze, show him I'm not afraid. But I *am* afraid, and my eyes keep slipping off of him.

I don't know what it means, me looking at an animal and feeling the itchy nervousness of looking at a person. Nothing good. I wish Granny was still around so I could ask her.

"Please don't be an evil trickster," I say under my breath.

After a moment that stretches into eternity, he slinks off into the brush, casual as a tumbleweed.

As soon as the coyote is out of sight, I run so fast that it feels like my feet don't even touch the ground. The milk Mama asked me to get slips from my hands, but I don't stop. Over the yellow hills, through the scruffy grass that grabs at my skirt, all the way back to town.

The smell hits me the instant I cross the town line. Not just the manure and human waste you get on a hot day, but a pungent stench of death and decay and evil.

It doesn't come from any one direction. It just *is*, everywhere.

The ladies walking outside the shops wrinkle their noses and the pastor gives a dirty look to the horses tied up outside his chapel, but I can't breathe. The smell permeates everything, winds its way up my nose and wraps itself around my brain until it's the only thought I can think.

I cover my face with my sleeve, but it's still there. Still an invisible cloud hanging over us.

The horses sense it, too. Animals can sense these things. They pace uneasily, pull at their reins tied to the hitching posts.

Something bad happened while I was out getting milk.

The milk. I look at my empty hands as if forgetting I dropped it. I shouldn't go home without it, but no way am I going back out to the ranches to get more.

"Miss Benally!" someone calls out.

I turn to see the sheriff striding across the street in his grey bowler hat. I skirt around the horses and hurry towards home. Maybe he won't follow me.

"Beck! Hold up, Beck!"

Reluctantly, I stop. I don't much like the sheriff; he stands too close and tries to touch my arm like we're friends. We *would* be friends if he stopped acting so... friendly. If he just let me be.

"Hello, Blue," I say. I keep my eyes on the ground, but I can tell he's upset. At me? I know he doesn't like my nicknames, but he knows I don't like *name*-names. I thought he'd accepted that he was Blue to me.

No, this is something more than me not calling him William. This is his *someone robbed a stagecoach* anger, not his *Beck Benally is being peculiar again* anger. A lot of people in Silver Valley have a specific kind of anger just for my peculiarities, and I'm good at telling the difference.

"You been out all morning?"

I nod. "I was gettin' on Mama's nerves, so she sent me to get milk from Cowman but then I saw a coyote with people eyes, so I don't have the milk. Why? What happened?"

He hesitates, but finally nods at me to follow, his hand hovering briefly near my elbow. "You'll find out soon enough, living next door. I was hoping you would have seen something."

"Just the coyote. It had people eyes."

"Yes, so you said, but nothing...more sinister?"

What could be more sinister than a coyote with people eyes? But I shake my head.

We come to the road where I live. The stench of evil is thicker here, and tinged with chaos as people flit around in a panic that's centered on our next-door neighbors' house. The doctor, deputies, nosy townsfolk... Everyone's here.

"Is Miss Cactus okay?" I ask. Blue doesn't answer, but his silence is answer enough.

Miss Cactus knew my granny, and she's looked out for me since Granny died. They escaped the Mexican armies together, way back before I was born. She's short and prickly, but sweet on the inside, and she never tells me to use her real name. Names are sacred things to Navajo.

I slip away from Blue and past the crowd, into Miss Cactus's kitchen that should smell of cornbread but smells like death instead.

There are two dead things on the floor.

One of them is Miss Cactus. At least, I think it's her. She doesn't exactly have a face anymore, and while I'm not great at faces, the complete lack of one is throwing me off.

I touch my own face in horror, feeling the shapes of muscle and bone. Is that what we look like without skin?

The other dead thing is a more familiar, but no less upsetting sight. A dog without its skin, like the fur traders sometimes sell to the butcher when they think nobody's looking. Dark red boot prints and pawprints trail in and around the pool of blood.

A hand comes down on my shoulder, and every inch of my body explodes in panic at the touch. I flinch away, fling myself against the wall and raise my hands to defend myself. Someone shrieks. It sounds like me.

"No, don't! She doesn't like that."

Blue quickly comes between me and the deputy, his arms surrounding but not touching me.

"You're fine," he says, his voice all soft and calm. "James didn't know; he just wanted to make sure you didn't step in the blood."

I nod, my breathing still fast and my shoulder still heavy with the echo of his touch. I try to talk but the words get stuck. Too many people around, too much death and the bad kind of magic Granny used to warn me about.

"You want to go outside?" Blue asks.

My neck almost breaks at the ferocity of my nod, and his arms act as a guard against the world as he guides me out the back to the garden. We sit on the steps, careful not to touch the bloody pawprints leading out of the house.

But that can't be right... If the dog is dead, why are there tracks leading away from the house?

Oh no. I think I know who killed her. Or *what* killed her, anyway—

Wait. Is Blue talking?

I look up, pushing my hair out of my face. "What?"

"I said I'll send someone to find your mother."

"No. She'll make me go home, but I need to be here to help you catch the killer."

"I have deputies for that."

"All your deputies are white."

If takes him a second to recover from what he thinks is an abrupt change of subject. "They are. But white deputies can still catch people who kill Indians, Beck."

"Not if you don't know what you're looking for."

He sits a little straighter. "You know who did this?"

I shrug. This kind of bad magic has to be done by a family member, and Miss Cactus only has the one son. But even if I could tell Blue his name, it wouldn't help because he could look like anything by now. Probably a coyote, but he might not stay in that body for long.

Did he recognize me when we met on the road? Is he going to come after me next?

I press my palms against the sides of my head. I'm thinking about this too much already. He'll sense it and use it to track me down.

"Beck?"

I have to stop thinking about coyotes with people eyes, people who walk on all fours. I have to, I *have* to. Thinking about these things invites them in. Thoughts and talk and names—it's all a powerful magic.

"Rebecca?" Blue asks. "If you know who did this, you need to tell me. We can stop him from hurting anyone else."

I look at the space between his eyebrows. That's as close to looking somebody in the eyes as I get.

He means it. This is his town, and one of his people got killed under his watch. Her being Navajo doesn't dampen his burning need for justice. Granny and Miss Cactus would have liked that about him.

I nod. Very slowly, but I nod.

The people who walk on all fours are practitioners of the worst kind of magic. Shamans who went bad in the sun and turned into witches. And they know when you're talking about them, so Granny never told me much.

I know more than I've told Blue, like the part about how the witch has to kill and sometimes eat a loved one to get the power to change themselves into an animal, but not a whole lot. Just what my granny and papa said when they thought I wasn't listening.

"I don't like any part of this," Blue says again as we walk through the silvery moonlight. "Especially not the part about you coming with me."

Neither do I, and neither did my mama. That's why I had to sneak out tonight, because she doesn't understand. Her family came from China with a whole different set of stories; she didn't grow up hearing about trickster coyotes and the witches that take animal shapes.

I can feel his eyes on us, the same way a rabbit can feel a wildcat lurking in the brush ready to pounce.

A high whistle cuts through the night. We whip around towards the sound, Blue's arm straight as an arrow with his revolver extending his silhouette. I wanted to have a gun when we set out but now I really don't.

Darkness eats up the wilderness after just a few yards. I can make out the jagged edge of the mountains where they cut into the starry sky, but even if we had a torch, the terrain is piles of red rocks anything could hide behind.

"At least—"

I jump at the sound of his voice and pull my hat down over my ears.

"Sorry," Blue whispers, relaxing his arm slightly. "At least we should be able to see eyeshine if there's a wildcat out here."

"Not if it has people eyes," I whisper back. "People eyes don't shine."

Blue looks at me. Not angry, but not happy, either. "Are you going to tell me who we're looking for?"

"Miss Cactus's son. River." I'm reluctant to say more, but Blue needs to be prepared. "He's a yeahnáglóshii." Another whistle, somehow both farther away and right beside us. I drop my voice even lower. "A *skin-walker*."

The words, the names of the thing, hang heavy in the cool night air. This lore is sacred and dangerous, not something to share with outsiders. Just talking about it draws evil to us like moths to a bonfire.

"They wear skins, and they become the animal. But they aren't... right. Too human to be animal, too animal to be human. They can never be right again." Miss Cactus's lack of a face flashes to my mind. Doing that to someone isn't something a person can do and still call themselves a person.

I open my mouth to say more, but a voice whispers my name in my ear, so close I can feel the breath on my neck.

I spin around, but no one's there.

"Beck?" Blue says, his gun following my line of sight. "I don't see anything. Where is it?"

A dark shape scampers across the landscape, a hunched figure with gangly arms darting from one shadow to the next. I take a step back, position myself behind Blue.

A coyote howls somewhere in the night, but the sound is all wrong. Like a human playing coyote. Then it's silent, too silent, just me and Blue and the whooshing sound of my heartbeat in my ears.

There are no footsteps, no heavy breaths before it happens. When the hand comes down on my shoulder, I'm so startled that I forget how to scream.

The panic lances out of its fingers like lightning, pulses into my body and squeezes my heart. I know Blue must be next to me, I know he's probably fighting it off, but I'm numb to the world.

I have to get the hand off me. I jerk away, but the nails dig into my sleeve. Not nails. *Claws.*

My voice finds its way back to me and I scream, flinging my fists at my attacker. The next few seconds are a flurry of shouts and movement and there's a shot and then I'm running through the night.

Shapes flick past in the darkness, barely illuminated by moonlight. I don't know where I'm going, just *away.*

Someone calls my name and it sounds like Blue, but Granny said they can mimic voices just like they can change their face. You gotta look them in the eye, real close, to tell if somebody's really somebody.

A rock hits my foot and then the ground hits my face and the world just kind of spins for a minute. When I scramble to a sitting position, Blue is standing beside me.

Even in the near total lack of light I can see the dark stain blooming on his chest.

It shot him. Oh god, the thing shot him.

Except he doesn't seem to have noticed. He just stands there motionless, like he isn't even breathing. The fact that some of his insides are becoming outsides doesn't bother him, nor does the excruciating pain he must be in.

I try to look him in the eye, but my gaze slips off his face and lands on his shoulder.

"We gotta go, Beck," he says. "It's coming."

I might not be good with tone or inflection, but I can tell that isn't his voice. Even when he's angry at me, Blue is patient and kind. This person, this *thing*, is rough and tired and... and just not Blue.

Which means Blue shot it.

Which means getting shot can't kill it.

"Beck. Let's go!"

His voice is like dynamite. I flinch but stay rooted to the spot, trying to remember Granny's whispers about skin-walkers and how to kill them. If they're too strong, if they're invincible to the things that should kill a normal man...

"Rebecca!"

*Names.*

Names are sacred things, especially to a witch trying to hide their identity. You name a skin-walker, and you take away its wicked power.

"Ri—" The word catches in my mouth, my mind too focused on where Blue is and if he's okay. I can barely breathe, let alone talk.

The witch takes long, purposeful strides towards me. I stumble backwards until I hit a boulder and can't go any further.

"Riv—Ri—"

Its face breaks into a grin full of sharp fangs stained with blood. It lunges forward and grabs me by the wrist and my neck tightens and it feels like I'm going to die, and I just have to make it stop and the word bursts out of me.

"River!"

The monster with Blue's face sneers, leans close to me. So close I can't look anywhere but its eyes. Yellow and horrible and staring right into my soul.

"That isn't my name," it taunts.

I know it isn't, and I know River always tried to force me to use his real name. But I can't.

I'm not being stubborn. My brain just rejects the sounds and I can't say it and the more I try the more it *won't come out*. His name is River. That's the only name I can call him. It's his *name*. It should count.

All my life, people have tried to make me say names, make me look them in the eye and touch them without flinching. They shame me into not being me. And all my life, I've tried not to be. Tried not to be me.

But this *is* me.

I'm peculiar and I can't be any other way if I tried, and I don't even want to try.

"River," I whisper, and the thing's eyes go dark. Human.

I squeeze my eyes shut so he can't look at me, and I hear Blue call my name.

No. No, no, no. He can't mimic anymore. He can't.

"Beck!" But it's really Blue this time. "Beck, get down!"

With River still in a daze from having his powers stripped away, I wrench my hand out of his grip and throw myself to the ground. A shot, and River falls down dead. He still has his face, but it's all bloody and has a new hole in it.

Blue's bleeding, big red claw marks across his abdomen, but he's smiling, and I think he'll be okay.

He offers me his hand to help me up, and I want to take it, but I can't. Maybe someday I will, but not tonight. I get myself to my feet and we walk home together. A real coyote sings out somewhere in the night, but it doesn't cross our path.

# MAFIA BUTTERFLY

## RAYMOND LUCZAK

No one who knows me will ever tell you this, but I'm a butterfly.

I'm not even talking about the clichéd hearing view of my hands signing as if they are pretty monarchs fluttering around, or the fact that I'm a full-grown Deaf woman who's full capital-D. People would say that at twenty-seven years old, I'm in the prime of my life. Guys especially notice me when I walk down the street. I am never sure if it's because of the way my hair flips about in the wind, or that I'm wearing clothes that fit me well. I never turn my head to look back. It's really nice to keep my hearing aids turned off when I'm outside. This way I don't overhear the catcalls.

No one makes a move to ask me out once they see I can't speak very well.

Let me retract that. They've certainly tried, but they keep looking down at my body. Uh-unh. I'm much more than the sum of my body parts. Oh, so much more. I'm always astonished at how men are willing to reduce themselves to the only body part that matters to them.

The minute I open my mouth to speak, everything changes in a second.

Suddenly, they're not in power.

I make it crystal clear that I don't need them to complete me.

That drives them nuts. Good!

They need to get over themselves.

It's the language, baby. If they don't know how to sign, I'm not interested.

It's clear on their faces that they assume just because I'm Deaf, I must be all about the body, as if my lack of speech has reduced me to the level of an animal ready to writhe about in the mud. I am tired of the joke that Deaf people are supposed to be great in bed because they don't know how to say no. Ha ha, right. They got that wrong. I am great in bed because I know *how* to say yes, and only when I'm ready.

Some people think I'm a woman of mystery. Having grown up in a hearing family has made it possible for me to keep myself cloaked on a need-to-know basis. I still keep in touch with my two sisters but only through email. They always look lost when we meet in person. They can't sign. They apologize again for not having the time to learn, but that's precisely when they know to stop talking about it. They know I'll remind them that I took fourteen years of speech therapy for their benefit. What could be so hard about taking classes? It's all about priorities, people.

Deaf people around here know who I am, but I don't hang out at Deaf events like I used to. I keep track of them on Facebook, but that's it.

I'm not going to name names here, but there's a Deaf man who still gives me dirty looks. He's in his sixties. Married with three kids and seven grandchildren. He talks about them all the time. People say he's very nice, and he's popular. But he's like the mafia boss of the Deaf community around here.

I'm not talking about the mafia that you see in the *Godfather* movies.

Little Italy's been long gone, you know.

The mafia doesn't need guns to exercise their power. The threat of excommunication is sufficient. It's a certain look that comes from having been in the community long enough to be considered worthy of respect, and who has been endowed the unassailable power of persuasion.

I'm talking about how Deaf people look to the mafia boss for guidance whether to accept a new Deaf member or not. They always invite him to their parties and into their homes for dinner. They always hug and take forever with their long goodbyes.

When I show up at a sign-interpreted theatre performance, they say hello and move on.

I try not to take it personally, but I do.

What have I done to merit dismissal?

I've never attacked anyone. Never!

I have a full-time job that I love. I design book covers and marketing materials for the biggest publisher in town. Visual language was mine long before I was allowed to learn Sign as a teenager.

When I tasted the forbidden fruit of Sign, I suddenly realized that I had been sleeping all my life in a cocoon.

I grasped the power of letting my hands out in the open.

I was announcing to the world that I was different. I didn't have to pretend to be hearing, or a hard of hearing person.

I wasn't just deaf; I was Deaf. Capital-D!

Yay, right?

I made my way to my first Deaf social gathering at a coffeehouse. At first I felt scared. I thought they'd accept me because I'd taken the time to learn Sign from videos online and read up on Deaf history. No one said hello to me when I sat two tables over. I didn't want to seem pushy. After all, I was a frightened teenager with pimples on my face.

Watching them carry on as if no one else existed, I wanted to die from my own stupidity.

I had hoped to say, "I know sign language, too," but watching them made me feel so small. There was no way I could possibly be as fluent as they were.

After I finished my bottle of soda, I slunk out of there.

To this day, I am amazed and yet angered that no one ever noticed the wide-eyed fear on my face. Did they think they didn't need another Deaf person in the community?

Apparently.

I cried every night until I felt nothing but stone in my heart.

When I graduated from high school, I decided not to go to Gallaudet University or National Technical Institute for the Deaf. The coldness of those people at the coffeehouse broke me into a thousand and one pieces. I went to Browell University right here. My parents aren't made of money, and neither was I.

I took ASL classes at Browell. Foreign language requirement, you know?

My teacher, Peggy Whitehead, was the best. She was so excited to have a Deaf student in her class for a change. She saw how quickly I mastered the vocabulary. The idioms and syntax were a bit difficult at first, but I discovered that as long as I didn't think about how I was signing, everything in Sign made perfect sense. Thinking in English was the problem.

I felt closer to home, but it kept drifting away each time I showed up at a Deaf event. Peggy and I became good friends after I graduated from college, and she introduced me to so many people.

I didn't know at first that the Deaf mafia boss had a thing against her when I met him. I didn't know how she had stood up to him years before. The fact that she'd grown up in a Deaf family made it impossible for him to dismiss her so easily. He mocked her behind her back, and she had learned about this from their mutual friends.

Before she finally introduced me to him after an ASL-interpreted show, she warned me about him. "Himself same-same m-a-f-i-a decide maybe you nothing. If happens, worry not. Himself run Deaf community not. Courtesy-show respect nice, that-all."

I recognized him from the first time I came to the Deaf social gathering. He was a bit older than I'd recalled. He had a nice smile. I liked him immediately. I wished he were my father.

Peggy beckoned me to come closer. "Want introduce you him." She told him my name, and we shook hands.

"Nice meet-you." I smiled.

"Herself learn Sign fast. My first Deaf ASL student. Proud her!" She squeezed my arm and hugged me.

A warm glow rose in me. I wished she were my real mother. "Thank-you," I said.

He gave me a look that said, *Oh, I see.* The slight distaste was clear in his eyes. "Go home now must. Sorry." He turned to Peggy. "Take-care."

She gave him a stony smile at his backside. "Bastard," she said, once he left the lobby and turned to me. "Warn you finish."

I nodded.

"Other friends find can."

So I did.

Each time I showed up with friends who signed, he and his friends looked away from me. Some of my friends were hearing ASL students; a few of them used to be my interpreters in college. I didn't believe in discriminating against friends who were hearing.

I began to notice something else about him.

You do know who I'm talking about, right?

Yep, that's him.

So you know how he walks around, like he's something of a politician, when he mingles among his friends. Sometimes a friend of his would introduce him to someone new. If the new person was truly fluent in ASL, or had come from a Deaf family, he would banter with his jokes.

If they weren't, tough luck.

Peggy is right. Why are we supposed to kiss the ring finger of the mafia? If we don't, is that so bad? Why are many Deaf people so afraid about being judged when they chose to befriend a new Deaf person? Can't they see that it isn't healthy to dismiss people they barely know? We need more Deaf friends.

I want to be accepted as I am. I used to be a lousy signer, but Peggy says that I'm very fluent in ASL now. She says I'm the best student she's ever had.

She's taught me so much.

She showed me how important it was to stay strong no matter what.

Strength isn't always contained in my hands. Strength comes from choosing how to use my hands in the most effective way possible.

I choose to mingle among my own friends. I do not worry about him or the fact that his Deaf friends have made a point of ignoring me or Peggy. They will eventually die.

It can be so hard, though, being a butterfly when no one tenders you a flower for you to perch on for a moment of respite. Isn't that what community is supposed to be about?

No matter what anyone says, I am a butterfly. I will continue to live my life as honestly as I can, and flit about, practicing my future powers of persuasion, so that one day I will live long enough, and be made mafia boss myself, and accept everyone no matter how badly they may sign.

It isn't just the language that matters. What's in your heart does, too.

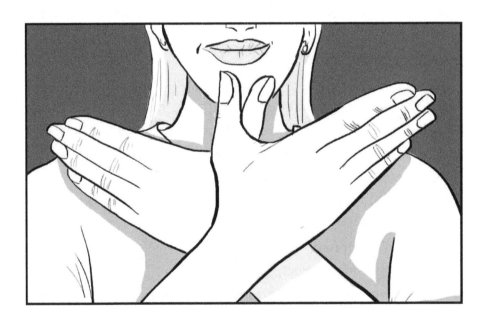

# DRESS REHEARSAL

## NICOLE ZELNIKER

Lizzie hated hospitals. She hated nurses and therapists and psychologists and especially doctors, anyone in a lab coat with a medical degree. That's why, when her sister suggested they go to the hospital together to say one last goodbye to their mother, Lizzie said no. It wasn't until Tess started to cry that Lizzie promised to get on an airplane, fly back to Florida, and at least drive with Tess so she wouldn't have to be alone.

"Don't you need to see your mom one last time?" Lizzie's roommate Jennifer asked late one night when both of them were in the kitchen. Lizzie had come downstairs around one in the morning carrying a sticker-covered computer in a baggy Gators T-shirt and grey sweatpants to apply for more jobs (her master's degree had earned her a job as a barmaid at the local bar and a cashier at the grocery store downtown) and found Jennifer already at the table in an overlarge blue sweater and black gym shorts, her dyed red hair up in a messy bun. On the table sat two mugs, two tea bags, two spoons, and a jar of honey. One of the mugs had a picture of a cocker spaniel. The other read "Perkatory: the anguished, prolonged period spent waiting for a fresh pot of coffee to be ready."

"I have photos," Lizzie said, stirring honey into her tea. She had just flipped through some of them yesterday, after Tess had requested she bring some, in a brown leather-bound photo album. There were several photos of her and Lizzie with matching dark, curly hair. In Lizzie's favorite, her mother was wearing black heels and a bright yellow blouse with red lipstick. When Lizzie was younger, she used to go through her mother's closet and try on her sweaters and long-sleeved shirts, pretending they were dresses. Several times, her mother caught her, but she never got mad. Once, she even showed Lizzie how to put on the lipstick.

Jennifer shrugged and left it alone.

Lizzie found Tess by the luggage in the airport, even though she hadn't checked any. She carried her multicolored plaid bag over her right shoulder. She had thrown her hair up in a ponytail at the airport in Virginia and wore Tess's old leggings that had somehow ended up in her possession, blue and white striped Toms, and a grey sweater with a white bird over the left breast. Tess, on the other hand, looked put together: she had her sandy-brown hair straightened down to her shoulders and wore a navy cardigan with a forest-green tank top under it, light-blue jeans, and black sandals that wrapped around her ankles. Lizzie put the bag down so they could hug.

"I missed you," Tess said.

"But now I'm here," Lizzie said.

Lizzie waited by Tess's car in the parking lot, a red 2012 Honda with Florida plates. Tess had insisted they go to the hospital right away, so Lizzie had said she would wait for Tess outside, in spite of Tess's pleas. She promised Tess to come back later, when she was ready. After Tess left, she had pulled off the sweater (it was still warm in Miami, even in November) and was lighting a cigarette when someone from behind said, "You know cancer's no joke." Lizzie turned around. There was a man there in a white jacket, a T-shirt with the blue Auburn Tigers logo on it, and ripped jeans. He had thick black hair.

"No one's laughing," she said. She put the lighter back in her pants pocket.

"You looked like you could be having a good time," the man said. "You have cancer?"

"Not yet. Do you?"

"Liver," he said and held out his hand. "Give me a stick." Lizzie took the cigarettes back out and lit a second one for the man in the Tigers shirt. "Why are you here, if you're not sick?"

"I didn't say I'm not sick, I said I didn't have cancer," Lizzie argued.

"Ah. Well, technicalities," the man said. "How old are you?" He put his lips on the cigarette and inhaled.

"Twenty-six," Lizzie said, exhaling smoke. The man grinned. "Do you think I'm lying?"

"I mean, kind of," he said. "I would've said, like, sixteen."

Lizzie smirked. "I'll age up when I get sick."

He stuck out his hand. "I'm Matt."

"Lizzie." She took it.

"Mom would really like to see you." Lizzie and Tess sat on their mother's porch swing in the evening, both wearing tank tops, Lizzie's sandy-brown and Tess's bubble-gum pink, and denim shorts. Both tank tops had been Lizzie's before she had moved to Virginia. Tess had just looked through Lizzie's photos. There were several of Lizzie and their mother.

"I'll go back soon," Lizzie said.

"You're leaving on Tuesday."

Lizzie shrugged and kicked off the porch with her feet. Her side of the swing wobbled gently. "I have time."

Tess raised her eyes and tilted her head forward. It was the same look she had used since she was little when she wanted their mother to tell the truth about whether or not there were monsters under the bed or if cauliflower really was as gross as she thought it would be. "It's Sunday."

"I'll go by tomorrow, while you're at work." Tess worked at the nail salon as a stylist.

"You don't have a car." Lizzie kicked off the ground again.

"I'll take the bus."

Tess raised her eyebrows again. "Lizzie."

"I'll go, don't worry about it." This time, when she kicked off, Tess lifted her feet off the ground and they both went flying.

"Where does your sister think you are?" Matt asked. They both lay in Matt's queen-sized bed, naked except for a thin blue sheet borrowed from the closet in the hall. They hadn't had sex, although they had done just about everything else.

"A friend's," Lizzie said, gazing up at the ceiling on her back. It was a pretty big room, with white walls and a blue carpet. There was a window looking out onto the street, a full-length mirror in the corner, and a dresser across from the bed. "I told her not to wait up for me."

"Will she?" Matt asked.

"Yeah, probably." When Lizzie was a junior in high school and Tess had just started her second year, their mother had gone out of state for work. There was a lot of snow that winter, too much for Lizzie to drive home in from a friend's that night. Tess had stayed up all night waiting to hear if Lizzie could get home.

Lizzie turned onto her side and traced a faint scar on Matt's shoulder. "Does it hurt?"

He smiled. "My shoulder?"

"The cancer."

Matt shrugged against the pillows. "Yeah, sometimes. I'm on a lot of drugs, though." Matt took her hand in his and kissed it. "What kind does your mom have?"

"Lymphoma."

"And that's the kind you'll get?"

"Probably." She stretched her arm and ran a finger through Matt's hair, catching soft strands between her fingers. They fell onto his shoulders in small clumps.

"You haven't seen her yet?" Jennifer asked. Lizzie's phone was sitting on the kitchen countertop on speaker, between her mother's old toaster and the blender she bought when solid foods started making her nauseous. Lizzie herself was boiling water, her hair still braided from before she went to sleep, dressed in black yoga pants and a light blue T-shirt from the night before.

"No. Why?" Lizzie ripped the top off a box of spaghetti and tipped the pasta into the pot.

"I don't get it, but whatever." Lizzie rolled her eyes and picked up the wooden spoon. "How's Tess?" Lizzie set the silverware beside the paper plates, the navy ones with the polka dots her mother had bought from Walmart since Lizzie's childhood. She heard a car door slam.

"I think she's home."

"Alright, I'll let you go," Jennifer said.

"Bye." Lizzie hit the off button as Tess walked in the door in a crisp white top, a black knee-length skirt, and black pumps. Her hair was pinned up at the sides.

"Thank god for lunch breaks," Tess said. "Did you see Mom yet?"

"It's noon," Lizzie said.

"So when are you going to?" Tess asked.

"Soon." Tess sat down at the kitchen table. "You wore that last time I saw you," Lizzie said.

"You're so obsessive." Lizzie stirred the pasta in the pot once. Tess drummed the table with her dark red manicured fingernails. "I'm going to psychoanalyze you."

"Go for it."

"You care so much about my outfit so you can distract me from the fact that you haven't seen Mom yet." She tilted her head and frowned. "Or you're distracting yourself. I haven't figured out which."

Lizzie stirred the pasta the other way. "Not even close," she said.

"What time do you leave tomorrow?" Matt asked.

"Twelve," Lizzie said. The two of them were getting coffee downtown at a Starbucks. Lizzie wore a red flannel top and the denim shorts she had worn yesterday. She had borrowed Tess's tan sandals for a change. Matt was wearing a dark blue sweatshirt and a pair of dark jeans.

"Come over tonight?" Matt asked. He kept his hand around his coffee cup.

Lizzie sipped her coffee, iced, extra milk and sugar, and said, "I can't. I'm watching a movie with my sister." Matt nodded. "But I can come over Tuesday morning? Just for a while?"

"I have chemo," Matt said, blowing on his drink, roasted, no milk or sugar. "But you could come."

"To chemo?"

"If you want to."

Lizzie crossed her legs. "I'll think about it."

Matt shrugged. "You'll have to do it someday."

"You're cutting it close," Tess said. Lizzie put her phone down between them, ignoring another message from Matt.

"Shut up and play the movie," Lizzie said. They were both sitting on the plum colored couch in the living room, the one their grandmother had given their mother when she died. They had found a box of old Disney movies, some of them so old they were on video tapes, and popped in the Brother Bear DVD Tess had gotten for Christmas one year. Lizzie had forgotten how small the TV was. Both wore old sweatpants. Lizzie wore another tank top (she was still readjusting to the Florida heat), Tess their mother's sweater. Both were sitting under their mother's old quilt. Her phone buzzed again with a text. Lizzie pretended she hadn't heard it.

"I just think she'd like it," Tess said, pressing play. The castle with the Disney logo came up on the screen.

"You know what, Tess, you're not going to get sick like her, so please just shut up."

Tess furrowed her eyebrows angrily and then burst into tears.

"Tess, I didn't mean that," Lizzie said.

"Yes you did." She started breathing in quick gasps.

Lizzie leaned over and hit the pause button. She took Tess's hand. "I did," she said.

"I know that," Tess said between breaths. "Just for one fucking second can you think about me? I'm going to be alone."

Lizzie pulled her close. Both of them cried into their mother's sweater.

The room was dark, despite the fluorescent lighting in the halls. The floor was checkered black and white and the walls were a lilac purple. on one side of the bed was a stand with a sandy brown bear holding a red heart that said "I Love You" in white script and three balloons, one red, one white, and one pink. The pink one was drooping slightly. On the other side was a machine that beeped every few seconds, mapping out the movements of Lizzie's mother's heart. Lizzie's mother lay on the bed. Her formerly dark and curly hair was gone. Her neck was swollen slightly, and her skin was pasty, almost white. Whereas her neck was puffed out, her cheeks had caved in, as though her body had redistributed all the weight. Lizzie pulled the door shut behind her. "Hi, Mom," she said.

Her mother turned her head slightly. "Did Tess make you come?" she rasped.

"No," Lizzie said, taking a few steps closer, slowly. "But she did let me borrow her car." Her legs shook slightly in her mother's old black heels. Lizzie wore black shorts and Tess's faded blue button-up short-sleeved shirt. Her mother wore a hospital gown.

"She said you were in town. I thought you would've come sooner."

"I know," Lizzie said. She was close enough now that she could've reached out and touched her mother if she wanted to. She settled for sitting in the chair beside her bed and putting her hand on the white sheet covering her mother's legs. "I was scared, I guess."

"Because it'll be you next."

"Yeah." Lizzie tried to grab her mother's hand but couldn't seem to get her arm to work.

"It's not so bad," Lizzie's mother said.

"You're lying," Lizzie laughed.

"Yeah." She inched her hand toward Lizzie's, and Lizzie took it. "That's what I do for you."

Lizzie rubbed her eye with the other hand. "I'm glad I came back," she said.

Her mother inhaled a shaky breath and nodded. She winced at the pain in her neck.

She was smoking on the hood of her sister's car by the entrance of the hospital when Matt came out of the building in a green Gators hoodie. "I might not get cancer," she said, handing him a cigarette.

He blinked. "Excuse me?" He took it.

"My mom and I had the same disease," she said, lighting his cigarette. "Have the same disease. It's genetic. Tess doesn't have it." Matt just stood there. "The treatment can cause lymphoma."

"So you've been blowing me off."

"So I've been blowing you off."

Matt shrugged. "At least you're honest."

"I just wanted you to know that," she said. "I don't really know why."

"I mean, I get it," he said. "Sometimes this woman comes into the room while I'm getting chemo and she's already lost her hair and she can barely talk and stuff. She has throat cancer."

She waved her cigarette in the air. "Probably from one of these." He laughed. "I'm moving back to Florida," she said.

"Why?" He blew the cigarette smoke out of his mouth. It smelled almost sweet.

"Tess."

"Does she know yet?"

Lizzie shook her head. "I have to talk to my roommate. And maybe I'll actually find a job here."

"If that's your reasoning, you'd better stay where you are." Lizzie laughed, too. "Maybe you can let me know when you get back?"

"Maybe," she said.

"You'll come back soon?" Tess said.

"I will." They were standing by the security line, watching the board overhead for any delays. "Maybe by then you'll have your own apartment."

"Yeah. Text me when you get there."

"I will." They hugged. "I love you."

"I love you, too." They broke apart. Tess picked up Lizzie's bag and handed it to her. "Don't be late," she said. They hugged one more time before Lizzie got in the security line and went back to Virginia. Lizzie looked back while someone checked her ticket and ID, but Tess was gone.

By the time Lizzie got home, it was dark outside. She went back to her room and saw Jennifer's sticky note stuck to her door: "Out to get groceries. Be back soon."

Lizzie opened the door and dumped her bag onto her bed. She leaned back against her pillow and opened her laptop to start looking for apartments in Florida. With one hand tapping on the keyboard, she fished her phone out of her pants pocket and saw five missed calls, three voicemails, and two texts from Tess. The first read: "Call when you can?" And the second: "Mom died. Call when you land."

She put her phone on the nightstand and studied her laptop. She had already pulled up an apartment complex not too far from Tess, both in her price range and with several openings. She closed the tab and her laptop. She scooted down off the pillow, lay back on her black and white striped blanket and stared up at the white celling, her laptop leaving hot marks on her stomach, rubbing the sides of her neck with her hands.

# THE DESCENT

## JAMIESON WOLF

He heard a *ding!* and stepped out of the elevator.

Looking around, the wizard had to admit appearances could be deceiving. Then again, oracles weren't necessarily obligated to dwell in shadowy places filled with refuse and cobwebs. Maybe this oracle liked to live amongst the luxury of plush carpets and walls done in a posh gray with a herringbone pattern. It's just that he had been expecting something... different.

All he saw was a long hallway and an old man sitting at a desk in front of the only door on the floor. Approaching it, the wizard tried to remain calm. His magic sparkled like stardust at his fingertips, and when he shook them to clear away the stardust, it flew up into the air with a whistling sound. He shushed it. He was nervous enough without drawing attention to himself.

The old man looked up from the book he read and smiled warmly. "Welcome. Here to see the Oracle, I presume? What's your name, friend?"

"Jefferson," he said. "My name is Jefferson." He walked towards his elder and realized that the man was much older than at first glance. Jefferson saw wrinkles covering his face, surrounding his eyes like the rings in a tree trunk. He wondered how long the man had been working here.

Taking another step towards him, Jefferson stumbled, his feet not wanting to cooperate tonight. The spasms ran up his left leg this time, making it feel as if that part of his body were humming a soft tune only he could hear. He wished he had brought his cane.

The old man's eyes softened. "Well friend, that is a fine name. Just take a seat here a moment, and I will get some details from you."

Jefferson looked around once again and then back at the older man. "I don't see a chair."

"Oh, my mistake, my mistake. Let me fix that."

The man took a wand out from his overcoat and gave it a gentle wave. A chair appeared in the air in front of him, a comfortable wingback in a soft and plush grey, much like the carpet and walls. Jefferson even saw a herringbone pattern on the chair's fabric. With a *poof!* the chair landed in front of him.

"Sorry about that. It's been a while since I've seen anyone here."

"Have there been many people to see the Oracle?"

The man nodded. "Oh yes. Yes indeed. Only problem is that none of them have come back."

"Back from where?"

"We'll pay that no mind just yet. I haven't introduced myself, have I? The name is Wallace."

Wallace held out a hand, and Jefferson took it. He was surprised by how warm it was. Jefferson had assumed it would be cold. "Pleased to meet you, Wallace."

"Oh, the pleasure is all mine, indeed it is. Now, we need to do one final thing before you go and see the Oracle. Just a formality, you understand." Wallace took out an old, leather-bound book from his desk and flipped it open. "I need you to sign your name here and then date it, if you would be so kind."

"Sure thing."

Jefferson signed his name and added the date. When he drew the last number in the year, the page glowed briefly, and his name and the date glowed brighter still before disappearing. Jefferson's fingers glowed, a shower of sparks falling onto the page. He brushed them away quickly and looked up at Wallace.

"You're all good to go. They're behind that door." Wallace said, pointing to a wooden door that looked almost as if it were breathing.

Jefferson watched Wallace close the book and put it away. "Why did my name disappear?"

Wallace shrugged. "That is the question." He stood and motioned to the door. "It's just a contract of sorts, keeping the Oracle covered should something happen. I'm sure you understand."

"Yes, but we're just going to have a conversation, right?"

"Yes, indeed. Better get moving. You don't want to keep the Oracle waiting too long."

Nodding, Jefferson pulled open the door. He saw a set of spiralling stairs. They were made of metal but had shining wooden railings. Jefferson went to the edge of the top landing and looked down. The stairs seemed to reach far below ground. Pulling his head back, he looked at Wallace.

"I thought I was going to see the Oracle?"

"And so you shall. They're just down there."

"I was expecting a boardroom or something."

Wallace gave a small chuckle. "You really expect the Oracle to sit in a boardroom? No, son. The journey to the Oracle is different for everyone. This way here"—he pointed at the stairs—"is yours."

Jefferson stared at the stairwell and the shadows that waited there. He nodded and swallowed thickly. "I can do this," he said. "I can do this."

"That's the spirit," Wallace said, kindly. "For what it's worth, I really think you'll succeed. I truly do."

Jefferson nodded and approached the stairs. He placed a hand on the bannister and was astounded when the door where Wallace stood began to close. He watched it as the opening to the foyer got smaller and smaller, but he didn't reach out to stop the door. Jefferson let it close and let the darkness claim him.

It wasn't truly dark, not really.

There was light coming in from what looked like a cavern ceiling, stalactites hanging downward, almost as if they were pointing the way. Looking down, Jefferson was pretty sure he was in his own personal hell.

He hated stairs and was cursing himself for not bringing his cane. "Wouldn't fucking help on stairs anyway," Jefferson said out loud. His voice echoed for what seemed like forever. He could almost see the soundwaves in the semi-darkness.

Looking down again, he watched as the stairs seemed to move and shift. He knew that this was his vertigo, and his fear was making his symptoms come to the surface. Knowing this didn't help matters. There was still a fuckload of stairs.

If someone had told him years ago that he would have multiple sclerosis, he would have laughed at them, not really understanding what it was. Now, almost six years later, it was as if multiple sclerosis was another person living inside of Jefferson, making him do things he didn't want to do.

At first, he thought that magic could fix it, could send the multiple sclerosis far away. After all, he could make lights appear in the dark, cause storms to crash down around him, and even ride on the wind if he so chose. He could put his hand into the arth and make trees grow and flowers bloom. Jefferson could even use his magic to make his every fantasy come to life.

The one thing he could not do was cure his multiple sclerosis with magic.

He had been enraged at this. What good was magic if it could not cure him? If it could not purge the monster that lived within his skin? In a drunken haze one evening, he had tried to cut it out of him, hoping that by releasing enough blood, the multiple sclerosis would flee his body as quickly as his life.

Jefferson didn't know how long he had lain there, or how much blood he had lost, when the door opened and a man had stepped into his apartment. He had gone to Jefferson's side and had placed his hands on Jefferson's chest. Too weak from the blood he had lost, Jefferson didn't have the strength to push him away.

A thrum had moved through Jefferson, sending shockwaves through his body and through the bed he lay upon. The very ground shook around him. As a soft gold light began to shine brighter and more brilliant around him, Jefferson felt a *pull* and watched as his blood began to move back into his veins. When it was done, Jefferson had looked at the man who had saved him. "Why?" he had asked.

The man shrugged. "Because it wasn't your time yet."

Thinking back on that first conversation with Mikhail gave Jefferson strength. It hurt knowing that Mikhail couldn't be here with him to help him though this, but Jefferson knew that he had to visit the Oracle alone.

Taking a step down while holding on to the railing, Jefferson just kept his eyes on the steps and made sure that his feet were hitting each one. It was slow work, getting his body to do what it didn't want to. However, Jefferson had learned to overcome many different obstacles since his diagnosis. "I can *do* this," Jefferson said aloud.

He was almost at the first landing when he heard a voice behind him. "You just keep telling yourself that, honey."

Turning to look over his shoulder, Jefferson saw Max standing at the top of the stairs.

"Oh, fuck you," said Jefferson. "Why are you even here?"

"Uh, hello? I'm inside you?"

Jefferson sighed and continued downward. In retrospect, he supposed it hadn't been a smart idea to give his multiple sclerosis a name. When he was trying to use magic to cure himself, Jefferson had called the disease Max Shadow. Over time, as the wizard had failed again and again to rid his body of the disease, Max became more and more defined. It was as if he were a real person.

Wiggling his fingers, Jefferson let his magic out. The stairwell was filled with a shower of sparks. He flung out his hand towards Max. There was a blinding flash and Jefferson could feel the heat form where he stood. Blinking his eyes, he turned his back on the returning darkness when he heard a voice speak.

"You didn't think it would be that easy, did you?"

Turning he saw Max Shadow, looking smug. "Fuck you," Jefferson barked, then turned away from him and began to go down the stairs, one at a time, while holding on to the railing. That didn't stop Jefferson from tripping or almost falling, but he continued his descent.

Max followed closely behind him, taking his leisurely time on the stairs. "I mean, you *do* know that I'm part of you, right?"

"Shut up," Jefferson spat.

"You tried to magic me and that didn't work. You tried offing yourself and that didn't work either."

"Would you please shut the fuck up?"

"Oh, big words from a man who was so scared that he tried to take his own life." Max said with a small chuckle.

Saying nothing for the time being, Jefferson continued, knowing that if he looked back at Max, he would lose his concentration. He began to count the stairs in his head: *twenty-six, twenty-seven, twenty-eight.* On twenty-nine, his foot slipped on the slick metal stair and he went down quite a few steps before he caught himself by grabbing on to the railing.

As Jefferson was working on getting up, Max's voice rang out behind him. "Are you sure that what you'll find at the bottom of the stairwell will be worth all of this?"

"It's gotta be," Jefferson said, hoisting himself up with a grunt. "It just has to be. I haven't come this far for nothing."

"You haven't gone very far. Just a bunch of steps," Max said.

"There was a lot of work beforehand. I had to learn to use my body all over again, be aware of what it could do—thanks to you. I don't expect you to understand."

The only sound that could be heard for a while were the sounds of Jefferson's footsteps going carefully down the stairs. Jefferson thought that Max wouldn't respond until he heard his voice: "I do, though. I do understand."

Jefferson kept going downward: *fifty-eight, fifty-nine, sixty.* "Yeah, right."

"C'mon, man. You made me. You think it's fun being inside your head all the time?"

"You think it's fun having you fuck with my body?" Jefferson retorted.

"You were the one who gave me a name, man. I didn't ask for this. I didn't ask to be alive inside of you. You were the one who gave me a face and an identity. Thanks for the great ass, by the way. Everyone loves a bubble butt."

Jefferson made a gagging sound. "Puh-*leeze*. I created an identity for you, so I could destroy you. Yet here you are." *Seventy-three, seventy-four, seventy-five.*

"Haven't you realized yet that we're one and the same? I have nowhere else to go. I live within you."

Jefferson's leg spasmed, and he fell down more steps, quite a few of them this time. He tried to stop himself, but his balance had been thrown off, and there was nothing to do but let himself fall. Finally coming to a halt, he pulled himself up and threw his head back.

"Fuck!" he screamed. His voice echoed in the stairwell, the word repeating back to him: "*Fuuuuck, fuuuck, fuuck...*" He had caught himself again, but his leg was still throbbing painfully. Sparkles and stars flew out of his fingers, and Jefferson pressed his hand to his right thigh where the spasms were coming from. He let the magic inside him increase, finding release, and it spread into his body. He might not be able to heal his multiple sclerosis, but he could ease his pain.

"Hey, we're almost there," Max said, pointing to the steps that remained.

"What's this 'we' shit? I'm the one doing all the work!"

"I'm your cheerleading section."

Jefferson could hear Max's grin. "Fuck you." He was almost there anyway. *Eighty-six, eighty-seven, eighty-nine.*

"Look man, we're in this together. You don't want me around, but we have a choice. We can fight each other, or we can learn to get along. It's really that simple."

"I can't believe you're trying to give me advice when I'm the one who made you up in my head." Another step and then another.

"I know. Pretty messed up, right?"

Jefferson took one last step down, and his feet left the slippery marble stairs with their shining wooden banisters. His soles hit dirt, and he could feel gravel and pieces of rock underneath his boots. *Ninety-nine.*

"See, man?" Max said cheerfully. "I told you that you could do it."

"Shut up; you did not." Quickly scanning the area, Jefferson saw many different entrances in the rock and counted seven entrances into different tunnels. "I wonder where the Oracle is. How do we find them?"

"We go that way." Max pointed at the entrance to the fifth tunnel.

"How can you be so sure?"

"Because I can feel the magic coming from there. Plus, can't you see the trail of dust left by magic on the ground?"

Jefferson shook his head. As a wizard, he knew all about the residue left behind by wizards, warlocks, and witches when magic was performed, but he couldn't see anything. There was something else that was bothering him as well. "I thought Wallace said that everyone's journey to see the Oracle was different. Why would there be magic here if this was *my* journey?"

Max shook his head. "I don't know, man, but that's the way we need to go."

"Okay," Jefferson relented, "okay." Steeling himself, he stepped forward with Max following him. Only Jefferson's footsteps made noise as they walked along on the dirt and gravel floor of the cave.

As they moved into the shadow of the entrance, Jefferson could hear a hum of magic, as if the air around him were singing a soft tune. They were on the right path. If he hadn't had Max with him, Jefferson would have spent a long time searching the tunnels for the right one, and who knows how long the tunnels went on for? He sighed inwardly. The irony wasn't lost on him.

The walls began to brighten, as if the rock itself was filled with light. As more light began to filter into the tunnel, Jefferson saw that it was not light that filled the walls of the tunnel, but stones and precious gems: amethyst, rose and clear quartz, labradorite, and moonstone. They covered the walls as if someone had placed the stones in some sort of haphazard pattern. Running his hand over the gems, Jefferson felt the hum of power that was running through him increase.

"Seer stones," he whispered. He didn't know why he was whispering, only that it seemed right. "This is clearly the place."

Max chuckled. "See, I told you I knew where I was going."

"Don't get too full of yourself."

They walked on, the sunlight growing brighter with each step. They were so close, so very close. Jefferson had been searching for the Oracle for such a long time; the fact that he was this close to it was almost too much to handle. The Oracle would know of a way to leech the multiple sclerosis from his body; he was sure of it.

A breeze came into the tunnel, and Jefferson could smell lavender flowers. He felt calmer and more himself because the very scent and the hum of the energy from the stones surrounding him had cleared his head of all of the fear he constantly carried within him. He was so tired all the time and so tired of being afraid.

Jefferson began to feel warmth on his skin and spared a look at Max Shadow. Nodding, Max indicated that he could feel it, too. Soon, the sunlight was all they could see. They were both blinded and warmed by it. When the light began to lessen, they found they were no longer in a tunnel, but at the edge of a field of lavender plants. What looked like a door waited for them, shining in the distance.

They walked on, the scent of lavender growing stronger. The sun shone off the door, making it seem like an eye in the distance. Jefferson could hear the rustle of the lavender, the whisper of the wind, and the hum of the magic that surrounded this place.

When they neared the end of the field, the door came into focus, except it wasn't a door. As they stood in front of it, Jefferson realized it was a mirror. On the top of the ornate wooden frame, three words were carved: The Mighty Oracle.

Jefferson regarded the mirror and their reflection in it for a moment. There was merely the sound of the breeze and the lavender plants whispering to each other. He had no idea what to say, how to articulate how far he had come to find this. "A mirror?" Jefferson said, almost lightly, like he was remarking on the weather. "A fucking mirror?"

"Listen, I know you're upset," Max said.

"Upset?! Upset is stubbing my toe in the dark. This is fucking pissed off!" Jefferson couldn't control the anger in his voice. "All this way, all that work, for this? A fucking mirror? What is it supposed to tell me?"

Max regarded him for a moment. "You know, for a wizard, you don't see a lot."

"What the fuck does that mean?"

"Well, don't you get it?" Max let out a sigh when Jefferson shook his head. "*You're* the Oracle. You get to decide where your life goes, you get to make your own choices. You don't need some mystical dickwad telling you what to do. You get to do it yourself."

Something clicked inside of Jefferson, and his magic started to spark at his fingertips. "Wait, what did you say?"

"Only that you get to make these decisions yourself. It's your life. You get to choose how it goes. It's up to you, after all."

The magic swelled within him. Jefferson could feel it move and shift within his body. "Thank you," he said.

"Hey, thank yourself. I am *you* after all."

Max placed his hands on either side of Jefferson's head. He looked Jefferson right in the eyes and said, "I'll be seeing you." Then Max Shadow began to slowly fade, and Jefferson knew that he was flowing back into him, and they were becoming one again.

The wizard walked alone back through the lavender field and the tunnel. He stood, watching the stairs that rose back up to freedom. He could have used magic to climb the stairs this time, but something made him plant one foot on that first step and begin his ascent.

It would be a long climb up, but he would not be doing it alone, and Mikhail was waiting for him.

# BUG HUNT

## JOANNA MARSH

Mina Tom was only a grunt. Technically. But she analyzed data as a hobby. Ran simulations. The capabilities, history, and battles of mechs were her special interests. She could recognize when a battle was hopeless. When a mission was doomed.

And this one was.

On one side, them: five rank-and-file soldiers. Mina didn't even recognize the names of the women she was due to die with. No commendations. No stand-out victories. Their mechs were similarly uninspired. Factory-standard. Tanks with legs. Cutting edge... about a decade before the War.

On the other side? Anna Hyde. The best pilot their Empire had ever seen. Their enemies called her the King of the War. Propaganda darling. Charmer. Celebrity.

Her mech? Could barely be called that. It had its own name and legend, just like its pilot. Godkiller. Pretentious? Yes. Effective? Very. The fluidity it displayed in battle was beyond mechanical capabilities. The way it responded to Hyde's commands! It did impossible things. Terrifying things.

And she'd gone rogue with it.

So the Empire had ordered Hyde's death. If Mina succeeded, she'd go down in history. Finally more than a footnote.

If.

But 'if' had her in a hanger of mechs, at attention with four other soldiers. Their commander explained that they were to deploy shortly. Passed them dossiers of info. Wished them luck.

Didn't say they'd dearly need it.

"We're all screwed, right?"

The first to speak was tallest of the four, though still shorter than Mina. Natural hair, regulation length. Earbuds—and Mina could hear very faint white noise. Sensory issues? Anxiety? Probably no one else could hear it, though. Her uniform said 'Albright'.

The other three—Winters, Cash, and Yoshi—didn't argue. Much. Cash gave a brief protest of "Not necessarily!" Nobody bought it. Not even Cash, from the way she trailed off. Wrapped one of her curls around her fingers awkwardly.

Mina stuck a thumb towards Winters. "Unless she's hiding a top secret mech that can beat the Godkiller in that chair."

Cash made a distressed noise. Looked between Mina and Winters like they were about to fist-fight.

Winters slapped the wheels on her chair. The move drew lots of attention to her impressive arms. Probably on purpose. "Shit, and here I'd thought I'd be fine to leave my badass mech-smuggling chair in the barracks today." She sniffed. Rubbed her nose. "But, yeah, she's right. On every level."

Mina let out a noise of consideration.

"Not *every* level. Technically, the Walkur units we'll be in have more guns than the Godkiller." She shrugged. "Not *better*—just more." She held up fingers as she listed, "Energy rifle, shoulder cannons, arm turrets."

"And the last time Hyde and the Godkiller needed more than that sword thing?"

The 'sword thing' wasn't really a sword, either. It resembled an insect's stinger more than a crafted weapon. If one was generous, they could call it a javelin. One of the many peculiar quirks of the mech.

But that wasn't the issue at hand. Mina shrugged again. "Hasn't happened yet."

Albright nodded.

"Thanks for sparing us the bullshit. Means you're in charge, far as I'm concerned."

What a gracious appointment on her part. What could Mina do but bow?

Cash mumbled. "We're really all the same rank. Private Tom is just part of our unit…"

Winters asked the question they'd probably all thought. Except Cash. She struck Mina as too goodie-goodie. "So if we're all screwed, why are we doing this?"

And Cash made another distressed noise. Mina wondered how long before she'd hyperventilate. Wondered the same of herself. Any second now, the 'I'm going to die' panic would start. Best to enjoy the numb while it lasted.

Yoshi looked around the hanger. There were no other soldiers on duty there. The maintenance workers had too much to do to listen in. But what did that matter? They all knew every inch of the Empire was under surveillance. They listened for traitors. Who cared if privacy didn't exist anymore? It was 'for the greater good'—a concept Mina had been chastised for neglecting over her own selfishness.

The Empire had more spy bugs than actual insects.

And Yoshi knew that, based on her quiet hiss.

"We're doing this because we'd get our own team of five nobodies to shoot us down if we desert. And none of *us* are Anna Hyde, so they'd actually do it."

Wait.

Mina tapped her index finger against her chin. "Would we each get five? Or would they send five for all of us?"

Yoshi paused. Considered the same question. Reached for the dossier she'd been given.

Cash laughed, high and nervous. Yeah, she knew there was someone who could hear their every word.

"But we wouldn't! We're all loyal subjects of the Empire!"

The other four recited as one, "Glory to Her." Natural as the alphabet.

After a moment of solemn silence at their invocation of the Empress, Albright said, "So was Hyde. Wasn't she? Wondered why *she* deserted."

It was a sensible question. Insight into Hyde's mindset might help to locate her. Maybe even help neutralize her. But that kind of insight wasn't Mina's strength.

She did throw in, "I heard she liked to anthropomorphize her mech. Called it her 'friend' and such. But plenty of neurotypical people do that. Might even have been a joke." That had never made sense to Mina.

(Assigning human traits to non-human items, not joking.)

Cash, surprisingly, gave that a half-way real answer instead of more propaganda.

"People always said she was...of a dramatic temperament." Mina knew that one—it was how people without mental illnesses tried to describe mental illness. When they weren't deliberately offensive.

"There was some rumour that she'd been diagnosed with a Cluster B personality disorder." Cash frowned. Gripped her copy of the dossier tightly. "I hope that doesn't make the Empire judge others with similar diagnoses so harshly. I'm a hard worker and loyal subject. Glory to Her."

Winters scoffed. "As if. Someone like Anna Hyde wouldn't go to therapy enough for a diagnosis. Not like us grunts. She'd get special treatment. Can't slow down the King with recuperation and mandated leaves." She paused. "That's probably the 'why' answered, huh? All work and no play made her a dull girl."

Seemed like Yoshi had a good head on her shoulders. She cut in, "We can ask her before she shoots us all down. Now let's fly."

They each got into their mechs without issue. Mina did a quick systems check—were the cameras at the brightness she liked? Was everything within arm's reach or did she need to adjust the seat's height? She assumed the others had similar adjustments and rituals. The Empire allowed such accommodations—after all, results mattered most.

And then....

"Albright, Walkur Uniform Charlie Five One, departing."

"Cash, Walkur Zulu Zulu Two Five, departing."

"Tom, Walkur Alpha Charlie Four Niner, departing."

"Winters, Walkur November Golf Echo One Three, departing."

"Yoshi, Walkur Sierra Delta Two Five, departing."

…not exactly the dramatic speeches prior to battles they'd all heard in propaganda films.

Regardless, they were off. Their immense grey mechs soared through the air, comets on a warpath.

Their dossiers had Hyde's last known location. If they got lucky, they could track her based on the Godkiller's fuel emissions. Even legendary mechs needed to put out energy to fly.

But a pilot as expert as Anna Hyde would probably guess they'd track her that way first. So…

The unlucky option was that the Godkiller would move on 'foot'. Easier to track visually, from the massive footprints. But the five wouldn't have time to process their mortality before they found Hyde. Very unlucky.

The team arrived at their destination nearly three hours after departure. They stood in silence, cameras taking in Olympus Mons before them. Four of them did, anyway. Mina wasn't impressed by a mountain, even the tallest in the Solar System. She'd been on Mars her entire life—big whoop.

"Spread out." Mina said over their closed communication system. They complied, thankfully—guess they'd all made the same decision as Albright. "Albright, Yoshi - switch from AV to TE. Cash, Winters - stay on cameras."

She flipped the sensors from audio-visual to thermal-and-energy-based. Mars looked black from its low temperatures. That meant even the slightest burn from rocket thrusters would be obvious.

Nothing on the ground. Nothing in the air.

Winters crackled in, "Found tracks, boss. She's not flying."

Damn.

Yoshi made a curious noise. Barely audible through the comms.

So Mina obviously called her on it.

"We might want to do TE checks at every track we find. She might be switching from flight to ground to throw us off." Then another noise. "Or…"

Mina finished the thought for her.

"Or she wants us to think she might, so we waste time in the search." How many plans could they make that Hyde couldn't expect? And how many levels deep could they go on plans that countered Hyde's plans for their plans?

What a headache.

Cash spoke up. "Private Tom… maybe we should just follow the tracks and not get ahead of ourselves?"

Not the worst idea.

Winters laughed. Maybe at the irony that she hadn't suggested that first.

The five grouped together at Winters's location. As a unit, they beheld the mark of the Godkiller's wake. It was a small canyon, marked with three fractures towards one end. Only one mech had feet like that. Only one mech had 'feet' at all.

"We are so dead."

It took Mina a second to realize she'd been the one to say that. Huh. Maybe she'd dissociated a bit. Silver lining—that would make it easier to go on.

Albright made a noise of faint agreement.

A moment of silence was the agreement all the others gave.

Yoshi broke it. Back to the mission.

"How far could the Godkiller jump from here?"

Mina paused. All mechs had documented data on their capabilities. A Walkur could make a horizontal jump of about fifty clicks. In her last recorded training session, Hyde had clocked a horizontal leap of four times that. Which meant...

"No clue."

Training was training. On the field, the Godkiller had the most annoying habit of blowing those numbers away. Witness testimonies were hyperbolic to an extreme. They described something like pyrotechnics during these times from the Godkiller's chassis. Impossible, of course. Why would you equip a military vessel with arbitrary lights? And why would you keep it off the record?

Mina had heard the exemplary field behaviour made higher-ups suspect Hyde was deliberately underperforming in training. To showboat? Maybe. She had the temperament for it.

Besides, Mars terrain had a lower gravity than the artificial gravity in training centres and Mina did not have the spoons for that kind of math before she died.

So Mina spat out the documented number. What else could she do? She couldn't factor for miracles.

"Based on the way the toes are pointed... let's go that way!" Cash pointed with her mech's unwieldy arm. Too caught up to remember cardinal directions? Or was she worried Hyde had hacked their comms?

No way.

The five moved, slowly and silently as the Walkur's block-legs allowed. There was little chance they could truly sneak up on Hyde. Still, even a second could make the difference.

They had only the loosest of formation—Mina literally led the unit at the front. Then, Albright and Winters flanked her. Yoshi and Cash were behind them, completing a pentagon. Again, it was about a second of difference. They all knew Hyde wouldn't sneak up on them.

Mina had punched in two hundred clicks into her mech's console. The number ticked down bit by bit. Close. Closer. Closer. The fake calm of dissociation was gone—her heart was in her throat. Every rock made her jump. And not just her—Cash had turned her comm off after five straight minutes of whimpers and yelps. That trademark Cluster B paranoia was doing her no favours.

Half an hour later, they came to a new track.

Cash moved her mech's cameras around. Fear was obvious in her voice as she asked, "Is that fresh?"

"How do you even tell?"

Both great questions.

Yoshi and Mina spoke as one, eerily enough.

"Assume it's fresh."

They'd probably had the same thought. Maybe one of them would survive if they all assumed everything was the worst-case scenario.

The track didn't look as deep as the first they'd found. That suggested...

"Oh, gosh! There's more over there!"

Maybe Mina'd spoken too soon about that paranoia doing Cash no favours.

Albright crackled in, "Hyde's on foot?" It *was* a bizarre turn. It would be easy for them to go from print to print without having to cover the vast distance of a leap. *That* suggested...

"She wants us to find her."

Damn.

[YOU ALREADY HAVE.]

Oh, no.

A flash of beetle-red across Mina's cameras.

Yoshi screamed at the top of her lungs. And, when the other four looked at her mech, they screamed too.

A Walkur was bulky in every inch of its chassis. It had to be, to support its own weight.

The thing in front of them was spindly. Limbs too long and too thin. They all extended from a cocoon-shaped middle that looked like it could only hold a pilot. If that. And one of those limbs had stabbed clean through the leg of Yoshi's Walkur. With a long stinger.

The Godkiller.

The 'head' of the thing, angular and lean, twisted from Yoshi to look at the others. No. It wasn't a head—it was a display for cameras. It was just a machine. It was hardly impossible - the way the neck bent and contorted. But it still made Mina a little sick.

[*THIS* IS ALL THEY SEND TO KILL ME? FIVE WALKURS?]

Mina might have been insulted if all five of them hadn't thought the same thing.

[YOU POOR SOULS.]

Okay, the pity felt a bit more insulting.

The limbs and torso snapped and twisted around to face the same direction as the head. Yoshi toppled, as if that thin arm was all that held her mech aloft. This was impossible.

But what had she expected?

Winters switched her screams from fear to fury. Her mech's arms extended, popped open—and let loose the turrets within. They fired physical bullets, hundreds of them—rare these days and meant as a last resort. But, if anything would take Hyde off guard...

The Godkiller moved almost faster than the eye could track. Its thin limbs stretched into a run and took off. Mina's brain had to make after-images of it in mid-travel to compensate. It was nauseating.

And it dodged every single damn bullet.

[STOP THIS AT ONCE.]

Oh, fuck that. They weren't about to die just standing there.

Mina pulled her energy rifle. Her mech's bulky hands cocked it. Aimed. FIRED.

It didn't even run to dodge that. Its long legs bent backwards. The entire Godkiller turned into a right angle and let the energy blast fly over.

Why didn't any of the reports mention that Anna Hyde was an asshole?

Maybe it had been subtext Mina had missed.

[WHO IS THE LEADER OF THIS UNIT?]

She lowered her rifle. Just enough to have the cocoon in her sights. "The one shooting at you, Hyde." And Mina fired again.

The blast hit!

But it didn't damage. Not as far as Mina could tell.

The red chitin-like metal of the Godkiller's exterior... shifted. The tiny segments extended outward. Like flowers—thousands of flowers. A contented noise resonated through the comms. Like... it had eaten the energy.

Like it was... No. No way.

From behind, Albright punched the Godkiller. No pomp—just violence.

The flower segments rippled around the point of contact. The Godkiller... No, *Hyde* groaned.

[DO NOT FIGHT ME. WE CAN HELP EACH OTHER.]

"Never, traitor!"

Cash punched it too, emboldened by Albright's success. But a long arm whipped out and caught her mech's fist.

[THE ONE YOU CALL 'TRAITOR', ANNA HYDE, IS DEAD.]

Something in Mina's brain felt like it broke at those words. They sounded like Anna Hyde had said them. But the voice said Anna Hyde was dead. That meant it had to be lying. Didn't it? But why lie about that?

"Then who are *you*?"

Yoshi, even downed, still cut to the point.

[I AM WHAT YOU CALL THE GODKILLER. I AM WHAT ATE HER.]

*What.*

"Wait... you're not a mech, are you?" Albright stepped in close to the Godkiller. Poked at the extended flower-like segments. "Are you... holy shit, are you an *alien*?"

The word seemed impossible. But what other option was there?

[AS ALIEN AS YOU ARE TO THIS PLANET.]

Huh. Fair.

It left a lot unsaid, though. How had it come to this planet? Had it been a spoil of the Empire's war somewhere else?

"So, if you... ate her, does that mean Anna Hyde *didn't* betray the Empire?"

No one bothered to point out to Cash how little that mattered at the moment. Not even the alien.

"What help can you give us?"

[THE HELP ANNA HYDE REFUSED: FREEDOM FROM THIS SYSTEM YOU CALL AN EMPIRE.]

The Godkiller's long limbs shifted forward to Yoshi's downed Walkur. The stinger jabbed, but without force-like a prodding finger.

[THESE MACHINES ARE NO MATCH FOR ME. YOU KNOW THIS. THE EMPIRE KNEW THIS. THEY SENT YOU AFTER ME TO DIE.]

The... head of the Godkiller twisted back to the four standing mechs.

[THEY DO NOT VALUE YOU. THEY SURVEIL YOU EVERY SECOND, WATCHING FOR BETRAYAL. YOU ARE TOOLS TO THEM, AS I WAS. WE DO NOT DESERVE THIS. WE CAN HELP EACH OTHER.]

Winters lowered her turrets at last.

"So you're helping us out of the goodness of your heart?"

That seemed inaccurate-did it even have a heart? (That was a joke.)

[NO. I AM DYING-SLOWLY, BUT SURELY. I NEED A PILOT.]

A groan of machinery failing to move echoed out from Yoshi's downed mech. "Because you *ate* your last one."

[SHE WANTED TO KEEP ME ENSLAVED. SHE CALLED IT THE GREATER GOOD.]

Mina kept up Yoshi's thread. "And how do we know you won't eat us? Whichever one of us becomes your new pilot."

[I COULD POTENTIALLY BOND WITH ALL OF YOU. I CAN DIVIDE—I WOULD BE EVEN MORE POWERFUL WITH MULTIPLE FOOD SOURCES.]

What did that even mean? And it wasn't an answer.

[I CAN TELL ALREADY WE WILL BE BETTER SUITED. YOU ARE LISTENING. CONSIDERING. WHY WOULD I TURN AGAINST YOU IF WE WANT THE SAME THING?]

"Do we?"

[I WANT TO LIVE, FREE AND WITHOUT FETTERS. DON'T YOU?]

Cash made a distressed noise.

Mina paused. If the five... maybe four... of them received upgrades with even a fraction of the Godkiller's power, nothing the Empire had could stand against them. No need to worry about twenty-five nobodies hunting them down.

And... if she destroyed the Empire, she'd definitely go down in history.

But she let the others go first.

Winters didn't hesitate.

"Fuck yes, I do!"

The Godkiller lunged forward, its curled flower-segments stretching out long and slimy. They latched onto Winters's mech and... changed it. The grey became tinted red, faceted like the chitin of an insect. The turrets changed too—thinner and more alive in appearance. Did they fire stingers now, Mina wondered?

And the voice of the Godkiller echoed from two sources.

[AHH. I FEEL BETTER ALREADY.]

But then there was a pause.

[HMM. YOU ARE NEUROLOGICALLY DIFFERENT FROM ANNA HYDE. IS THIS HUMAN AVERAGE?]

Winters laughed.

"Absolutely not. Her brain worked—mine's shit." Mina could nearly hear the smirk in Winters's tone. "ADHD, baby."

Mina cut in.

"And hers isn't the only one. I'm autistic. Albright has sensory processing issues. Yoshi?"

"Schizophrenia."

[I FEED OFF OF THE ELECTRICITY OF THE BRAIN. FOR ANNA HYDE, THERE WAS NO RISK. BUT, FOR YOU ALL, IT MAY BE IMPERATIVE THAT YOU ALL BECOME MY PILOTS SO I DO NOT TAKE TOO MUCH FROM ANY ONE BODY.]

Looked like they were stuck together, then. They'd worked pretty well as a team so far. Why not?

Winters turned to Cash. Raised a turret.

"Look...we don't want to hurt you—"

Cash's voice came out over the comms, harsh and hard.

"The Empire betrayed *us*. We should strike back. Hurt them."

Well. Look who wasn't such a goodie-goodie when she knew she could get away with it?

Cash turned to Mina.

"Right, boss?"

She *was* the leader, she supposed. She could already imagine the history books. The data on her impossible unit of Godkillers.

It sounded great.

"Then let's strike."

# OLIVER GUTIERREZ AND THE WALKING STICK OF DESTINY

### ELLIOTT DUNSTAN

Oliver Gutierrez glared at the cane in the corner of xyr room with a quiet rage, considered stuffing it into the back of the closet where it wouldn't taunt xem, and wondered why on earth xe couldn't be normal. Xe'd given up hope of really fitting the definition a long time ago. Once you stopped checking the boxes, you could do pretty much whatever you wanted—get an undercut, pierce your nose, tattoo Pink Floyd album covers on yourself—nobody would be able to see past the hearing aids anyway. 'Normal' had never been an option to begin with.

But one still had to ask, at some point, *how* many things one person could have wrong with them.

Maybe it was the cane. It was *stalking* xem. Hadn't Oliver seen identical canes at every Shoppers Drug Mart for the last year? Coincidence? Xe thought *not*. So that answered the question. It was the *cane*'s fault, clearly, that xe had rheumatoid arthritis and not something nice and fixable, like a broken leg.

Oliver sat up in bed with a sigh, blowing a few strands of dyed-green hair out of xyr face and wondering if xe should change out of the flannel shirt and sweats xe'd been wearing all day. "You couldn't have waited until I was like, fifty? Or some otherwise respectable age?" Xe complained to the empty, still air of xyr room. Xe wasn't sure who xe was complaining *to*. The *Transformers* posters, maybe. Or the framed picture of Montreal xe'd gotten from xyr ex-girlfriend ten years ago and never thrown away.

"Don't be silly," echoed a voice in response, and Oliver started in shock, hands flying up in front of xyr face. "You know it doesn't work that way."

Xe looked around the room, wondering if xe was being pranked.

"Over *here*. In the corner." It was an older voice, friendly, sort of Julie-Andrews-ish.

Oliver's eyes settled on the cane.

"Oh fuck," xe groaned. "Not again."

The thing was, kids didn't ever get called crazy. They were *imaginative,* and *creative,* and occasionally a bit, you know, *odd.* So when Oliver was handed xyr first pair of hearing aids at four years old, xe had no idea that they weren't supposed to talk to xem.

Xe'd been left alone with xyr hearing aids, supposedly to *adjust.* Oliver wasn't sure what xe was supposed to be adjusting to, but xe didn't know enough to be surprised when one of the flesh-coloured devices spoke up.

"Don't worry," said Left. "We don't bite."

"Are you sure?" Oliver said nervously. "You do look kind of

weird."

"I suppose that's true," Right mused.

"How can I hear you so clearly? Everybody else is so fuzzy."

"We're hearing aids!" Right sounded more than a little indignant. He was lower-pitched than Left, Oliver noticed, a little more bassy. "Our entire job is to help you *hear* things. Can't do that if you can't hear *us.*"

"I don't know if that makes any sense."

"Oh, just put us in."

So xe did—and suddenly, sound unfolded in front of xem, bright and clear and loud, so *unbelievably* loud—

Oliver jerked them out again, and consequently dropped them down the edge of xyr bed. Sound was overrated.

"No," Oliver pronounced to the cane in the corner. "No, we're not doing this."

"Doing what, dear?"

"You are *not* the first inanimate object to lecture me."

"I haven't lectured you about anything—"

"Yet," Oliver seethed. Xe got to xyr feet, ignoring the pain in xyr knee long enough to march to the kitchen and grab a bag of ice. Xe stuck it to xyr forehead—ice was supposed to help chase off stupid delusions and hallucinations, and where *had* xe put xyr meds—

Ugh. Right. Xe'd run out. Because... oh, that was the kicker, Oliver remembered as xyr knee began to ache again. The walk to the pharmacy was fine one way. The idea of walking *home* again was too much to bear. So xe hadn't done it, and as such, xe'd been on half-meds for about three days. No wonder xyr cane was talking to xem.

Oliver banged xyr head against the fridge door. So xyr choices were walk to the pharmacy and cry in pain, or talk to the cane in the bedroom.

Oliver was stubborn. But not that stubborn.

Xe hobbled back into the bedroom and collapsed back onto the bed, glaring daggers at the cane in the corner. "What do you want?"

"I just want to help, dear."

"Talking to me is not helping. I'm *supposed* to be *medicated.*"

"There's nothing wrong with-"

"Being bipolar?" Oliver drawled. "Or did you mean the part where I have an old person disease?"

"Both are true," the cane added glibly.

"Ugh." Oliver flopped back onto the bed, throwing a hand over xyr eyes. "Look, I wouldn't—I don't—I wouldn't mind using a cane."

"Except?"

"Except I'm already deaf. And crazy. *And* queer."

"I noticed you don't have your hearing aids in."

"I'm at *home.* I don't need them."

"I see. And that wouldn't have anything to do with you shoving them down the side of the bed when you were little?"

Oliver spluttered, and chucked a pillow in the general direction of the cane. "It's bad enough that you're a hallucination, stop reading my mind!"

The only response xe got that time was a wry, cheerful chuckle.

Oliver hadn't slept very well the night after xe got xyr hearing aids...

mostly because they wouldn't shut up. Even from down by the wall, xe could hear them bickering—sometimes about the virtues of tone vs. pitch, and then later into the night about the left and right brain. Xe didn't understand most of it. Xe just knew it was really annoying.

So by the time morning came, Oliver stuck xyr hand down the edge of the bed and picked them up again. Xe cradled the hearing aids in xyr palm, tracing the clear tubing, the indentations in the flesh-coloured molds shaped to xyr ears. "I can lip-read just fine," xe said finally. "Why do I gotta have hearing aids?"

"You don't have to," Left said kindly.

Right sighed. "You don't *have* to," he said, "but it's going to make things easier. Not everybody is going to look you in the eye, and not every word is easy to read."

"But it hurts."

"Only for a little. But then there's music, and laughter, and windchimes. "

"All of which are optional," Left added.

"But they're an awful lot of fun."

Oliver considered this quietly, warming up the hearing aids in xyr hands. Then xe nodded. "Okay," xe whispered. Then Oliver put the hearing aids back into xyr ears, and let the sound flow back into xyr brain, and sat there in the quiet room for a little while, taking it all in.

Oliver glanced over at the cane, turning it over quietly in xyr mind. Xe'd bought it on a whim a week ago, before the diagnosis had been confirmed. All xe'd known is that xyr knee wouldn't stop hurting, and maybe a cane would help. That, and the purple flowers had

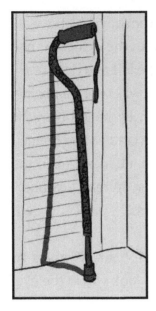

appealed to Oliver's genderweird aesthetic.

It had been a fun experiment, a week ago. Oliver just wished it had stayed that way.

"Why are you torturing me?" Xe sat up and gazed at the cane, half expecting it to move. "This is hard enough without a relapse."

"Not every one of your delusions is trying to hurt you, dearie."

"They're *delusions.* By definition, that's bad. And if your next act is to tell me going off my meds is a good thing—"

"No, no," The cane sounded horrified. Good. Oliver could give it *that* much credit, at least. If xe had to hear about how xyr mental illness made xyr mind more *open to possibility* one more time, xe'd probably just snap the damn thing over xyr leg. "But we *are* your mind talking to you."

"Cool. Next time I hallucinate a horde of bugs swarming across the floor or bloodstains all over the carpet I'll be sure to sit down and have a discussion."

The cane sighed with such disappointment that Oliver had to shake xyr head a bit. "That isn't what I mean."

"Listen, Flora—I'm gonna call you Flora—"

"I suppose it's as good a name as any."

"I just got diagnosed with rheumatoid arthritis at the age of twenty-nine. I don't want your sympathy. I don't want to hear about how you're my fairy godmother. I want to be *left alone.*" Suddenly, Oliver couldn't seem to swallow the lump in xyr throat. Xyr eyes were burning, but xe blinked the tears back. Deaf. Crazy. Queer. And now xe had a lifetime of not being able to *walk* ahead of xem as well.

The room went silent for a moment. Oliver didn't feel any happier. Xe wanted to be left alone, yes, but actually *being* alone was just as depressing. Who on earth was xe supposed to call? Xyr friends would sound sad and offer help. Maybe one of them could offer a lift for groceries. Xyr parents had given up the right to know anything about xyr life a long time ago. And not a single person could take the diagnosis back.

"I may not be your fairy godmother," Flora said, "but I *can* help you walk. That's what I'm for."

Oliver stared down at xyr knees, covered in the black denim of xyr jeans. "What if it doesn't work? What if I still can't do it?"

"You bought me for a reason. You saw me in the store and took me home with you."

Xe couldn't help being a little resentful at the gentle, reassuring tone in Flora's voice. It was the same way the nurses during xyr hospital visits sounded when they were encouraging Oliver to, quote, Make the Best of Things, or to Have a Positive Attitude. But at the same time...

"I have to go to the pharmacy," Oliver murmured. "I have meds there. And a new prescription that *might* help."

"You don't sound very hopeful."

"Hope is extremely frustrating and not always terribly productive."

"A little bit of hope might get you out of the door."

"You sound like somebody's grandmother."

Flora laughed. "Perhaps I am! Now come on, you. You've got meds to get."

"You're definitely not my own mind talking to me. You are *way* too chirpy."

Oliver leaned forward onto xyr knees, wincing as xe did. Then xe reached out and grabbed xyr hearing aids. They didn't say anything at first, but when xe put them into xyr ears, they sparked to life with a happy chime.

"Are we going out?" Left asked.

"Of course we are. Oliver doesn't wear us in the house," Right replied.

Oliver crossed the floor, wincing as the pain started in xyr knees again. Maybe the meds *would* help. Maybe. It was easier to say that this time, it wasn't worth it—that xe might as well just suffer through it, to resign xyrself to no way out.

Oliver took hold of Flora's handle, bracing her against xyr leg. Even standing up, xe could tell it helped. Three legs instead of two.

"Come on," xe said to the hearing aids and the cane, the support systems that kept xem going. "Time to go." They didn't respond this time, but that was okay.

Shoes. Check. Purse. Check. Coat. Check.

Oliver opened the door and exhaled.

# CRUTCH. CAGE. SWORD. KERFUFFLE

## DOROTHY ELLEN PALMER

*Act One: Friday, June 25, 2010*

In the Roman Britain Wing, it's 6:00 pm. It's closing time.

Nellie lays a shielding hand over her nine-month double baby bump and clenches her crutch.

When the sword in the stone display case begins to speak, she doesn't question her sanity, only its motives. In Fortress Toronto, all speech is suspect. On the brink of the G20 Summit, this weapon is either opportune or an opportunist, a saviour or a sleeper sword. It's foisted no jab until today: 'Behold the once and future sting! Take me up; cast me away!'

Nellie concludes the obvious: this sword wants to be stolen. Wants it bad.

In pun and proclamation, it's valiantly Arthurian, a rusty blade still rasping to qualify as sharp. But, if stealing anything from any museum is unwise, pinching an artifact that can scream bloody murder is docent suicide. This should, but does not, give her cause for pause.

"You're quite the cut up," she whispers back, carefully lowering her empty guitar case to the creaky hardwood. "But if you want me to break you out of here, cut the rapier wit."

Thus engaged, the blade finds the full tang of its tongue.

"List close, my fecund lady fair! To win my freedom, I'll spin you a tale. A Camelot of mists and spires, of knights so bold and ladies bolder. I'll thrust it in vernacular yours, not mine, to ensure its hearing: Arthur was an asshole; Lancelot a pedophile, and Merlin a charlatan in a stolen hat. But Mordred, my sweet Mordred, now there was magic! There was a boy worth stabbing."

Nellie winks. "That's one slick pick-up line. You had me at *list*."

"Then, milady, perhaps you are too easily had?"

Nellie snorts. She glances at Sherm in his uniform, as usual, protecting nothing but his phone.

"Milady, you need a champion, not a chump. As your Excalibur, I say: Behold the once and future sting! The issue of a man's sting may serve fittingly to sting the stinger."

Nellie raps on the case. "I don't have forever here, sword. Get a grip!"

"I have one, milady. It is yours I question. But I promise, my triple-hearted one, take me up and I will not cast you away. Unlike chumps, I am good for more than one night of riposte and repartee. I am your keen blade. Because, you have one, do you not? A boy worth stabbing?"

Years of improv at Blakkat kick in. She must 'advance the scene,' must 'say yes to the drama.'

"Yes, my pointed friend. Let's prick that little prick together."

All improvisers talk to themselves; it's the answers that matter.

Slipping into Sherm's security cubby, Nellie grabs Windex, a ShamWow, and a set of keys.

In dedicated polishing, she notes the curator's error. They've labeled the case, *Weapons of Roman Britain*, but Excalibur is not a Roman gladius, which is a legionnaire's short sword of twenty-six inches. It lacks the typical bronze scabbard of twins Romulus and Remus suckling the she-wolf. Its 'standing man' pommel marks it as Celtic. But war makes strange bedfellows. Excalibur sleeps with his enemies, weapons of Roman mass destruction: a shield or *scutum*, a heavy javelin or *pila*, and a double fan of daggers and darts—missiles that sound like appetizers at Bar Italia—*pugio* and *plumbatae*. A legionnaire threw his pila first. When a giant pila protrudes from your scutum, you drop it quick. Even shieldless, a legionnaire still hacks and chops at feet with his gladius.

Nellie hears: *Cut them. Lame them. This is how you bring a standing army down. This may be their home, but protesting Britons are barbarians, not our citizens. Fight hard. Fight dirty.*

**Meanwhile, back at grand theft Excalibur, 'Cheese it! Da cops!'...**

"Hold up, Ms. Wolfe." Sherm gets in her face. "I'll be taking that back from you, please."

Nellie feels a rising gorge of fight or flight, until she realizes he's holding out his hands for the keys, Windex and ShamWow. Then he lifts her guitar case, full of freshly-burgled booty.

"I'll take this to Blakkat for you, Nellie. But, geesh, what've you got in here, rocks?"

"No, I've just stolen a deadly sword, one I plan to use for murder most foul on Saturday."

Sherm nods. "I get it. You're nervous. Tonight and Saturday are your last shows with Kerfuffle before... Don't worry. I've got your back." With a sly glance around, he slides his hand down her arm, past the elbow cuff, to her wrist. Gently, he cups the hand that grips the crutch.

Nellie shivers. It is old code between them, runes from the ruins.

It's a hot gesture that nearly thaws her icy resolve. Nearly. Not really. Not at all.

The impulsive offer of a moment's comfort is what got her in trouble in the first place. Such boys mean well, but they're puppies. They climb all over you with sloppy kisses, until the next thing that smells good catches their eye. When their heat is spent, their warmth is fleeting. When this little pup magnanimously pats her hand nine months later, it's the cold comfort of far too little, far too late.

Screw him. Excalibur is right. She has been too easily had.

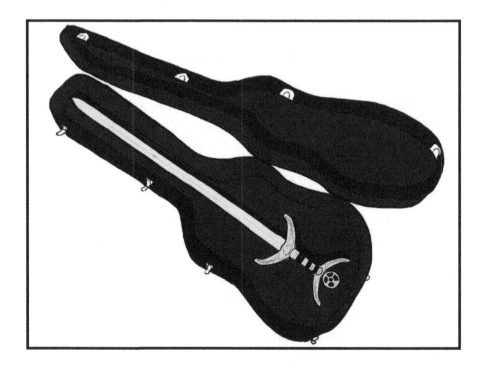

***Meanwhile, because a pregnant woman's bladder shrinks to the size of a walnut***

Of course it's raining. Her text to Connie at Blakkat reads: *late, blame it on the rain.*

In a rush of subway hot air, the train arrives. Damn. If this station had an elevator, she'd have made it. She pushes down stairs faster than pain allows. A crutch length away, the doors whiz shut.

Nellie reminds herself not to say whiz. The walnut is brimming.

Yet again, she wonders how much of life she has lost to being left behind. Inaccessibility is a cruel irony for an improviser. It relegates her to a life of bad timing, perpetually missing all offers. Always too late to 'say yes to the drama,' she must watch the fun advance without her.

When the world constantly forces you to stop and smell the daisies, they fucking stink.

***Meanwhile, under constant surveillance ...***

The new subway security guard likes to pose with one little black boot up on the bench, scanning commuters with the all the contempt of a Nazi commandant. At the 'life unworthy of life' combination of Nellie's crutch and baby bump, all pretense evaporates. He sneers.

She longs to fall on her knees, to confess to Mr. Mini-Pig that she's not really pregnant. She's a single sleeper cell, planted by al-Qaeda via the impregnation of a terrorist doula from Melfort, Saskatchewan and a jihadi Baptist Minister from Bancroft. She's a baby left sleeping in Toronto on the remote chance that three decades later, the city might host the G20, when she would cunningly inflate and burst into ricin gas at their remote command. Now beyond the grave remote, since her mother and father were both unmercifully awake when murdered by an underage drunk driver.

On June 26, 2009—exactly one year ago tomorrow.

Intrusive commuting eyes flit a predictable circuit from face, to crutch, to belly.

In the script in their heads, they want to star as smiling subway philanthropists. They want to offer up the sympathy that sprouts like a thin spring flower in the first heat of their conviction that 'the poor thing didn't know any better,' that 'some pervert must have taken advantage of her.' They supply their own deflowering frost when Nellie won't follow their lead. Her face belongs to a proudly lame crip on a crutch. Her intelligent glare burns their script to cinders.

But Nellie still hears: *Look at that ugly thing. Such criminal stupidity, to bring another lameo spaz into the world. Then she has the gall to ride our subway and throw it in our faces. Bet she's on welfare. Living high on our taxes. Got pregnant for the baby bonus. The fat gimpy bitch.*

This is not the Madonna worship her doula mother has taught her.

But Nellie grins. Tomorrow night, to honour her parents in her last show, a chump will get stung by the spawn of his own ineffectual little stinger. Excalibur nailed it, bang on. What else do you use to carve up a great big chicken, an indiscriminately rutting rooster? To serve up the most fowl member of the species—the philandering pullet? Ex can ex-member her ex most excellently.

Two more stops to Queen Street. Twenty more stairs. She's late, but all warmed up. As she sways white-knuckled on her crutch, there's only one thing hotter—the fragrant L'Eau de Walnut cascading down her thighs and pooling in her fluffy white socks.

### Act Two: Saturday, June 25, 2010
#### Meanwhile, in the wee hours of morning...

Having missed Friday's show, Nellie stands in what was her mother's bathroom, in her underwear, practicing her best Xena Warrior Princess moves in the full-length mirror. Framed by dainty rosebud wallpaper, she twists sword overhead. Time to make Joxer soil his boxers. As exquisitely lawless as the exquisite Lucy Lawless, Excalibur agrees, she's a law unto herself.

"See my magical chimeras, milady, beginnings that are endings, carved like the Roman Janus, facing past and future on either side of my blade? *Take me up; cast me away*, are more than words; they're prophesy. You have taken me up. You must be your own true knight, then cast me away."

But when the mighty Xena whacks the mirror, it explodes into pugio and plumbatae. The mystical Xena tells herself it's an accident, not an omen. But, in a broken mirror, rosebuds wither.

She mutters, "What the Jesus fuck were you thinking?"

Dropping her crutch, Nellie reaches with both hands for her massive bra. She rips open the eight Velcro straps strapping her torso. It takes a brutal tug to yank out the plug between her legs.

When the jutting foam breasts of the Simu-Twin Empathy Belly slip away, she sighs.

As the sixty-pound saline pouch slides free, she giggles.

When two Simu-Babies crack their little heads on the bathroom tile, she lurches for the toilet.

Her father holds her glasses. Her mother holds her hair.

***Meanwhile, that afternoon, hunting and gathering pinkos at Queen's Park …***

When a re-costumed pregnant Nellie reaches the Legislature at Queen's Park—a dull chocolate brown her entire life until its recent sandblasting—she thinks what she always does at its eye-popping makeover: "Who knew it had such playful brickwork? Who the hell knew it was pink?"

She navigates a roiling sea of protestors, looking for her equally pink friends.

Twitter puts the People First March at some 40,000 pairs of feet. She gets jostled non-stop. When the police stop her, quoting The Public Works Protection Act and The Trespass to Property Act, both sound more Monty Python than Metropolitan Toronto. Then, a musician gets arrested for waving his trombone in, quote, 'a threatening, weapon-like manner, like a light saber.'

Nellie hears: *Seventy-six trombones fled the big parade. With this cornet close behind.*

She passes three Goth kids, pale, thin and maybe seventeen. They blend into a black blanket, looking wan, as if today was the only exercise these poor little emos had seen since birth and they needed a good long sit down. When Nellie stumbles, the boy with a bolt in his face jumps up.

"Please take my seat. You look fuckin' shit-stomped."

Nellie laughs. "Yep, that sums it up. Thank you. I appreciate it."

The crowd thickens. A ring of riot police on horseback cinch the park.

Two not-so-jolly giant officers leer over the blanket. When they see Bolt Boy, they don't see the Little Bean Sprout. Nellie looks for nametags, but they are covered in Velcro strips.

Before she can speak, horses charge their blanket.

Giant hairy beasts chomp at the bit to get at them.

**Meanwhile, this is not the kerfuffle she has hoped for ...**

It's smaller than Blakkat's washroom. With an orange Port-a-Potty without a door. No sink. No water. She asks for water. An officer squirts a water bottle in her face. Her hair is soaked. Her neck and shoulders are freezing, but her crotch is colder. She is 'one smelly bitch,' caged in a dog run.

Each cage has four seats. Each cage jails twenty human beings. She can't count the cages.

So far, no one has touched her belly. They have taken her glasses.

In a shifting kaleidoscope of shapes and colours, some five hundred bodies are forced to alternate standing and sitting on the floor. The 'other bitch' thrown into her cage is an older Indigenous woman, one who is weeping. She also, quite obviously, has a broken arm.

Cops laugh. "Well, then, it's a good thing you're too drunk to feel it, isn't it?"

When Nellie offers to use the woman's scarf to tie an improvised sling, a female guard yells, "Quit your squawking, squaw! And you, Gimp Girl, get away from her."

Nellie does not join the waves of meowing, barking, and cage-shaking to drown out her captors. She has stopped seeing the clever words of resistance pressed into chain-link cages by Styrofoam cups. She sees her childhood Lite-Brite, pegs poked into holes to make glowing words and pictures. And loss hits again. It's always a blind side: no set of twins will play with her toys.

They will all be left behind, untouched and alone in the basement.

A handsome young officer smiles into her cage. "Only a total retard would screw a fugly broken cunt like you. Maybe I should show you how it's really done?"

And Nellie gets truly *Meanwhiled*. She's not on a metal seat in a cage; it's an examination table. It's cold. It's as cold as January, when she told everyone she was sick. Sick of death and sick to death. When the ultrasound technician falls silent, she keeps breathing. When he looks up into her face, she longs to be anywhere and anyone, that doesn't have to meet his gaze.

"There is no easy way to say this. We have exhausted all our medical capabilities and can find no heartbeats.' He gives her a moment. "We must conclude that both pregnancies are no longer viable. For the sake of your health, they must be terminated. As soon as possible."

She does not cry. She simply ceases to live in her body. She tells no one.

At the clinic, old scars on her bare feet push down on metal stirrups. When she gets home to the emptiest house on Russell Street, she turns off her phone and lies flat on her back in her parents' bed for two days. Then she opens her mother's closet and finds their blessing.

Her doula mother smiles. "Women who miscarry should be able to grieve any way they want."

When the Empathy Belly fits, her father nods. "Whatever you need, pumpkin."

*Meanwhile, behold the brain of a dragonfly's dick ...*

Four hours later, they unlock her cage. It takes twenty minutes to find her crutch.

She has to run a police gauntlet, past a wall of centurions with tempers up and visors down.

Dodging scutum after scutum, Nellie tenses for the slice of gladius at her ankles.

She hears: *Lame them. Shame them. Toronto may be their home, but protestors are barbarians. Fight dirty. Throw them in dog cages. It's how you bring an army of young people down.*

It's raining, but she can't stop to clean her glasses. She falls repeatedly, tripped by water bottles, bricks, and a splintering two-by-four. Her crutch catches the jutting legs of an overturned mailbox. The shattered glass of pugio and plumbatae re-weaponize the sidewalk.

She's hyperventilating, pushing past judgement, fear and pain. When she arrives at Blakkat, she stares at the offer it is making: a shattered window, the old stripped awning bleeding on the sidewalk, a door that has lost a fight with an axe. It is small solace to find her guitar case in the prop pile, right where Sherm has left it, in another life, in a sane city, in a Toronto not under siege by centurions.

At the sound of a crutch in the wings, Connie makes herself an exit from play.

"Are you, okay? We phoned and phoned. Nobody would tell us

anything."

"Yeah. A cop with the brain of a dragonfly's dick called my crutch a concealed weapon."

"Anarchists hid weapons in our awning. Used 'em to smash up storefronts."

"It appears cops think improvisors are the enemy. Good."

Connie's radar pings. "Did they hurt you? My god, did they hurt the babies?"

"No. I'm fine, but I need in this show. Now. Fill me in."

"We asked for an occupation, got 'washerwoman.' Asked for a location, got 'Up Against the Wall.' Sherm is Lord Wall. I'm his suffragette daughter, Pandora. Andy's a union organizer, Mr. Hadrian. Cal's a bomb-making anarchist, Wallcrushington."

Nellie sighs. "Let me guess: get left behind and you get leftovers. I get the laundry."

**_Meanwhile, back at the raunchy launch of the show...._**

Kerfuffle has planned to ridicule the G20 fake lake and its insulting security wall.

As Lord Wall, Sherm has established himself as arrogantly out of touch, bragging about his noble family, the Berlin Walls, the great Walls of China and his Yankee cousins, the Cuban Blockades. He's moved his fake lake three times, a foot to the left, two feet right, and back to center. Spending more than it costs to feed his workers, he builds a wall to keep them out. When they starve, he feels guilty, then orders them to build it higher.

His daughter, Pandora, meets behind the wall with Wallcrushington, to build bombs.

In an inept attempt to woo Pandora, the union organizer goes full throttle Scottish hooligan.

"I'm a Hadrian, like the fookin' wall the fookin' Romans built in my country. I'm a big blue Pict with a big pink haggis in me sporran. I'd jump a lassie like you at a fookin' single bound."

Connie, of course, has out-jumped horny Hadrian each time. Her Emma Goldman line gets the best laugh: "If I can't dance, I don't want to be part of your revolution."

Through all this boiling and roiling, a very-pregnant washerwoman has passed through their scenes in self-imposed silence. A witnessing apparition, a far-from-blithe spirit, she clutches a guitar case held flat, established as her laundry basket. She is silent when flirted with, silent when asked a direct question, silent when ordered to speak by her lord. Even when hugged by a loving Pandora.

Her body is on stage, but Nellie sees only the last truth she is hiding.

**_Meanwhile, behold a Warrior Princess...._**

When you enter an abortion clinic, you arrive with a future inside you; you leave without it.

Of course, a fetus isn't a baby. It's no more a person than an egg is a chicken, or a chrysalis is a butterfly. But neither is it nothing. It's an offer your body is making. A completed offer. With all the foundations. It's a loved one waiting in the wings. It will advance into play, unless you act to cancel it, decide to draw the curtain. That's improv. That's life. One offer must end for another to progress. It's a choice a woman has every right to make. But there can be loss. And lasting consequences.

Nellie counts back from ten, in the first and only moment she is glad her parents are dead.

**Meanwhile, back at Blakkat....**

A washerwoman throws down her crutch. Cold as stone, she lifts sword from laundry basket.

Chimeras glow. Their mouths spit fire.

A sword scrapes along Sherm's chest. Nellie pauses, then, "AIEEEEEEYAAAAA!" Clutching the hilt with both hands, she lifts Excalibur aloft and stabs down, straight into her womb.

Two eight-pound bouncing babies launch into the audience.

The audience recoils. A girl in the front row, spattered in saline, retches and runs for the washroom. Only Sherm stands his ground, waiting for Nellie to complete her offer.

"They died, too. I couldn't face it. For just a little longer, I wanted to keep them with me."

**Act Three: Sunday, June 27, 2010**

**Meanwhile, when you kettle people, they keep boiling ...**

By Sunday night, all of Canada is glued to the drama advancing on their TV screens. Some 1,100 citizens have been arrested, more than any mass arrest since the 1919 Winnipeg General Strike.

On the couch, upstairs at Russell Street, Nellie feels her parents beside her. Her father says Jesus would have been in the front lines; her mother says Mother Mary would rage beside him.

They all agree. Canada does not need to be protected from an improvising minister's daughter.

We all need to see young protestors wielding swords and crutches as our own children.

# IRON BONE

## J. IVANEL JOHNSON

It has been suggested—even directly to my face on occasion—that I might have an unyielding metal rod up my backside. This less-than-complimentary indignity is usually bestowed upon me by some pubescent pimply in one of my classes, at a moment when they find me particularly inflexible on some point, almost always in direct relevance to their own behaviour. Ironically, these students don't know how literal they are being. I do indeed have a magnet board of rods, screws, pins, and clamps below my waist.

However, with all the assertiveness training courses available to teachers, especially women, when it comes to confrontations with the Royal family, doctors, employers, or parents, I remain spineless. I have no real backbone at all.

I was born breech. Means I tend to do things ass-first. I don't like to follow trends or fads, so many *ass*-ume I'm socially inept, but it just means I'd rather go backwards than forwards. If you *tell* me to go somewhere, I'll want to dig in my heels and not move at all. I was also born with spondylolisthesis, and when the good doctor gave a tug on my legs to try and 'straighten me out,' he also weakened my knees. So, frequently I can't move at all.

This symbolism of the physicality of my actual birth also suggests I inadvertently cause trouble or pain wherever I go. (Sorry again, Mom! It was a hell of a delivery, I know. Despite your best efforts, no amount of straightening up ever occurred, did it? Physically or otherwise.)

When Queen Elizabeth II gave me, as a disabled member of the Commonwealth who had contributed to her own nation in sport, an S.O.T. medal of honour, I felt like such a hypocrite. I couldn't, of course, tell her the many 'interferences' I'd had with members of her own family in the past. At this moment, no backbone meant no courage.

I just bowed my head as she approached, more with guilt than courtesy. Being a wheelchair-user at that time, I could hardly curtsey. The admin over with and the medal awarded, Her Majesty then almost gave me an *opening*, saying wittily, "There, that should counteract any misdeeds you've done in the past!"

What was I supposed to have answered? "I once believed I was put on earth to disturb royalty and tilt the cosmos, Ma'am?" Thank goodness her husband Prince Philip wasn't behind her as he often was. His queries tended to be more along the lines of asking Gandhi why he was wearing his pajamas, or asking a blind recipient of the medal why he'd put two different-coloured socks on for such an important occasion. If he'd known I once smacked his grand-daughter with a riding crop, or picked a fight with his son-in-law, he'd have had a lot more inappropriate things to blurt out at me.

The first time I relocated to England was the day before Princess Diana was killed. My inaugural teaching job began the day following this momentous event, and the country was in shock and mourning. Counsellors expecting a crisis in every classroom thought the new Canadian teacher utterly disrespectful when they heard unmitigated howls of laughter emanating from behind my door. I was simply trying to come to grips with the fact that I'd mentioned to a couple of wiseacre students that I kept extra pencils in my fanny pack. That was apparently like saying, "Go look in my vagina," to a classroom of British twelve-year-olds. I left soon after that to come back to Canada for the first in a series of back surgeries, but I'm sure that incident has been discussed among those children almost more than the shattering death of their future king's mother.

"Remember that teacher that told Nigel to look in her fanny?"

"Fiona the Fanny Packer, we called her! Oh, yeah..."

My second teaching job a few years and much rehab later, at a school in Maryland, USA, began on the morning of September 11, 2001. We were only a half-hour from Washington. The day before had been a Professional Development Day and a complete waste of time, considering what was to occur.

"Teachers, you will need to be aware of the explicit necessity of following the curriculum *exactly* as it is laid out this year, in Report 24 C. Our school has been chosen by the school board to be tailored as an example of rudimentary testing procedures for the new fundamentals..."

Indeed, we would all soon find that none of the nonsense they spouted to us that day prepared us for the type of 'development' we would need, both for ourselves and our traumatized students, in the weeks to follow. My own developing sounded like near-paranoia: *Because I came out of the womb askew, am I to continually have the same effect on the universe, every place I go? It is not that I dare disturb it; in my case it is when will I CEASE disturbing it? Am I to always feel at least partly responsible for this frightening phenomenon that some would call merely coincidence? Straighten UP, Fiona! Straighten up!*

Generally, I felt like the spiritual bull in the china-shop, inadvertently crashing around the Earth and causing things to fall off the shelf and break. Some said these coincidences developed into superstition that metamorphosed into self-fulfilling prophecy. (And by some, I mean a long line of trying-too-hard therapists).

Three different co-competitors of mine on the horse trials circuit died whilst riding at the same events at which I was competing. Two of them were Olympic candidates, and the other had been competing for more than 30 years, virtually unscathed, until she crossed my jagged path. And I'm supposed to believe I am not a jinx?

When I competed a variety of colourful geldings in the dangerous equestrian triathlons, I would win if I was given the bib-number 3 or 7 to wear... but lost if I had any multiple of five, and came to grief in a thunderstorm on top of a picnic table jump in the middle of the muddy forest when I once had to wear the number 13. Thirteen different hospitals, five surgeries, and all the jokes about 'Ms. C. has a rod up her backside,' or how I'm now completely 'spineless,' added insult to literal injury. Mind you, I *was* pretty spineless when it came to turning down the S.O.T. medal or explaining to the Queen that I'd been the cause of more consternation than concern-for-nation.

Part of the time I taught in England, I also worked for a disabled duchess in Lancashire who needed an enema every morning and evening. I think she hired me because she thought I'd understand what it was like to be disabled, especially as a keen rider, which she had also been. But I couldn't seem to get past the enemas. I was lousy at their applications—they made pony poo-picking seem like paradise. I didn't last long, working for the duchess; however, it was through Lady Delham that I taught a Pony Club clinic in which the young Zara Phillips (future eventing World Champion) was riding. And when she had sassed me about her stirrups not being too long, I jokingly tapped her riding boot with my crop and said she was to put them up two holes for jumping, anyway. I only found out that evening to whom the energetic and outspoken child was related. Had I known at the time, I would have been a spineless, stammering servant, as is my wont.

But there was a time when I was both flexible and aggressively brave with the Royals. This is the aforementioned argument with Princess Anne's ex, father of the sassy Zara. Standing in a queue behind Captain Mark Phillips, awaiting a breakfast sausage (all I could afford), I grinned and cheekily blurted: "That tricky coffin of yours won't stop me, shadows or no."

The venue was Bromont, Quebec, home of the 1976 Olympic equestrian three-day event in which both he and his royal wife had competed. I'd been there on their Olympic cross-country day as a teenaged spectator, so of course it was inevitable that Princess Anne should fall at the water jump. Again, later apologies to her mother should have been made, had I had a bit of backbone! But at this time, 15 years later, the captain was there in his capacity as course designer, and I was more than ready to ride it on my chunky dun cow-horse cross, Harvest Gold.

"It's placed in the woods for a reason. Just make sure when you walk the course you remember your ride time, and where the sun will be casting the most shade," advised the captain.

He stepped up to the caterer and ordered five breakfast sausages as I replied, "But the ditch portion is very dark in there, from a horse's perspective, and when he's never seen it before!"

Thinking back on this now, I still can't believe I spoke up like that. So, I did have some backbone once upon a time…

"You'll be fine," said the course designer matter-of-factly and strode away with his loaded paper plate.

I fumbled in my breeches pocket for the small amount of change I'd allotted for protein before the big day. But the caterer informed me that the man who'd just left had taken the last of the sausages and did I want some fried steak? I had a bagel instead but was always rather resentful that the captain couldn't have left me one bit of inexpensive meat.

We didn't need it though, as it turned out. I had plenty of energy

to burn that weekend, and Harvest Gold was a star. He flew through the water jump (same one at which Princess Anne had fallen 15 years before) and the coffin's ditch in the woods harboured no scary threats in its dark depths for my boy. Like me, Harvey was unathletic but got over life's obstacles with sheer determination. After that glorious weekend, we were ranked fourteenth provincially, and I was to have many more heady periods of adrenalin-injected moments that same season with my beloved and incomparable Harvey, whom I'd rescued 'off a meat-truck' (or, in the UK, 'from the knacker's yard.') Though he never refused a jump, Harvey did however always go right to the base of it and then would chip-in with an extra little step. He was brave but didn't quite have the scope or ability to jump fences in stride. It always struck me as a good metaphor for how I went about life as well.

However, when I next rode a Mark Phillips course, many years later after the turn of the millennium (and this time far across the continent in Montana) I'd already undergone two of my three spinal surgeries. I'd had to leave England and my teaching post there, sell most of my horses, keeping only the one youngster I'd bred myself, and move to partake of a 'less-stressful' life. Doctor's orders... I wasn't to do anything strenuous or overactive. This consisted, in part, of living in a log cabin in the Rockies and teaching high school on a Blackfeet reservation where class size was smaller and supposedly less intense.

The grandson of the tribal chief I was dating then had a nickname for me: Iron Bone. He knew about my disabilities and all the metal in my spine. He had listened to my symbolism about not ever being able to 'straighten up,' and he knew about Harvest Gold and the metaphor about us not quite being able to take life in stride. Indigenous peoples love their legends, and symbolism is an important part of many of these traditional stories. Thus, it was Connor's encouragement of my bravery that helped me make the decision. He said I was nearly as stubborn and as courageous as his once-famous ancestor. So, despite the cautions of surgeon and family, I had to try competing again. It wasn't just the adrenalin rush, nor the heady floating of galloping across waving oceans of green current. It was the joy of packing and preparing for a four-day camping trip with one's horse, the harmony and fluidity of the dressage ballet—when one got it right and our pasture's moose calf wasn't playing tag with his mama while we were practicing. It was the countdown to 'Go' in the start box while one's partner, anticipating what was coming, could barely contain his excitement, adding doubly to one's own. And of course, it was the intensity and often pure luck of the show-jumping course to add to the overall score, with coloured rails that would tumble down if the horse so much as farted.

All of these and many more fed my addiction for eventing, one of the few equestrian disciplines which, in the 'good ole days' could be achieved inexpensively on your backyard horse, provided the proper conditioning and training was at hand. So, with my home-bred-and-schooled youngster, Arrow Straight (Connor had helped me name him, because of his love of my straightening-up metaphor), I drove my ancient horse-van through the treacherous mountain pass that day on the way to the show grounds at the inaugural Kalispell Horse Trials, beautifully decked out in the splendour of the sunny valley beneath the snow-peaks. I was the Canadian Mountie, mounted up in the Mountains of Montana.

Arrow and I set up camp—well, I did most of it. He just stood tied to the horse van and tugged at his hay net. Not only was my truck an antique, with a home-made interior, but I'd never been able to afford a groom like most other competitors at our level. So, though I might once more eat breakfast this weekend with the father of a princess and reigning World Champion, I would be dressed in second-hand dressage breeches with re-sewn suede patches and my uncle's too-large leather boots whilst I stood on my crooked legs on an upturned bucket and braided my own horse's mane.

We did not, however, dine with Mark Phillips this time, and maybe it was just because I was getting older, but his latest course scared those second-hand breeches right off my bottom. (That's 'fanny' in the USA!) After walking it early the next morning, I could barely concentrate on the first phase—our dressage test—but I managed to guide Arrow Straight through a passable example. His extended trot across the second diagonal was a little strung out, and our final salute at "X" wasn't quite square. But after the results were in, we placed ninth out of 26 in the division, going into the cross-country phase.

"Three, two, one...GO! Good luck!" chanted the start box official, in the same tone as every other start box official around the world. (This consistency gave one a wonderful sense of calming familiarity before the death-defying act about to be produced. And the one to which I'd been specifically restricted, of course.)

We shot out of the box and launched easily over the oak barrels with flowers planted on top, then raced up the hill to the stone wall, and down through the quarry, galloping over two ditches. Unlike Harvest Gold, Arrow had the athletic ability to take everything in stride. If he felt like it. But he also liked to take things askew, just as I'd entered the world. And so it was that at a simple chicken coop under a red maple tree (more Canadian irony for me), Arrow Straight lost his straightness for one instant that could have cost me my life, or at least, as it did to Christopher Reeve at a similar fence, my mobility. And I was no Superman.

He stumbled in the shade of the tree as it was a thoroughly trampled bit of mud underfoot by now, then righted himself to jump but realized the angle was wrong. I leaned forward and yanked hard to the left, and he managed to scramble over the coop anyway. And though I felt a marginal tug in my lower back, old Iron Bone kicked on.

After the cross-country, we were now in fourth place, going into the stadium jumping phase; however, it was not to be. When I dismounted after the last straw-bale-with-scare-crows jump and walked gently to cool out my glistening bay horse, I bent to pick up his pail of water and SNAP! Whatever pins were still holding my spinal column together at this point let loose, and I passed out on the ground.

Three weeks, a five-hour surgery and quarts of morphine later, my spine had sufficiently mended to return home. Here, for the third time in a decade, my poor mother spent the next two months nursing me back to where I could at least manage to get to the toilet and lower myself to the raised oval seat alone. Slowly recovering with physiotherapy, I was told I could be almost 'normal' once more. I would have to go back to wearing braces on my legs much of the time. I was also told I would often have to sit and rest both back and legs. But jumping and galloping a horse? Never! Not ever again, they said—or I would risk becoming paraplegic.

My beloved Arrow Straight was sold, Connor and I broke up, and though I tried to return to teaching school after four months of rehabilitation, I felt lost. My soul had been snatched away. I was forced to move to a city closer to medical care and so despised everything about this new so-called life, desperation drove me to answer an advertisement which of necessity I kept secreted from my family.

*Equestrian centre in heart of Yorkshire Dales seeks riding guide/instructor. Stone cottage plus fair salary.* As a certified riding instructor and competitor, I was offered the post almost immediately, with just an emailed CV and a few telephone exchanges.

However, I was spineless, still—figuratively at least. I had no backbone to stand up to my loving sister, my doting mother, the principal of my school, the surgeon. Everyone's voices, their strict advice, kept whirling in my head. I needed pastoral countryside again.

I left behind job, family, household belongings...and seven months after the surgery on my spine, I was back up on a horse, another stocky buckskin (Fjord) like my first wonderful Harvest Gold. And as we slowly, gently cantered to the top of a heather-brushed hill, looking down on my little stone cottage in the twilight, with a roe deer bounding past on one side and the sun setting on the other, I knew I was truly recovered. All the physical bits can be pieced back together, but if the soul is lost, this must also be repaired, no matter the risk or the cost. I gave up on my superstitions and the tilting-the-cosmos coincidences. I was only responsible for my own actions, but of this I was most whole-heartedly and happily responsible indeed! *Only* me. And thus, magically, I don't seem to have caused any more catastrophic world losses since moving back to the UK. I take one obstacle at a time now, as it comes to me. Taking it in stride is rarely an option in this life, but chip-ins before every obstacle to gain a bit more balance, strength and determination are commendable. And it was for this, (as much as my instructing several British Olympic riders in the decade to follow) that the Queen saw fit to come pin a medal on me.

I will never jump again, I know. I often have to coach in the ring from my wheelchair. But one special season, I travelled to Gatcombe Horse Trials, sleeping in a student's horse van high on a grassy hill in the Cotswolds above Princess Anne's residence, excited as always, just to know a three-day event was about to begin, and that I was on the premises. Perhaps in the morning I'd split a breakfast sausage with Mark Phillips. Maybe I could even convince him he owed it to me to spring for it.

Iron Bone will kick on.

# SOMETIMES YOU...

## TONYA LIBURD

...fly.

Lying down on the grass in College Park in downtown Toronto, high, but not on drugs, memories of lazy beer-fed summer evenings swimming in your head...

Then they show up in your vision. Three of them.

The first one, a young man with a corned beef complexion, with far too much blonde hair for one human being...

The second: carroty hair matted over his face. Some pimples.

The third. Eyes that are sharp, that are flinty, that don't waver.

Said the first: "He looks like a guy trying to figure out how to open a bottle of whiskey from the inside." Rough laughter. A mean smile.

A cool breeze set the foliage in the park whispering.

You feel an exhausted gravity weigh itself around you.

*Why?*

You paste on a smile. This is the pain of being alive...

You have the prerogative to remain silent, but not the ability.

"Well, hello, gentlemen."

The first one's face betrays annoyance.

The meal of a while ago is a warm memory in your stomach. Too bad you may be bringing it up soon...

"Let's get this one over with, shall we?"

The second one's face fists angrily.

The look on the third's face... to know that someone is a knife—sharp, deadly—and to watch that knife turn against you...

Falcon-like eyes good for hunting narrow. He gives you a penetrating look as if wanting to peel away the skin to see what is underneath.

A tune escapes you in a hum. You can't help it. It's a coping reflex.

The first's expression changes from annoyance to a cold, glittering readiness.

*Here it comes.*

"Fuck you, you crazy freak."

Hands grasp you and lift you up from the grass.

You pass a blur of walls and cars and enter the throat of an alley.

There, they beat you up.

Even among the already discarded, lost and hungry, you are reminded that you are *different*, that you are *other*, that you are unwanted and crazy...

You try and smile past the busted, bloody lip.

*Why?*

The first passes a hand to pull back his bangs from his face and looks down at you on the ground.

"Fuck you." *Kick.*

A shoe adds to the hurt you already feel in your side.

"Crazy fucker."

Are they afraid of the unknown?

They are all looking down on you.

The second spits on you.

A little snowfall of cigarette ash. The third flicks until nothing falls.

Then you are alone.

Alone with your thoughts.

With the pain.

You stand, alone with the almost-autumn air, the garbage and recycling bins put out for emptying; sick with tension, you throw up.

...hurt.

You gather your battered, bruised body and head to the youth shelter you're currently staying at by Gerrard and Yonge Street, literally across Yonge from College Park, at the Four Seasons of shelters—especially for youth—thinking longingly of your bed.

But Sandra's on staff today. She sees you, blood crusting redly on your shirt and mouth. And makes a beeline straight for you.

"What happened to you?" she asks, her gentle voice full of alarm.

"Nothing." And you try and walk past her.

She doesn't move. She isn't taking that for an answer.

You look at the white walls, at the comfortable blue and pink pastel sofas behind her. You don't want trouble. It'll make things worse for when the staff isn't around...

"C'mon. You can tell me. You're supposed to be *safe* here..." She takes you gently by the arm. "Come. We can talk alone in an office..."

You shrug her off. Silently, you shake your head.

"You're *sure?*"

Stiffly, you nod.

She sighs. "Okay. But if you change your mind..."

You limp to your room. You open the door.

Guy number two is in there. He turns around to look at the door.

*He got the empty bed across from you!*

He sees you. His eyes narrow. "What the fuck...?!"

You stumble away, your head mutely shaking side to side...

Where to go? Where to run?

You head down the beige-carpeted hallway onto the bare stairs and crumple into a heap halfway down. You're whimpering uncontrollably.

*Stop. Stop...*

Guess who's coming up the stairs.

Sandra.

"Robin? *Robin?!* What's wrong...?!"

She takes you by the shoulders and tries eye contact, but you're not there. You're not looking at her. You're floating, you're humming a song to yourself...

"Who's 'in there'? Your room?"

You must have spoken. She knows.

She takes you into her arms. "Oh, baby," she says, rocking you.

If it weren't for the fact that you're well known in the shelter, and especially to her, there wouldn't be physical contact. She's taking a job risk...

But it works. Human contact. Like you had with your mother. You hear yourself talking.

"The guys who beat me up... one of them's in there..."

"Oh my god."

You stop, reminded of the threat of the situation. Your words run, hide. You choke up. You... start crying.

"Okay," she says. "Come... come."

Sandra manages to get you to your feet, and this time you and she go to a small meeting room. And you tell all.

"Do you want to press charges?"

Emphatically, you shake your head no.

She sighs again. You know she'd prefer you to. But it's your choice.

She's got a determined look on her face when she leaves the room, instructing you to stay put.

Eventually, you're informed the person's been kicked out of the shelter, the other bed in your room's now empty, and it's safe for you to enter. But maybe you want to go get some dinner first?

Numbly, you nod. You eat dinner, the scent of the roasted chicken not even rousing you, then make a beeline for your room.

This is the pain of being alive...

Alive, unlike your mother.

What it's been now, three months? Six? You're not missing time, but you have a bad sense of it passing.

You have absolutely no idea if you have any surviving family. It's always been just you and her. In the apartment. And it was... a *mess* when the building staff came in after she died. Your mom isolated herself quite a bit. You couldn't tell where even her acquaintances lived. Not even the woman down the hall really counted. Then you were 18, and you just... wandered off.

You fold yourself into bed.

*Folding yourself... like you reflexively did when they were beating you, kicking you...*

You burden your tissues with sadness.

...want revenge.

A couple of days later you are on your feet, sharking around the room.

The fear after the beating has gone; emotions not linked to fight or flight have risen to the surface. Like anger.

You feel like having revenge.

It fills your head, it presses into the bones of your skull. Pounding, pushing it apart...

You pass by the door for the umpteenth time. Unconsciously, you open it and march right out into the hallway. You somehow find yourself, in your pacing, back in your room again.

You imagine guy number two, he who had been assigned the bed across from yours. You imagine finding him alone in an alleyway, not unlike the one they dragged you to. You imagine telling him off. You dip away from reality; you feel energized. In real life, you start talking out loud, talking to yourself. You imagine taking him on, taking him out. Swing, punch. Punch again. He falls. You spit on him, the memory of the warm wet saliva hitting your face as he spat on you in the alley. Tit for tat.

You imagine his life struggling redly out of him in bubbles.

"Robin..."

You think for a moment he is trying to say your name with his last breath...

"Robin!"

No. Someone's talking to you. In the hostel.

You snap back to reality.

Sandra.

Why is she always there when you screw up? Doesn't she have days off?

"Robin. Are you okay?"

Your gaze drops to the floor.

"Are you here with us now?"

You nod mutely.

"Okay. You're assigned to me again. I'm doing overnight today. I'll... talk with you after dinner, okay?"

You mumble. "All right." And she walks away from your door.

You slump to your bed. Take a deep, shuddering breath.

Later, after dinner, next to a wall by a bulletin board stuffed with notices, Sandra sits down opposite you on some chairs off in a corner of the main floor of the hostel, where no one can overhear the two of you. She gives you a long, deep look. Sandra. A woman with fox-sharp eyes. Her smile pierces you.

"How are you doing."

You shrug, looking to your feet, shifting in your seat. "All right, I guess."

"I don't think you're doing as well as you should or can be. I think we should talk about finding you a doctor, Robin."

"A shrink?"

"Yeah." She pauses, looking at you.

She sees right through you, and you don't like it one bit.

"I wonder what you are thinking. Can you tell me?"

"Uh..."

She tilts her head, waiting patiently.

"Are they going to screw me over? People don't like crazy people, even the shrinks. I had a bad therapist once..."

"How about this. We go to check out the psychiatrists and the therapists together. So you won't be alone. I promise I'll do everything in my power to make sure you're not screwed over."

You take this in, nodding.

"Another thing. This might be harder. You'll have to consider that the doctor would think you might function better day-to-day taking some medication, and prescribe some for you. For what it's worth...

I think you can benefit from taking some regularly." She let that sit.

Quite frankly, you're tired of fighting to stay moored when things get hairy. It didn't used to be this way when you were a young kid. But then you hit twelve...

"Okay."

"Just okay? No questions? No second thoughts?"

"No." And this time you look her in the eye.

Her expression grows studious, olive green eyes narrowing thoughtfully. "Okay. We'll talk more tomorrow. I have a couple days off after that, then I'm back for the weekend. How's that sound?"

"Sounds okay," you mumble.

"Have a good night's sleep." She gives you a pat on the shoulder and gets up.

In your room at bedtime, your mind races, as it is wont to do.

You feel a chapter of your life ending, and a page turning to a new one.

You lie still and feel the moment.

It informs your dreams as you sleep.

...feel everything shift.

So you're accompanied by Sandra, just like she promised, when it's time to pick a shrink and a therapist. The fear is real, the stakes feel insurmountable, but...somehow you get in the groove of confiding your thoughts, wishes...pain.

And being heard.

This is wild. They believe you. They respect you. They teach you to be aware of your own boundaries.

Boundaries.

You also don't... feel alone.

After a good while, you'd rather trust them than not, and risk end up feeling alone, vulnerable, paranoid...

Yes. This is better.

So this *was* the pain of being alive... being alone.

So what do you do now?

You talk with Sandra. "I hate how abuse victims are always told that forgiveness is the key to recovery," she says, fire in her eyes, "because maybe that's true, but it's not the type of forgiveness they're thinking of. Listen. You don't have to forgive *anyone*, ever. It's not your job. Okay?"

"Okay."

So that question's resolved...

So you go on disability. You start going to a drop-in. One day, leftovers from dinner at 5 p.m. are on plates, wrapped up in plastic wrap and displayed on the counter for a price. It's a talent night. You can sign up to sing. Somehow, one of the staff convinces you to put your name down.

It's your turn. You stand before them in the converted cafeteria, a mic stand in front of you. You start singing.

A prolonged silence.

So this is what humiliation feels like...

You feel ashamed. "I'm sorry." You start to walk off...

Fervent applause.

Applause!

"Hold on. Hold on! Wait a minute."

You freeze in place.

A staff member walks up to you, touches one of your long sleeves reverently.

"That was good. *Really* good. We weren't silent for a bit there because you were bad or anything. I think I can speak for everyone when I say we were shocked at the beauty of your singing..."

He turns around for assent. And there it is. In smiles. Heads nodding. A fist pumped in the air.

"You've got a *fantastic* voice. Are you planning to do anything professional with it?"

*What?*

"What? Um..."

"Hey, hey, you don't have to answer," he says, smiling. "That was very good," he says again. He claps and the audience does again too.

Your mind swims. You think of your mother, singing as she opens cans of food for dinner.

"I got it from my mother..."

"That's wonderful. Do you still talk to her?"

Your eyes mist up. "She's dead."

"Oh, I'm so sorry to hear that. Here, have some water." And he scurries off to a nearby tap.

You're still stunned. No one has ever commented on your voice before...

So you drink water, think, and smile at others saying hello and complimenting you on your singing.

At home, you're floating on a cloud. But not like before. You can still see your feet on the ground.

Medication.

It's... working...

...heal.

You start at the beginning.

You try and see if they've held any of the belongings from the apartment building for anyone who wants to collect.

The superintendent hasn't, but he tells you of a neighbour down the hall who'd saved several personal effects. Relieved, you head to her door.

The woman down the hall.

She'd saved the pictures.

The pictures.

That was a good beginning... you thank her.

"I always wondered about your mom. I'd say hi, but she sticks to herself. How are you now?"

"Better," you say, a lump in your throat.

"Try and... make friends. There's no reason to be that alone... get support. Find someone to advocate for you. I know you don't know me well, but... I'm here if you need anything. I'll do my best to help."

*A stranger is this kind?* Your eyes threaten to mist up. What would it have been like if your mother had admitted friends into her life?

Or was she so hurt by the stigma of mental illness that she decided to let nobody in?

"I...take...medication now." Might as well get it out in the open. See if she'll run.

"*Good*, good." She nods emphatically. "Like I said, I'm willing to help you out if I can. Here's my number." She hands you a piece of paper. Clearly, she has been waiting for this moment for several months now. "I don't want to scare you or anything but...we were worried, some of us in the building. No one could find you. I think someone tried calling the police? We didn't know if people had decided not to bother with her belongings. I couldn't save it all...but I knew the pictures might matter."

Your head bows in shame. Then you decide, why be ashamed? You couldn't have done any different then. You look her in the eye. "Yeah. I'm sorry about that. I wasn't well, then. I'm...better now. And thank you."

Later:

"Hey," someone tells you. "You know those guys who beat you up?"

"Yeah," you say, cautious.

"I heard one of them got into trouble with the police," they say. "Got aggressive. Got arrested."

You take that in. You take a deep breath.

You're moving on in a much more productive path; he's, they're, moving along in a more destructive path. Their tendencies will hang them on their own petard.

"What about the others," you ask.

"They're hiding or something," you're told.

You nod.

You were targeted because you were displaying signs of mental illness.

They hurt you. They scared you.

You lift your head.

*I will not forgive*, you think. *I will not forget. But I will not fight you, either.*

You know now that you have psychosis. Your mother likely was schizophrenic. It still didn't justify some of the things that she'd done, didn't justify completely the way she lived. But you choose to keep her in your heart all the same.

You look through the pictures and visit her resting place from time to time.

You've decided to walk though Allan Gardens to clear your head; your appointments with your psychiatrist and therapist are both downtown.

You've just seen your therapist. Your psychiatrist is quite busy and tries to make extra time to talk, but all he essentially does is clock in to make sure you are still stable. Your therapist digs deep.

You come out of Allan Gardens, the scent of flowers departing.

You start to hum a tune. You stop yourself.

Why stop? You are musically inclined. You have perfect pitch, you've discovered.

So you start up singing a song, low, under your breath.

This is the joy of being alive...

The chapter's page turns.

# SEARCH AND SEIZURE

## SHANNON BARNSLEY

**NEUROLOGY DEPARTMENT, ANSELM MEDICAL CENTRE, JUNE 15, 2004, 1:55 P.M.**

It was happening again. Cassie felt the disappointment, not like a wave crashing down on her as she once had, but like a sinking feeling, one that leadened her bones. The emotions straining at her chest packed themselves into a tight ball that she buried as deep as it would go, even as she tried to float away. She wanted to yell. She wanted to protest. She wanted to tell him he was wrong. But all she could do was go still, nodding here and there, as this doctor, too, told her it was all in her head.

"You're just working yourself into a tizzy over natural fluctuations," he told her, regarding her ability to go from hypertension to hypotension and from bradycardia to tachycardia (and back) in mere seconds.

She'd heard it all before. It was a virus. It was growing pains. It was iron deficiency. It was normal. No, it was stress. No, it was hormones. No, it was anxiety. No, it was her looking for attention. No, it was all in her head.

If only she'd focus on something else and not dwell on it. Go live her life. No, she wasn't having seizures. She was just making that up. Or she was just crazy. And, when she got her friend Jess to film her having a seizure, then it was "Okay, they're real, but they're psychogenic."

Just stop thinking about it. Just stop focusing on it. Just stop obsessing over it. Just stop researching it. Just stop seeing me. Just stop calling me. Just stop.

The test results were all normal again. She didn't have epilepsy. So what if the other doctor had told her not to drive until she was seizure-free for three months? There was no reason she couldn't. She was just afraid. Just letting her fear control her. Just using her 'health problems' as an excuse. Just trying to avoid real life.

We can't help you, Cassie. There's nothing physically wrong, Cassie. The results are normal, Cassie. It's you, Cassie. It's all in your head, Cassie. You're not trying hard enough, Cassie. Stop looking for attention, Cassie. Stop trawling for sympathy, Cassie. Stop looking for problems where they don't exist, Cassie. Stop making excuses, Cassie. Stop missing school, Cassie. Stop falling behind, Cassie. Stop wasting the money on tests and co-pays, Cassie. Just stop talking about it, Cassie. Stop getting yourself so wound up over it, Cassie. Just go away, Cassie. Just stop.

She didn't make eye contact with anyone. She kept her head down. Her parents thanked Dr. Gates for his time. Cassie all but ran from the building, fighting back hot tears as she bolted to the car. She felt the heat of the metal door that had been cooking between the sun and the asphalt for the last several hours. Her black *Prisoner of Azkaban* t-shirt soon grew warm as well, but she felt numb and cold and unreal, floating between realities, wanting desperately to float away or sink into the earth.

If she cried, they were right. She was just weak. She was just overly emotional. She was just hysterical. An overly-dramatic teenage girl making a big deal of nothing. No one should cry because they aren't sick. If she was disappointed, it was proof she wanted to be sick. It was hypochondria. Psychosomatic. Munchausen's. All in her head. All her.

She shut the car door behind her, the oppressive heat making her feel even weaker. She leaned her head against the window and didn't move it again, feeling every bump and twist in the road as she passively absorbed the college towns, crumbling stone walls, country roads, and country stores they wound through on their way back home. It wasn't until they pulled into the driveway that she realized she'd left her copy of *The Hobbit* in the waiting room.

### *EMERGENCY ROOM, ANSELM MEDICAL CENTRE, OCTOBER 9, 2004, 9:47 P.M.*

Cassie remembered the blue flashing lights. She remembered the EMTs. The ambulance lights. She went in and out. Someone was talking to her. Or near her. Or about her. She felt weightless.

She'd felt out of body a lot since her health problems had started. Some nights she had laid awake, feeling like she was going to fall through the bed. Many nights she had fallen asleep, unsure if she would wake up, her heart rate in the 30s or 40s and her BP hovering somewhere near 50/90. This just felt like that.

It wasn't until the ambulance got to the hospital that the truth began to dawn on her. When they pulled the gurney from the ambulance and left her inside. Her feet and mind numb, she followed after them, watching as the girl in the gurney was wheeled into the ER.

The girl in her torn-up hoodie over her Sirius Black t-shirt and thumb-holed undershirt. Her jeans. Her knockoff Converses. The girl with her strawberry blonde hair, now spilling siren-like over the white gurney. The girl with her medic alert bracelet. A single silver snake glinted under the bright fluorescent lights.

She heard the EMTs and the doctors. Car accident. Seventeen-year-old female. Seizure.

The seizure. She remembered the seizure. The flashing lights. Linkin Park on the radio. The other car swerving. The tree. The sound of the metal crunching. The radio going dead. Something hitting her chest. The airbag, maybe? Or the car itself? The smell of rain and earth. Someone shouting. The lights.

It wasn't the first time her head swam and her legs went weak under fluorescent lighting. But this wasn't like the others. The room spun. This couldn't be real. This couldn't be happening.

She watched her vitals on the screen. She watched as the line went straight with an augural screech. She watched as they tried and failed to resuscitate her. She watched as Cassie Pryor was pronounced dead. Time of death: 10:22 p.m.

"No!" she cried out to the doctors. "No, stop! Wait! Wait!"

She tried to grab the arm of the nearest doctor, a blonde woman in her early forties. Yet Cassie's hand went through her like a sword through mist. Cassie reeled back in horror.

"Please!" She turned to the next closest doctor, a young man with shiny black hair and brown skin. "Please, won't you listen! Please! Listen to me!"

The man neither saw nor heard her.

"Please, won't somebody listen, please!"

Cassie ran from the room and tore down the hall. She would have run right into an older black nurse in brightly coloured scrubs, but instead she seemed to fade right through her. Once more, Cassie drew back in horror.

"No." She backed up against the white hallway wall. "No, no, no, no, no, no."

Cassie slid to the ground, still in the zip-up hoodie she'd watched them cut from her body. Her shoes squeaked against the polished floor. The snake on her medic alert bracelet glinted in the harsh lighting. She buried her face in her sleeve-covered hands, sobbing.

"I just want to go home," she cried. "I just wanna go home. Please. Just let me go home. I just wanna go back. I wanna go back."

### EMERGENCY ROOM, ANSELM MEDICAL CENTRE, UNKNOWN

It was hard to tell the passage of time. She noticed the little things more than she felt it herself. The *Order of the Phoenix* t-shirt on the ten-year-old boy with a twisted ankle. The Class of 2009 Beanie Baby on the new phlebotomist's desk. The change in clothing and hair and slang. The songs on the radio. The cars she could see from the windows.

The cell phones getting smaller and smaller and then bigger and bigger. The screens they watched in the ER waiting room and then tucked into their purses and bags like books. The watches that counted heartbeats like minutes. The nurses and interns and doctors that came and went. The patients that came back older or never came back at all.

She wasn't all there, but she wasn't all here either. She was somewhere in between. Between lives, between realities, between the world of the living and the land of the dead, between corporeality and nothingness, between the end and some new beginning she couldn't yet find her way to, between memory and oblivion. Floating through a life that had stopped short as time still spun on for everyone else like grains through an ever faster hourglass. She learned new words, new explanations, new red flags she should have picked up on, new connections her doctor should have made. The diagnoses she had never gotten herself.

Yet still she waited, haunting the halls, going from hospital room to hospital room, waiting. For what, she couldn't say. Jess had come in once, when her fiancé had broken her leg hiking. But she hadn't seen Cassie. Neither had Cassie's first boyfriend when his appendix burst. Or Cassie's sister when she was wheeled into the ER in labour. Or her grandfather when he'd come in with a heart attack.

Every once in a while, she thought someone might have seen her. A glimpse seen here. A whisper heard there. She'd see eyes on her and freeze. Sometimes they were seeing something behind her. Sometimes they weren't. Sometimes she wasn't sure.

She tried to talk to them sometimes. But they usually chalked it up to a dream or good drugs. Or bad drugs, depending on the person. Or they didn't realize she wasn't a 'regular' patient. She looked so real, so 'normal.' A healthy teenager in the prime of life. No one would have thought twice.

There were others like her sometimes. They'd linger for a few days or weeks or months, but usually they were only passing through. They got a glimpse at her in-between life, but then they moved on. They weren't permanent residents.

There were some waiting room veterans, like her, here and there. They recognized one another in the halls, nodding as they passed. There were some that had been here far longer. Ones with diagnoses like *hysteria, nervous constitution, domestic illness,* and *Briquet's syndrome.* People who seemed to hate her as much as they did the doctors.

Cassie tried to give them a wide berth. They scared her. But the longer she was here, the more she found herself understanding them. That scared her even more.

Some days she would pick a patient or an employee and follow them. She hated following doctors, though. Either they listened to their patients, and she would pine away the day wishing things had gone differently, or they didn't listen to their patients, and she'd spend the rest of the day screaming at them to no avail. Most days she just explored the hospital. She found her copy of *The Hobbit* in the lost and found, then the nurses' lounge, then the children's ward.

And so, she stood there in the children's ward one night, staring at the book. It was hers. It was still hers. She reached out to trace its spine, as she'd done so many times when she'd tired of reading over dying children's shoulders. But this time, her fingers felt resistance. She had touched the book. It was solid again. Or perhaps she was.

She pulled it from the shelf. Felt the faded cover and yellowing paper between her fingers. Her name was still scrawled inside in gel pen ink. The pages flipped for her. Her grip tightened on the book and she pressed it to her chest, feeling the cool weight of it against her.

Clutching it like the most precious treasure, she took a tentative step away. The book was still in her grasp. She took another. She left the room, with its bookshelves and bleach-scented toys, behind. The book was still with her.

She made her way down the halls of Pediatrics and turned the corner. She kept going, wondering how far the book could come with her. How far she herself could go. She'd never made it farther than the ER front doors before, but she hadn't tried the other ways out.

She paused, her eyes on a doorway. Familiar, but from long ago. Like something from a dream. Or a picture in a storybook. She pushed open the door and found herself alone in the dark room.

The computer was off. But the wooden bird hanging from the ceiling she remembered. This was where she'd seen Dr. Gates that day—the last time she'd been here before the very last time she'd ever come to Anselm Medical Centre. The day he'd told her she was just letting her fears and her silly overreactions about her non-existent health problems dictate her life. The day he'd told her there was no reason not to drive.

In the morning, they found the computer fried from a power surge. A few days later, they found the old, beat-up paperback on top of a neuroscience journal, last year's *Farmer's Almanac*, and an old *Country Living* magazine stacked on the edge of the desk. The nurse practitioner who found it figured it must have been left by a patient. She asked Dr. Gates for the contact information for a patient named Cassie Pryor, but when he went to look it up, his eyes went wide and he left in a hurry.

"He didn't even remember me," said Cassie.

But he did now.

After that, she dogged his steps. He began to shiver after she'd stand over him for hours on end, but he'd always just adjust the heat or put on a sweater. She tried to pick up the phone, to call home a thousand times, but the one time she finally managed it, someone else picked up. It wasn't her phone number anymore. She tried to log into his computer to find the patient info for her family, assuming they were even still in the system, but it never seemed to work. Keys only registered her at random. It was like using sticky keys through thick mittens wrapped in oily cotton.

Eventually, she gave up. Her family had moved and likely moved on. Though, no matter how many times the copy of *The Hobbit* was re-shelved in the children's wing, it always found its way back. Finally, Dr. Gates stuffed it into his drawer and locked it, just to stop the rumours.

**EMERGENCY ROOM, ANSELM MEDICAL CENTRE, NOVEMBER 11, 2017, 8:32 P.M.**

"Rate your pain on a scale of one to ten, one being no pain at all and ten being the worst pain you can imagine," said the doctor.

Cassie had heard it a thousand times. She looked to the patient. Curly brown hair. Willowy build. Olive complexion. Amos, Sandra, DOB: 03/06/90, according to her hospital bracelet. Her medic alert bracelet was the newer stamped kind Cassie had seen more and more of. It bore the diagnoses she'd never gotten: Postural Orthostatic Tachycardia Syndrome, Ehlers-Danlos Syndrome, Mast Cell Activation Syndrome.

"Nine," said the woman, her forehead knit in obvious pain. "It feels like when I had spinal headaches. I have chronic pain and I get migraines, so when I say I'm in pain, I really mean it."

"So, this is a migraine?"

"No," said the woman. "It hurts more than anything I've ever—"

"This happens often then?" he said.

"No, this isn't my normal. I just mentioned the chronic pain so you have a baseline for what I mean when I say I'm in pain," she said.

"And do you get the migraines when you're under a lot of stress?"

"You're not listening to her," said Cassie.

She watched as the doctor continued to ignore Sandra and then left. Once alone behind the curtain, surrounded by the beeping and the hissing and the moaning all around her, the woman began to cry. Cassie tried to put her hand on her shoulder but couldn't.

Cassie had always thought if she'd just been diagnosed, things would have turned out differently for her. But this girl *had* been diagnosed. They knew she wasn't 'working herself into a tizzy over natural fluctuations.' They knew the answer wasn't to put her on anti-psychotics and 'up the dosage until something happens.' Yet they still weren't listening.

They came back with a migraine cocktail that contained a drug Cassie knew they weren't supposed to give to people with histories of seizures, even though Sandra had mentioned her seizures twice, and the snake-branded cuff on her wrist bore witness to it as well. Then, after several hours, the doctor returned and told the woman if she was really in as much pain as she claimed, she wouldn't be so poised and polite and healthy looking. The doctor who had told her to go to the ER immediately was probably just trying to get rid of her, he said. A headache wasn't an emergency, he assured.

"You aren't listening to her," Cassie growled.

"If it persists, you can follow up with a neurologist or your primary care," he said.

"You aren't listening!" Cassie shouted. The computer nearby in the hall blipped and the light above flickered. "Listen to her!"

The doctor turned to go.

"LISTEN!" Cassie roared.

Sparks flew and the place went dark. People screamed. Cassie grabbed the doctor by the arm.

"Ma'am, you're going to have to calm down," he chided.

In a few minutes, the generator kicked in and the lights flickered back into life. The doctor disappeared in the frenzy. But it wasn't him Cassie was really mad at. No, she knew who she was mad it. And she haunted his every move after that.

Every time Dr. Gates turned his computer on, he saw a document that contained seemingly random numbers. Blood pressures. Heart rates. High and low and high and low and extremely high and dangerously low. Or, the screen displayed 'Postural OrthostaticTachycardiaSyndromePosturalOrthostaticTachycardiaS yndromePosturalOrthostaticTachycardiaSyndrome' over and over and over again. Or, there were search results for 'Cassie Pryor car accident' and image results for 'yellow wallpaper' or 'gaslight.' Or, information appeared about other patients, whose symptoms he had overlooked, ignored, or willfully dismissed.

One morning, he found the glass on his family portrait shattered. One night, the police were called when the window was broken. They found nothing and chalked it up to bored teens causing trouble or looking for attention. Another day he found the lock on his desk drawer torn open and the book on his chair. The handwritten Cassie Pryor inscription was underlined in red. October 9 was circled again and again on his wall calendar and datebook.

He shivered more and more, no matter how much he turned up the heat or how many layers he wore. He knew it wasn't just a draft.

He started calling in sick and canceling appointments. He lost weight. His skin grew pale and ashen, his hair white. His wife started calling a lot to check in on him. Then she called less and less until she stopped calling altogether. His co-workers kept inquiring about his own health and giving him all manner of advice he didn't need and hadn't asked for.

### NEUROLOGY DEPARTMENT, ANSELM MEDICAL CENTRE, DECEMBER 21, 2018, 10:22 P.M.

Then, one night, when he was working late, trying to make up for his absences, it happened. Finally happened. He saw her. Just a glimpse. A shadow. Motion. Out of the corner of his eye.

He ran from the room, his own heart pounding. She followed, in no particular hurry. Alone in the bathroom, in the eerie silence of a noisy building that's gone quiet, he bent over the sink. Cold water dripped down his face and neck.

"Get it together, Jake," he said. "Get it together. You're just overworked. It's the divorce. Get it together. It's not real."

He wiped his face and looked up. Horror twisted his reflection as he caught sight of Cassie in the bathroom mirror. Not a shadow. Not a glimpse. Cassie. Sneakers and Sirius Black t-shirt and torn hoodie and all. Not a day over seventeen. Standing in the doorway. Real as could be.

"Don't worry, doctor." A grin spread across her face. "I'm sure it's just all in your head."

# BACKBONE

## MADONA SKAFF

I lay on the floor covered with blood that wasn't my own. The cop reached for me with a beefy hand, undisguised anger on his face. Only one thought registered clearly through my fear.

My best friend Lucas's last words to me: "You won't get away with this."

As long as no one panicked, and they stayed quiet about what had happened here, it would be okay. But watching the cop's boiling anger as he got closer to me in frighteningly slow motion, I was beginning to think that Lucas was right.

*Why the hell did I do it?* A simple question... whose answer began years ago, in elementary school.

Lucas and I had been friends since junior kindergarten. He was the kid that everything came easily to: good at sports and always got the lead roles in school plays. I was the scrawny boy, born with a limp in both legs, which I always thought should've evened things out and helped me walk straight. But by the time I got to grade two, I needed to use a walker.

Lucas and I had a lot in common. We had the same taste in movies, books, and especially video games. Another thing we had in common was that everyone treated us like we were special. Him, because he was the popular kid and me, the one with the 'special needs.' You know, the 'need' to be treated gently, as though I might break. Everyone was always asking if they could help me with, well, everything. As though I couldn't be trusted to get from the door to my desk without help.

I expected that kind of treatment from the teachers. But what really bugged the hell out of me was that the kids did the same thing. Maybe the teachers made them do it, I don't know. But even the class bully, Jordan, was nice to me. Okay, to be honest, he just ignored me. I hated it. I always smiled, said thanks, when all I wanted to do was scream. I hated it.

Then Petra arrived in grade three. She had round dark eyes and the brightest red hair I had ever seen. She passed me in the hall, walking slowly, probably looking for her classroom. I caught up to her at the closed double doors. She took a step back and turned to wait for me. Great! The teachers had already ordered her to be super nice to me.

"Well?" she said, frowning at me like I'd done something wrong.

"Uh, what?" I asked.

"A gentleman opens the door for a lady, y'know." Man, for an eight-year-old she really sounded mature.

With one hand holding the walker for balance, I grabbed and pulled the door open. Geez, it was heavy, but I got it open enough for her to go through. Then I shuffled through, dragging my walker with me. It was going great until the door started to close and my backpack that was hanging on the walker got stuck. And of course, that's when I remembered the door button. After a lot of grumbling and grunting, I yanked everything free. The next time we met at that door, I used the button.

Petra treated everyone, including me, the same. If you did

something wrong she'd let you know. She was always impatient. Whenever I thought she was behind me, a little hard to miss those loud sighs, I'd move over to let her pass. I even accidently rolled over her foot a few times.

"Ian!" she always scolded, harshly.

"Sorry," I always added, timidly. It was like a game we played.

In grade six, there was one time when she yelled at me for crashing into her, but she'd stopped so suddenly in front of me. I grinned at her, grateful that never babied me. She leaned in to whisper. I thought she was going to apologize for yelling.

"Just because you got the entire school fooled into doing everything for you, doesn't mean I'm going to fall for your act." Then she stomped away, throwing a knowing glance over her shoulder.

What the hell was she talking about? I despised the way people treated me. A couple of the teachers also tended to speak louder and slower when they talked to me as though my weak legs somehow affected my ability to understand.

By the time I got to class, she was already at her desk in the middle of the room. Seating was alphabetical by surname, and I should have been on the far side at the back, next to the class bully, Jordan. Instead, I took my assigned desk nearest the door. I guess it was easier with the walker.

"Ruben!" Mr. Halibut's voice boomed. "Help Ian to his desk!"

"Yes, sir," Ruben said, as he got up from in front of mine and, robot-like, took my backpack off the walker. Put it on the floor by my desk. Waited until I sat down, then parked it by the wall.

But before he'd fully sat down, the teacher's voice again shook the silence. "Ruben! Help Ian get his books out!"

With a tiny sigh, Ruben returned to open my backpack, pulled out a notebook, and placed it on my desk. I gave him a tiny, "Sorry." One side of his mouth curved up before he sat down. This had been going on for four months. Mr. Halibut was also one of the loud, 'let me speak slowly' teachers.

As Mr. Halibut started writing on the blackboard, I realized Ruben had forgotten my pencil case. I reached for my backpack. Unfortunately, that's when the teacher turned around.

"Ruben!" the voice boomed from the front of the room. So that's how they got the expression 'jump out of your skin.' "Help Ian with his backpack!"

I'm not sure why. Maybe it was his irritating voice. Or maybe Petra's painful words. All I know is that I lost it.

"I got it! Thanks!" I boomed right back. Wide-eyed, Ruben turned in slow motion to return to his seat, but not before both sides of his mouth curved up slightly and he winked at me. With a loud, exaggerated sigh, I picked up my backpack. Slammed it on my desk. Rummaged through it. Pulled out my pencil case. Threw the bag to the floor then waved the case at the teacher and added, "See? Not that heavy."

I opened my notebook, noisily flicked page after page until I found a blank one. Grabbed a pen and sat there waiting for Mr. Halibut to start teaching. For several seconds he just stared back, his face turning an interesting shade of red. He pinched the chalk in his fingers as though he was trying to turn it into dust and his mouth moved silently like a fish gulping for air. Several awkward seconds later the math class resumed.

The next day, no booming voice ordered poor Ruben to be my indentured servant. Though Ruben did turn around and silently mouthed, "You okay?" I nodded, and he turned back to his text book. I took the backpack off my walker and put it on the floor near my desk. Parked it by the wall then limped the four steps to my desk—just like a 'regular' person.

Before I knew it—lunch time. I was starved. Having a desk near the door also meant I was first out of it.

Lucas had play practice at lunch, so without him to make me hurry, I guess I took longer to empty the books from my backpack and put in my lunch bag. By the time I hung the bag on my walker the hall was empty.

I shut the locker and gasped when I saw the class bully standing there. Jordan was examining me with unblinking blue eyes from beneath bushy black eyebrows. He reminded me of a snake about to spring on its prey.

I reached for my walker not sure if I should say something. Without warning he shoved me hard, knocking me to the ground.

"Tough guy, eh?"

He blinked once. Do snakes blink? Do snakes even have eyelids? Funny what goes through your mind when you think you're about to die. With no witnesses.

I shrank away when he took a step forward. But instead of pounding the crap out of me, he just pulled my walker close and yanked me to my feet. "About time you got a fucking backbone."

"Uh..."

"You made Halibut treat you with fucking respect." He lightly punched my arm before walking away. He never ignored me after that. Not that we became best buds or anything, but at least I wasn't invisible to him anymore.

By the time we got to high school, Lucas and I stayed close, even though we didn't share the same circle of friends. Lucas really loved the drama group, so I hardly ever saw him at lunch. I wasn't really interested in most of the clubs, so I usually just hung out with friends. I occasionally met up with both Petra and Jordan for lunch to catch up on things.

Petra was a top student making the honour roll, as Lucas and I did, year after year. Though not a top student, Jordan was putting effort into school. He had friends and was turning into a really nice guy. In grade nine he joined the school band playing saxophone and by grade eleven was so good that he got the chance for a big solo during the Christmas concert.

Show time!

Lucas and I arrived early to get a good seat in the gymnasium, which had been set up with chairs like an auditorium. Only a couple of band members were on stage practicing. Jordan was also there holding his saxophone in his arms like it was a baby and talking with Petra. He wore a huge smile, and when he saw us he gave a big thumbs up. I returned the gesture, while Lucas just waved.

"Save me a seat, please?" Petra called to us. Lucas rushed ahead to grab three chairs on the aisle, just behind the rows reserved for parents.

I sat on the aisle, while Lucas moved in to save the middle seat for Petra. He said, "Jordan looks so calm. I thought he'd be nervous."

"He's really ready. I've seen him in the music room practicing every lunch period."

"Hey, I heard his dad is coming," Lucas said.

"Really? I don't think he's ever been here before," I said. Jordan was always so close-mouthed about his family.

When the lights dimmed, Petra rushed to take her seat next to me.

The band played a couple of nice Christmas tunes, then we came to Jordan's solo. He stood up, and started to play. The crowd was silent. No coughing or little kids whining. Just his music. Normally, I'd prefer listening to modern rock or things like that, but his classical solo reached deep inside of me. I'd never been the emotional type, but my eyes actually started to tear up.

Loud voices shattered the mood. An angry man shouted incoherent obscenities at the band. I heard chairs scraping on the floor. Then several parents in the first row jumped out of their seats and stood protectively in front of young children. Chairs were flung everywhere as a man made his way past whimpering children. A few slurred words floated above the chaos.

"That's what you're wasting time on at school? Goddamn music?" Then he stumbled out, still cursing and waving his fist at the band.

"Oh, my God," Petra whispered.

Only now I realized that the music had stopped. Jordan clutched the saxophone protectively to his chest a look of horror and pain on his face.

"What happened?" I asked Petra, who was trying to get past without knocking me over.

"That's his dad. Drunk like always." She ran to the front, climbed up on stage to go to Jordan's side. He'd sat down and was slumped forward in his chair, his shoulders quivering as band members to either side comforted him.

The lights came up as the principal came on stage to announce that there'd be a short break. It took about twenty minutes before things calmed down enough to continue the concert.

Without Jordan.

He quit the band the very next day and soon reverted to his old ways. He isolated himself and picked fights with anyone that dared to look at him. And then the arrests started. Mostly minor offences.

He barely graduated high school.

I'd never known how noxious his home life was.

By university my walker and I had become just another one of the sleep-deprived masses, wandering zombie-like in the halls. I'd almost forgotten what it was like to be treated 'special.'

After graduating from university, Lucas and I started up a computer gaming company that grew so fast, we could afford to buy a house together within a year. I kept in touch with Petra and Jordan. I was relieved when he left his abusive home. Finally free of his father, he managed to turn his life around. He took a few night courses to get his marks up and was accepted into a music program the next fall.

Petra was excelling in medical school. Three months ago she'd met a hockey player, and they'd fallen in love immediately. She was ecstatic and so was I.

Then last month her posts changed. The light-hearted banter was replaced by dark, foreboding imagery. They were worse today. When her cell went straight to voicemail, I really got worried. I had to find out what was going on. Being an expert with computers had some advantages.

I was concentrating so hard I didn't notice Lucas come into my room

"What are you doing?" He peered over my shoulder. "Seriously? You're hacking someone's computer?"

"I'm not..." I broke off and added, "Remember Petra's boyfriend, the one I told you about?"

"The star hockey player big teams were interested in?"

"That's right," I said. "I read in one of her posts that he'd failed the team's drug test. She said that it started so gradually that she didn't realize what was happening. Constant arguments, a shove.

But on the weekend he beat her and broke a couple of ribs. Tonight she wrote, 'I'll be totally free.' And the ones before this..." I scrolled for him to read.

Lucas leaned in close to read one aloud. "'The sun is gone forever. There is no light, only tunnel.' That doesn't sound like her. She should call the cops, or we should."

I turned back to the computer keyboard as he asked, "What're you looking for?"

He was right, the computer couldn't help me. I got up, limped to get my walker from the far corner and was on my way to the garage before he even reacted.

Fortunately, there weren't any cops around to see Lucas run a few red lights, and made the forty-minute drive to her apartment in fifteen. As soon as the elevator doors opened, shouts and screams echoed down the hall. Lucas raced ahead while adrenaline helped me almost keep up. He skidded to a stop at the open door as everything became eerily quiet.

I got to the door, my stomach knotted sharply at the scene. Jordan stood over a man who lay face down on the floor. In the corner, Petra huddled in a fetal position, her arms protecting her head. I finally shook off my stupor and rushed inside.

I went first to Jordan's side and that's when I noticed the bloody hockey stick in his hand. There was a pool of blood on the floor near the man's head.

"Jordan?" I said, gently. He turned to face me. Tears flowed unchecked down his face and neck.

"I didn't mean to," he whispered, in a small and vulnerable voice that I'd never heard before. It frightened me. "We waited until he was out of town for me to come over to help Petra move her stuff out. But he came back. Screamed that he knew she was cheating on him. Started punching her. I pulled him off. But then he grabbed a knife." He pointed at the knife block on the kitchen counter. "Went after her again. I, I just grabbed something." He looked down at the hockey stick in his hands in surprise. "I only hit him once."

Lucas knelt down to check the man's pulse. "He's dead," he reported, quietly. Then went to Petra. As soon as he touched her she curled up into a tighter ball, her terrified whimpers audible now. He leaned close to whisper to her and she calmed down enough to sit up.

"Petra," I cried. One eye was swollen shut. She was bleeding from her mouth and nose.

"I didn't mean to kill him," Jordan told her. "He had a knife…"

I looked at these two friends from elementary school. She'd made the mistake of choosing the wrong man. Jordan had made countless mistakes in his life, especially with the law. Now this. I knew juvenile police records were sealed, but he was still getting into trouble long after he'd turned eighteen. He finally found the right path. But with his tainted reputation… It wasn't fair. I turned to my best friend.

"Lucas, get him out of here," I said.

"Who?" he looked at the body.

"Jordan. The neighbours have probably called 911 by now."

"Are you crazy? It was self-defence," Lucas insisted. "He'll be okay. But if he runs..."

"He's not going to run." I took the hockey stick and rubbed my hands on it making sure my fingerprints covered his. "With his past they might not believe him." Looking at his clothes, I added, "I can't fake the blood splatter." I shoved the walker back and let myself drop to the floor to land next to the body making sure I landed in the blood. No need to worry about a pattern now.

"Why are you doing this?" Jordan asked.

"We can talk about that later." To Lucas I pleaded urgently, "Please."

Lucas shook his head at me, then sighed adding, "If we're doing this, better do it right." He took off his coat, handed it to Jordan. "Put this on to cover the blood." To me he said, "You won't get away with this." Then he dragged Jordan still protesting out of the apartment.

"Petra," I said. She was still sitting in the corner, hugging her knees to her chest, staring at the body. "Petra, can you hear me?" She nodded. "This is important. You have to tell the police I'm the one that came over to help you move. I'm the one that hit him. It's important. Okay?"

Her one good eye blinked slowly, then it seemed to focus on me. We could hear the police sirens getting closer. I wasn't sure, but I thought she nodded.

I looked up at the cop who wore an expression of undisguised anger as he reached for me with a beefy hand. Gently, he took my arm and helped me to my feet. I didn't have to fake the extra trembling in my legs as he guided me to sit on the sofa next to Petra. She clutched the blanket tightly around her as she rocked back and forth.

"You'll be okay," the cop said. "An ambulance is on its way. Miss, do you need some water? Sir, do you?"

Before either of us answered he called the other constable. "Get a couple of glasses of water here." Then he joined the medical examiner kneeling by the body. Even though they whispered, I heard them.

"I can't believe this guy attacked a girl and a cripple," the cop said. I glanced at Petra, wondering if she got the irony of the situation. I'd never forgotten how she'd scolded me when she thought I was using my disability to make people cater to me. But this was different.

"From what I've been told, failing a drug test for some hockey team is what set him off. I won't know till I do the autopsy, but I'm sure it's steroids. Roid rage. It's lucky that young man was able to stop him with one blow."

"I guess using a walker really helped develop his upper body strength," the cop said. "If he'd missed, I doubt he and the girl would still be alive."

I wonder if Jordan would ever know how much he'd affected me that day in grade six. Perhaps part of him would realize that although my spine makes it hard to walk, I do have a backbone.

# THE CASE OF THE SILENCO SCIENTIST

## MAVERICK SMITH

I approached the entrance apprehensively, wishing for the billionth time that my business partner had asked for my input before taking this case.

*Are you sure the door isn't booby-trapped?* I signed to Tia. My scanner indicated the door was not electrified but, like all Silenco children, I had grown up on a steady diet of stories where scientists like the man who lived here were the proverbial creatures that went bump in the night.

*Yes.* Tia signed with one hand while they searched for the keys in the many pockets of her red Silenco jacket. *Our client's husband rented these apartments less than seven days ago, so he hasn't had time to add any security measures. Plus, even if he wanted to, the rental contract on file at the Tenant and Landlord Office explicitly prohibits enhanced security systems.*

*Let's just hope he didn't change the locks,* I signed as Tia brandished the keys triumphantly. *I know our client said it was an amicable separation, but I still think it's odd the missing man gave his ex his spare set of keys.*

*I suppose it had something to do with the fact that they share custody of a little kid.* Tia turned the key in the lock and pushed the door open. *You know, in case she forgot her schoolbooks or finished class early or something.*

*If you say so. You're the one with nieces and nephews.* Like me, Tia had been raised in a family compound. Unlike me, her family included older as well as younger siblings, many of whom had children.

Tia put the keys away and unholstered her gun. *Now that I've re-established our client's trustworthiness, shall we go find out why his husband and their kid have disappeared?*

*Fine.* Although I drew my own gun, given how my hands were shaking, I made sure my finger was nowhere near the trigger. Taking a deep breath, I stepped across the threshold, prepared for laser beams. Nothing happened and I expelled my breath in relief.

*Told you it was safe,* Tia signed, striding past me to press their palm to a switch beside the front hall table. As she headed deeper into the dwelling, the solar-powered lights in the hallway flicked to life, glinting off the shiny metal hairclips which indicated Tia's usage of both 'they' and 'her' pronouns.

I resisted the urge to make an immature gesture at her back. Instead, as she turned into one of the rooms and out of my line of sight, I did the mature thing and increased the volume on my BatEars™. I was the half of our two-person investigative agency with some hearing, which meant it was my responsibility to keep an ear out in case Tia ran into trouble and couldn't hit the alarm on her belt.

Just above the light switch, a gauge indicated how much charge was left in the dwelling's solar battery. I frowned and used my fingers to magnify the display, hoping I was wrong. Due to the frequent brownouts, city council guidelines required private residences to store energy based on a schedule where the battery stores were replenished every seventh day. This one would have turned once the rental agreement was signed and would have been automatically replenished two days ago. According to this gauge, no one had used it since. I texted my findings to Tia, then opened the drawer of the front hall table. The plain, unlabelled file folder in it made my eyebrows rise and they rose higher when I opened it.

The folder contained mail. Some of it consisted of individual letters from magazines arranged together to convey different sentiments, while others were written out in crude slanted writing. There were tons of pages and, as I flipped through them, I realized they were all unflattering. Most of them seemed to describe exactly what the authors thought of scientists in general and Silenco scientists who tinkered with genes in particular. I was still sorting them into piles of general to specific threats when Tia returned from searching the rest of the dwelling.

*Did you find anything?* I asked her.

*Nothing useful,* Tia signed in reply. *I found loads of half-written letters in his study, all apologies where he asks for forgiveness and wants to get back together when, as he writes, 'it is safe.' He didn't elaborate on what that means, though.*

*I may have found the answer out here.* I gestured at the letters I had spread out across the hall table. *It seems this is a cache of hate mail. The client's husband was helpful enough to date each one as it arrived. The earliest one is from three months ago, and the most recent is from two days ago.*

*Then that is the one we should look at, since the solar battery gauges indicated that no one has been home for two days.*

*I agree.* I found that one in the pile of specific threats and handed it to Tia. *What do you think the lines 'we know everything' and 'will collect what we are owed' mean?*

*Non-recycled paper indicates money.* Tia rubbed the glossy paper between the tips of her gloves. *An off-world consortium would be interested in the work of a geneticist. Since this picture was on the fridge, I think we can guess what sort of genes he works with.*

The picture she handed me was a child's drawing of an iguana, equal in size to the kid with braids and a red jacket who stood next to it. The iguana had been coloured in three different shades of red, which made sense, given that the drawing was titled 'Big Red.'

*Breeders are always looking for an edge in iguana racing,* I named one of the archipelago's popular tourist attractions. *If this size is accurate, some off-world consortiums would kill to get their hands on this specimen or its offspring. The drawing also indicates he took his daughter to the lab at least once.*

*We need to find that lab,* Tia signed. *Our client had no success at the Land Grants office, since his husband kept the business in his*

*name, but I bet you can convince the receptionist to let you see the listings.*

*What? Why?* Of the two of us, Tia was more known for her charm than I was.

*You'll see,* my business partner promised.

Sure enough, when we entered the Land Grants office, the Silenco receptionist at the counter looked inordinately pleased to see me. When I explained our request to see the business holdings of our client's husband, he leaned forward, running one hand over the shiny new pronoun hairclip pinning his braids back. His signed his reply quickly, his fingers moving almost too fast for me follow.

*You want the name of my surgeon?* I touched my newly flat chest.

*As long as they did good work.*

*She promised a 'reduction with sensitivity.'* I transferred the surgeon's contact information to his personal TextTalk™ device. *I've yet to write a review, but so far her results fulfill that promise.*

*Wonderful.* The smile showed dimples in the young man's cheeks. *Here's the lab address.* He passed me a slip of recycled paper. *I added the Global Positioning Coordinates, in case that helps.*

It depends on if the satellite signals were clouded by atmospheric debris or not, I thought, but did not share. Instead, I signed a thank you, and the two of us headed off again.

The buildings in what was widely known as the scientist's sector of the barrio were a veritable warren of addresses. Twice we got turned around and had to retrace our steps before finding the correct building number. The first sign something was wrong came when the door was closed but not latched. The second came as we made our way into the building, where the hallway mirrors that allowed Silenco to look around corners had been covered with black spray paint.

*Off-worlders,* Tia signed and I nodded agreement, grateful my soft soled shoes made no sound on the tile floor. The black spray paint made it difficult to make quick progress through the winding hallway, since we were forced to take turns peering cautiously around every corner before continuing. Once we located the laboratory, the presence of off-worlders who communicated orally meant that I had to assume the role of translator as I took cautious glimpses around the corner and into the laboratory. It was difficult to read complete sentences off the lips of the people from across the room, but their threatening demeanour and body language made it easy to take stock of the situation.

*They want him to engineer them an iguana to win some race, or else they will kill his kid?* Tia summed up the situation when the type of threats switched from specifics to impossible feats involving anatomy.

*Yes. At least we know where the kid is.* I gestured at the glassed enclosure where a young girl was attempting to organize a clutch of young iguanas by size while their hatch mother looked on indulgently. *She seems to be fine.*

*Yes.* Tia pushed the bright red button at her waist, an action she had been repeating every minute for the past twenty minutes. *If only the fracking grid was up, then we could summon emergency services. I didn't think this through. I should have brought a different gun. I don't want to take the chance of firing a loaded weapon of this calibre in a lab. If I hit something volatile, I could kill us all.*

*If you don't, those off-worlders are likely to kill the scientist and the kid. Especially because he keeps telling them he can't do what they want.* I glanced down at her gun. *That model you brought, it holds six bullets, right?*

*Nine.*

*That's good. There's six off-worlders, so that leaves you three extra bullets. Not that you'll need them. You are an excellent shot. And I can provide a distraction so they will be less likely to return fire.*

Tia narrowed her eyes at me. *What kind of distraction?*

I reassured her that it didn't involve me risking myself unnecessarily. Then I reached above our heads and pulled the fire alarm.

There are hundreds, if not thousands, of species of iguanas, all evolved to inhabit particular geographical environs of the planet's archipelagos. Iguana racing is a tourist attraction and a sport that mainly takes place on land where the scaly skin of iguanas is very susceptible to changes in heat. For scientists like our client's husband, who tinker with how to build a better racing iguana, a fire would be catastrophic, and he would have put corresponding safeguards in place. That much I knew before I pulled the fire alarm. What I didn't know was how distracting those safeguards would be.

The front of every enclosure slid into the ground simultaneously. Seawater began to fall from nozzles in the ceiling. Emergency lights flashed a muted purple and a screen announced the fire services had been summoned. Dozens of iguanas of various sizes sought shelter under the lab table and benches. For me, it was a silent exodus but then, in the large enclosure just behind the off-worlders, something I had thought was a sandy hill uncurled and roared.

The sound was loud enough that with my BatEars™ augmenting my limited hearing, the roar registered as a low-pitched buzz. For the off-worlders, who presumably had better hearing than I, the roar punctured their threatening demeanour like a burst balloon. In a huddle, they shuffled away from the scientist and the enclosure. The iguana lowered itself to all six legs and stepped beyond the bounds of its enclosure, nails leaving gouges in the tile. The beast opened its maw, showing rows of sharp teeth and a long black tongue. I heard nothing but, based on how the creature's neck pouch bulged, I assumed it had roared again.

Tia, who had been observing the scene at my elbow, chose this moment to step around the corner, gun drawn. The off-worlders looked between her, the iguana, and the scientist. Then they broke ranks, retreating up a passageway at the back of the lab. The scientist immediately pressed a series of buttons in the corner of the lab table where the off-worlders had been standing. A metal door slid down from the ceiling to seal that passageway and a heartbeat later, the sprinklers shut off. Once the water stopped spraying from the ceiling, the giant iguana slowly turned and lumbered back into its now open enclosure and stretched out on the sandy floor. The beast barely raised its head when the scientist pressed still another button, one which caused the glass door of its enclosure to close once more. That done, the scientist sagged against the lab table, weariness etched unto his features.

*It's okay, Abbie. These people are here to help us... sorry, to help you get home to Daddy.* His first signs were on a downward angle as opposed to at us, and I realized that sometime since I pulled the fire alarm his daughter had attached herself to one of the legs of the lab table like a limpet. *That is why you are here, right?*

For this question, he extended his arms across the top of the table, presumably so his daughter could not see the conversation.

*Yes, yes, that is why we are here,* Tia signed, then pointed a finger at the metal door. *Tell me about that passageway. Where it does it lead?*

*Nowhere. It just leads to lab storage. No windows, no other way out. It should hold them until the planetary police get here.*

*This button is finally working.* Tia waved the hand at the flashing button on her belt. *They should be here momentarily.*

*That's great. The last two days-* He broke off his sentence and ran a hand over his face. The movement reopened up a cut on his forehead that looked like it was made by a knife. *Let's just say, I am really glad you came. But who sent you?*

*It is not our policy to divulge a client's name,* I answered, falling back on the rules of client confidentiality. The scientist lifted his hands to sign a reply then stopped, staring past me. I turned to see police and paramedics filing into the room. As was typical of emergency personnel, their uniform jackets were a special reflective hue of Silenco red. But these distinctive jackets were not what had the scientist mesmerized. Rather, he was staring at the man in their midst wearing a regular Silenco jacket as well as glasses with red rims.

I felt my mouth drop open in surprise and recognition.

*That's our client?* I nudged Tia, who spared a moment to nod at me before explaining the situation to the new arrivals. Before she was half-way through the first sentence of her explanation, our client, one of the most famous Silenco on the planet, was striding past me, nimbly avoiding the iguanas to enfold his husband then his daughter in a hug. I felt satisfied at the sight of this small family reunited, and more satisfied still when I considered how having had such a high-profile client would increase our business.

*Are you still upset I didn't tell you who our client was?* Tia asked a few minutes later, after we had accepted the thanks of the police and promise to stop by in the morning to give a formal statement.

*No,* I reassured them. *I wouldn't have been able to concentrate, had I known.*

*Good. Want to celebrate a successful case? I know a place by the water that sells ice fresh from the 'poles.*

*Lead on,* I replied and the two of us headed off into the humid evening, arm-in-arm.

# FLIGHT

## GEORGE ZANCOLA

A cigarette burned close to Tom Harold's fingers. Nicotine stains spread out on his hands like a crude road map. He was embarrassed by their distinction as the prominent feature on his person. They flared at his knuckles like botched tattoos. Tom's pensiveness was at a broil. The sun was raging mercilessly. Heat warnings had been in effect all week. All along the length of the boulevard, there was no respite from the torrid temperature. Searing like brands, the chrome and the coloured metals of the parked cars on the roadway stamped their reflected light into Tom's eyes. The street, and the heavy traffic roar from it, brought to his mind the image of a smelting furnace.

Tom was walking with an associate who was into falsetto wailing. Tom had become inspired enough to answer his companion's shrill song with a plaintive howl that was part hum, and part cry. Both of them were dressed in clothes that were too heavy for them, as if they meant to be armoured against the stuff of summer. The lament that issued from them was pitiful.

Tom, and his friend, were heading to the streetcar loop west of Kipling avenue. The heat, the blinding light, and the unkind surroundings along Lake Shore Boulevard combined to bring their high spirits into a downward spiral. Hospitable cafes, user-friendly restaurants, and beer establishments were in short supply. As well there being a lack of places to imbibe, they hadn't enough money to buy a cold drink for themselves.

For over an hour they walked in the abusive heat of this roadway crucible. They must have appeared an odd pair as they stalked Lakeshore Boulevard. They prowled along this road like a pair of hungry wolves. Their focus was on what they needed to accomplish, which wasn't very complicated. The objective was to create a safe distance between themselves, and their point of departure.

As they neared the streetcar hub, Tom's companion began to interrupt a growing silence between them by speaking incomprehensible, mumbled phrases. The sing-song they had been engaging in ceased. The unexpected fly from detention began to carry more the feel of a doomed event than a celebration of sudden, unexpected liberty. Unmerited favour became a burden they did not know how to handle.

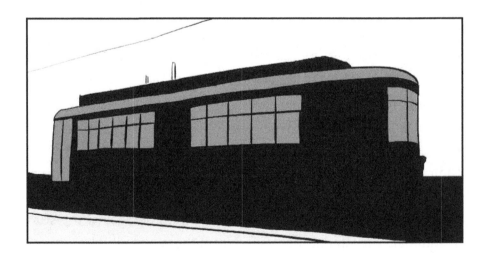

This happened on a late summer day in 1976. Tom and his sidekick had just escaped from the Lakeview Psychiatric Hospital through a door that had been carelessly left open. Unlike any other young dude walking about in the city on that day, Tom Harold's thinking was extremely unconventional. His ideas never moved in a straight line. His partner in this flight was burdened with an even greater dysfunction. They both identified as misfits.

As they walked away from the hospital grounds that morning, Tom's fellow fugitive revealed that she used pseudonyms. A few were given mention. Since Tom seemed a nice guy, she said he could call her Cathy. She told him that all her friends knew her by that name.

Tom and Cathy met for the first time on the ward the previous evening. She was not new to the place. Tom had seen her around before. A kinship sprang up between them. Cathy had been readmitted to the hospital shortly prior to dinner that evening due to a return of her paranoid symptoms. She believed she was being followed about by the murkier button men of an organized crime syndicate. This belief was her peculiar delusion. There were many such mistaken hypotheses put forward as fact by the residents, past and present, of the Lakeview Psychiatric Hospital. Presumption abounded and was given form in the diagnostic manuals of psychiatry. Cathy was in the parlance of the doctors, a paranoid schizophrenic.

Cathy was understandably frightened of Tom when she met him. The dodging of the men who trailed her created complications in her life. Where was it she could place Tom in this grand scheme of things? She had a task simply recognizing the bad guys. The scramble to figure this out lead to name changes, identity shifts, and an irreality of personal identification. There were constant moves from one apartment to another, an ever-changing realignment of friends, and acquaintances. Deep, and abiding, suspicions did not allow her a safe world.

Cathy and Tom hit it off well. He related to her dread because of a similar chronicle of his own. In his fantastic thought he was followed about, too. At times he believed that unspecified powers were doing their best to steal his more brilliant ideas. On a good day, Tom was able to talk himself out of this peculiar mode of reflection. He had achieved some cogency of thought. Or so he believed.

Cathy, on the other hand, was not able to let go of the drama that played out in her head, even when she was deemed to be doing well by the doctors. A sadness covered her. She struggled to find peace. Their connection began over dinner the evening before their escape. Cathy was looking for a place to sit down with her food. Withdrawn and timorous, as shy as a child of three at her mother's skirts, she approached Tom.

"Do you mind if I join you?" she asked. She appeared to tremble as she spoke. Her question was a good one. The place was full of people strange enough that one or two among them might object if Cathy sat down with them.

"Sure. Pull up a chair. Your name is written on it."

She looked at the back of the chair, as if her name might actually be written there.

"Oh, yes. I see it now. They misspelled it again!"

She was in a good mood. The safety of the hospital brought forth a better perspective in her.

Laughing, Tom pushed out a chair from the table for her to sit down on. They talked freely about their past experiences as hospital inpatients. At one point she swilled the orange drink as if it were a fine wine, and declared it a vintage brew of water and drink crystals. The hilarity of it was in the delivery. Tom loved it. He appreciated her sense of humour.

She didn't then tell him her name, and Tom didn't ask. Never too sure of how quickly to allow himself to get to know someone he met in the hospital, he had not come up with any rules for establishing such bonds.

Making new acquaintances created only wariness in Tom. He could never figure out another person easily, especially in the wards. Everybody was weird to him, including the doctors. Cathy probably felt the same way about introductions, too. It had been a rough life, likely for both of them. Cathy and Tom each hoped, perhaps unrealistically, that the recouping of the losses they had sustained in life could begin in one another.

Aimless wandering turned out to be a tiring endeavour. Only exhaustion seemed to result from their pointless stroll. Disquiet of mind began to grip Tom because of the mission's flagging purpose. Cathy and Tom had been thinking in grand terms. They were going to find a new way of life for themselves. They would be leaving the institution of the hospital far behind. Finding Shangri-La, though, did not come with adequate directions.

Tom became afraid. The saunter away from the hospital grounds became a case when life fell short of having a concrete objective. The lack of a clear destination made Tom uneasy. He hated uncertainty. He did not know how to handle it. Going nowhere wasn't his cup of tea. He needed a straightforward and happy outcome for everything, particularly for an effort at bolting from detention in a sanatorium. The better option seemed to him to be for Cathy and himself to return to the ward. A reluctance to express this to Cathy determined silence from Tom on the matter. He didn't want to lose face before her.

Cathy was no longer a comedian. Tom was no longer laughing.

He wanted out. In spite of the good times they had together the evening before, he was ready to leave Cathy on the boulevard to struggle against the heat and the din of the traffic on her own. Increasingly stranger thoughts began running through his head. He couldn't blame her, but everything had changed for him.

Tom could not make himself leave Cathy. Not yet. The argument became complex within himself. The voices in his head chattered, asking him if he should leave, or if he should stay? The debate going on within him had to be settled. Tom's natural inclination was to want everything tied up neatly, with holiday bows. Indecision was his hallmark. This benchmark wavering of mind was now fluttering like a large flag. The need to make a decision was building up in Tom like pressure in a kettle about to whistle.

Cathy would have to deal with the increasing discomfort of their little escapade without Tom. Bafflement, high temperatures, and clamour were not his idea of a good time. Taking a last look at Cathy before deserting her, Tom believed his decision was irrevocable. She wasn't bad looking. The sweat and the youthful glistening on her skin were enough to warrant his continuing to walk with her. Her face, round and pretty, conveyed a dream-like and desirable aspect. His salvation became buoyed in her again. Changing his mind another time was entirely foolish, and unreasonable. Cathy was not able to succor him, or anyone. He knew he was chasing his tail in another romantic delusion, but he persisted. One of his weaknesses was the pursuit of phantoms in love, or pretty much anything else.

Cathy ceased her soprano lilting. Her mumbled monologues increased as they progressed farther away from the hospital. The repetitive droning of her muffled words was beginning to madden him. All the while she kept the pace of a hiker late to make camp.

She was wearing him down physically, and mentally.

Her lips slid about as though she were uttering a prayer calling forth the universe. Her blue jean jacket, too big for her, made her look cuter than the average hospital detainee. This made it difficult for him not to have his heart go out to her. Her hair was shiny and black, shoulder-length. She had it tied back with a red bandana. Her feet stepped in green Adidas runners. His best pretense was to offer himself the notion that he was content with his life, as it was unfolding in that moment.

With each step he took, doubt replaced his clear-headedness. Discouraged of reaching a safe haven with Cathy, he couldn't handle much more of what was turning out to be a purposeless wandering.

At the streetcar loop, the noise of the traffic became a caustic din. The colours on the street were pressing against him like an ill-fitting glove. He felt as though he were aflame. The heat burned the air, the air set his skin ablaze. A yet greater depression gripped him. He was going to turn back. This time the choice he made was final.

Crying was an option, but he didn't go near it. Tears didn't make sense to him. A display of sensitivity wasn't going to help anyone. Turning his back on Cathy, he headed in the direction of the hospital. Being superstitious, he did not look behind him. Fear had him think he might turn into a pillar of salt. Denial kept him from seeing the situation in its stark reality. He felt like a rat for abandoning her. Explaining himself to her was not difficult. She understood by looking at the consternation displaying on his face. There was no need for him to say a word.

There was enough coin in his pocket to make up transit fare. A streetcar was heading east along the boulevard. Tom ran to catch it. The jog did him good, but the feeling of well-being quickly dissipated. Out of breath, he sat down behind the driver. The streetcar was filthy. The image of Cathy shrugging, and slowly walking away from him, was rending his heart. He told himself that life would have been worse for both of them if he had continued walking with her.

He began hearing voices that kept up through the rage of time. The summer turned to winter, and the winter to the passing of years. The boarding houses came and went, so did his buddies. By their own hand, by the way of drugs and alcohol, one by one they passed. The voices continued, streaming harsh and hard. *Where is Cathy? What happened to Cathy?*

# PANIC IN PARADISE

## DIANE KOERNER

I would dream my car was underwater, but these weren't nightmares. Mermaids would be swimming around my silvery blue sports car, which blended into the colour of the sea, beckoning me. But to where exactly?

I found out, after struggling up fifteen flights of stairs to the doctor's office (the elevator would have trapped me in a small space, fogging my brain with perfume and machine oil fumes, exacerbating my Multiple Chemical Sensitivities or MCS). Collapsing on the waiting room sofa, I picked up a copy of a New Age magazine that fell open to an 'old age' mind-body healing retreat. The picture of the class swimming with dolphins sold me. Tropical island life, here I came.

The workshop lasted a week, but I stayed for the last ten years in the botanical garden-like jungle by the ocean. I found a small house of my own by the ocean, at the easternmost edge of the island, which feels like the edge of the world. I am safe here. I can breathe in the warm, salty air year-round…a mermaid.

My best friends are the turtles relaxing in the warm waters inside the reef, who wink at me when I snorkel by, as I repeat the mantra that keeps me calm, "I am happy, healthy, and safe," over and over again in my head. I've escaped into a hermit's life. One day, I will get over my toxic chemical exposure, and I might be safe in the world at large; but here in my own paradise found, it's true now.

My only neighbour, Nathan, does most of my local shopping for me. Why? Because, when I drive, my vision could be blurred with a zig-zagging migraine aura caused by the herbicides sprayed on all the roadsides. Nathan is a big, bald, burly, scary-looking Vietnam veteran, who is the gentlest soul on earth and my caregiver of sorts. He also became my matchmaker. He introduced me to Hank, a hippy horticulturist who planted my permaculture garden, patiently teaching me about organic gardening and using medicinal herbs to help my body detox and to alleviate some of my symptoms. I embraced Hank's organic food, and even got used to his untamed beard. When he embraced my toxin-free existence, he permanently moved into my bedroom.

But wait—all was not perfect in my piece of paradise. A geothermal plant was constructed, desecrating the earth's mantle with chemicals, fracking to reach the volcanic energy deep within and transform it into electricity. Nathan wanted me to join the protests, carrying a sign that said, "Don't Mess with Mother Earth." But I avoid crowds and especially a plant spewing chemical fumes. I just had to email in my protest letter.

One day, enough was enough. The holes drilled deep into the earth caused unsustainable instability and we were thrown off our feet by a 6.9 magnitude earthquake.

I rushed over to see what had flown out of my kitchen cabinets— white and yellow hibiscus-decorated dishes, my favourite green goblets, everything that could break, smashed on the white tile floor. I walked on the cut glass before realizing I was leaving bloody footprints. The effect left a mosaic that looked like a woman's face to me—the face of Mother Earth? She was blowing off steam, and this was just the start. In the days and weeks to follow, the island jumped and shook with 200 to 400 earthquakes a day.

Fissures and more fissures appeared near the geothermal plant and hundreds of people were displaced when steam and then lava started spurting out like no one had seen in millennia. Every photo of the lava seemed to have the face of a woman in it... Mother Earth?

Even though I never thought we were in danger eight miles from the fissures, the roads to town might be closed by the lava flow, so Nathan stood with many others in line at the supermarket to buy what he always stocked if a natural disaster might be coming— bread, canned beans and tuna, paper goods, bottled water, batteries, and rum. Hank thought the rum was the most useful purchase (and drank most of it), although he denied it. Hey, we all have to cope, right?

But the one thing I forgot to do was devise a safe exit plan if the lava reached the shores of our bay... something I never thought would happen. Denial?

Well, the sirens went off at 2 a.m. one morning when a fissure started spurting madly in our direction. Bull horns shouted out the message to head to the Red Cross Evacuation Center, a high school gym crowded with everything that would shut down my lungs, give me dizzy spells, migraines, and more.

We joined all our neighbours as well as Nathan, who started a caravan with his dog to the pet-friendly cacophony of the center. There, we were given cots, and I made a tent on top of one with the organic cotton blankets we had brought and put on my portable oxygen—my own improvised oxygen tent. I rarely ventured away from home, but when I did, I wore my charcoal mask over my special plastic-free oxygen tubing. It was sure coming in handy; I would just need a hundred more oxygen tanks.

The next morning, my blankets had been pulled off by Nathan's dog. It wasn't Hank I was spooning; it was Murphy, licking my face. He knew and liked me, but the tofu and veggies in our cooler wouldn't pass for the bones Nathan fed him.

"Sorry, Murphy," I said as I rubbed his neck and looked around for Nathan. It was only later we found out he had snuck home past the road block to sleep in his own bed and that's where he was found the next morning... cold, alone, and without a pulse. Too much for his heart? Knowing him, I suspect that he was ready to evacuate his life, but not his home.

Smoke from burning houses and trees started mixing with the rotten-egg smell of sulphur dioxide fumes released by the lava. I coughed fitfully, begging for sleep, only to have nightmares of drowning in toxic fumes.

My safe haven was gone. My sliver of safety on the ocean cliffs, gone. The chemicals in the air at the evacuation center, lava and man-made, were making my migraine auras (lightning bolts inside my eyes) appear every day, with pain pulsing from my head to my toes.

After several nights, Hank and I were told to evacuate the evacuation center because my screams were keeping everyone awake. I was screaming in my sleep? To make matters worse, we had no safe place to go. The east side hotels and vacation rentals were filled to bursting with other evacuees, so we headed to the west side of the island where vog (volcanic smog) posed a serious but not fiery danger.

On our drive over the moon-like, eerie road that crossed the middle of the island, the vog became so thick we had to pull the car over onto an ancient lava field. I jumped out and ran to a large rock that was shaped in comforting curves like my idea of an earth mother. I sat down and leaned against it and asked her what was happening, and when it would stop, but no words came, just an eerie whistle carried on the wind.

I refused to budge, even with Hank trying to pull me up. My nerves were shot, I just wanted to rest. I slapped away the pill he tried to put in my mouth but must have taken one or maybe two in the end, because the next thing I knew I woke up in an ocean-front campsite.

It would be another interminable two weeks before Hank and I would learn our personal fate… when lava headed to the ocean. In the meantime, we moved from one grubby, overfilled county campsite to another, mostly eating canned tuna, beans and crackers.

We drank coffee nonstop at an air-conditioned cafe like we were at an AA meeting, so I could escape the vog and Hank could use their Wi-Fi to check the videos of the lava explosions.

On June 7, an unlucky number of a day, the local TV station showed a flyover of my house in flames, its metal roof crumpled like an accordion. So, there would be no going home for us.

That night I dreamt Nathan was flung unceremoniously out of his burning house. Was his spirit staying there until the lava actually took it? OMG, where was Murphy? I forgot to take his dog with us.

During the day, I frequently saw Nathan out of the corner of my eye. I knew it was him by his tattoos. When I blinked or turned my head around, he'd be gone.

Crazy talk? Wait…. Have you ever looked at the bark of a tree or the shading on a rock and seen a face, a nature spirit? Well, I started seeing not only the usual shape of nature spirits, but Nathan's spirit too.

Hank and I began camping in deserted stretches of beach where the freshest air could be found. We were officially a homeless couple, living in a discarded tent, waiting to find out if the government would offer us any assistance. Disaster relief and insurance claims were a choke of red tape that led nowhere but to frustration, angst, and anger.

One night I dreamt I was back home with my family, in Wacky Woods, and epic earthquakes were opening the earth's bowels there too.

I opened my eyes, my face slick with sweat, my sister Susan holding my hand. "Are you okay? You look like shit and smell like the devil," she said.

"How did you get here?" I asked her.

"You mean 'How did *you* get to Vancouver,' sweetie. Hank put you on a nonstop flight. I've got you, and you're safe now."

"Is Wacky Woods okay?" I asked aloud.

"What does that have to do with anything? You are worse than I thought, Patty. Walked off the plane like a zombie. Well, Hank said he had no choice but to give you sleeping pills he got from the Red Cross. But you're here where it's safe, and I'm making breakfast, so rise and shine. I can never remember whether you like two 3-minute eggs or three 2-minute eggs."

"Actually, I'm allergic to eggs."

After some sisterly hand-wringing and comfort cuddles, I settled for a cup of steaming green tea and oatmeal with apples and walnut chunks.

"Where is Hank?" I asked, "and why am I seeing him in my tea leaves with another woman?"

She laughed, "That hillbilly… here? No, he stayed on the island to volunteer at the shelter. But we both thought it best if you came here to chill out and recover. I've put away all our fragrant shampoos, laundry soap, cleansers, and everything else that made you sick here before."

"Suze, I might be safe, but I'm just miserable."

"Think positively, Patricia."

"Okay, I'll try to pretend my loser life is not real. That I haven't lost my home, my boyfriend, my paradise."

Susan sighed then opened her laptop. I saw her searching under 'psychiatrists in Vancouver.' Before she could start making calls, I said, "I need to go to Wacky Woods. Can you drive me to the ferry?"

"No, I've gotta take Jessica to kindergarten, then I have work. But here's some of your overdue bills and other mail Hank had forwarded to this address. He said your post office closed due to lava smoke."

In the mail, there was confirmation that my house had actually burned down. So, I spent the day crying over the piles of insurance paperwork I had to fill out, while I waited to see if my plan would cover the damage. The house was insured for fire but not for lava, and it was debatable which came first, the chicken or the egg.

The rest of the day was not the calm, serene scene Hank would expect me to be having, I'm sure. But how would I know, since I had no way to reach him? Cell service was obviously down in the lava zone. Or at his new girlfriend's house. The girlfriend without chemical sensitivities. The one who could be a Red Cross volunteer.

After a few hours of wiping away tears and blowing my nose, I started ranting and raving over the phone to the already-frazzled insurance agent, screamed at my sister's video-gaming kids, and lay on the couch in my spare time, shivering under a blanket in 59-degree weather (freezing compared to my island home).

When Susan got back, once again I said, "I need to go to Wacky Woods. Can you drive me to the ferry or not?"

"What are you, nuts? Sorry, Patty, I didn't mean that literally."

"I've got magical things to do there."

"Magical or mysterious?" She sneered. "Okay, okay. I'll drive you to the ferry tomorrow. You can take the tourist bus to Wacky Woods from the Vancouver Island landing."

I thought tomorrow would never come. Somehow, I felt the nature spirits in the woods would tell me what to do. I didn't love the diesel fumes on the ferry or the smelly gas exhaust on the bus, but I wore my charcoal mask—the only sign to others that I have a disability, other than my dizzy attacks, when I drop the words in my head, and anything in my hands.

Once we got to magical misty Wacky Woods, there were trees cooling their roots in the fresh water underground and lifting their branches through the fog up toward the sun. These Wacky Woods, created by George Sawchuk, who was disabled by a logging accident, were filled with pieces of art and poster prose that I knew would help me connect with the 'all-knowing presence' and maybe give me a clue on how to move forward.

Maybe there was a message there just for me.

Moving away from the rest of the tour group, I looked at every poster, then every knothole in the tree barks and saw nothing of help. Finally, I saw one nature spirit in a tree trunk that looked benevolent and hugged it for so long that a woman came over and tapped me on the back.

"You're a tree hugger with no boundaries, I see. But the bus is getting ready to take us back to the ferry."

Believe me or not, but this woman was the spitting image of *my image* of Mother Earth. Flowing curly dark hair, a long green diaphanous dress swirling over a voluptuous figure, and a flowery necklace around her neck. I sat with her on the bus. She didn't back away because I put on my mask, like others do. They assume they'll catch something from me, not realizing I'm protecting myself from them: their chemical perfumes, cigarette smoke, and other 'normal' things that make me unable to function.

For the next few hours, I told her my story, shaking whenever the bus hit a bump in the road, or the ferry hit a wave.

After she held my hand to steady my walk off the boat, she handed me her card. Her name was Sapphire, and all the card had was her phone number and the words EFT TO THE RESCUE.

"What is this?" I asked.

"EFT is Emotional Freedom Technique, to help people with trauma, anxiety, depression, whatever. Give me a call if you want to give it a try, okay?"

"Oh, I don't have an emotional issue. It's a physical disability. So…"

"Which probably gets worse from stress, right? I'll give you a free first session, what do you have to lose?"

Susan was beeping her car horn, so I gave Sapphire a hug and ran to the car.

The next week, Susan finally thought I looked calm enough, so she lent me her car to drive to see Sapphire. Her house sat next to a small, serene lake and had a xeriscape garden of wild grasses, interspersed with green statues of fairies. At her front door, I reached up and spun the wind chime and she opened the door in a swirl of blue silk this time, with her hair up in a braided knot and crystals around her neck and on all her fingers.

After I downed a warm cup of chai while describing how many times I had to make U-turns to find her home, she chuckled, "Call me Sapphy. Everyone else does."

"So, what exactly is EFT supposed to do for me?" I asked.

"EFT is like psychological acupressure that can help you get to the root of your trauma and let it go."

"Ever since my chemical exposure at work years ago, I've felt traumatized by the world, the 'world made better by chemistry.' Now, after all the lava explosions, I feel like I've been in a war zone."

"It could be PTSD," she said. So Sapphy showed me how to tap with my fingertips, explaining that I was signaling specific meridians on my head and chest to clear any emotional blocks from my energy system, to restore calm and balance to my mind and body.

Shit, the lava flows had probably added PTSD to my list of invisible disabilities, a new social stigma. But wait, the website I read said it's essentially just like choking, but not a death sentence. "When emotions created by an intensely negative experience don't get digested correctly, negative emotions can continue to emerge, creating nightmares, outbursts, and more," I read, nodding in agreement.

I have to say I did feel happier after tapping. I became obsessed with EFT and even signed up for teacher training. I needed full-time distraction while I waited to find out if I had a home, boyfriend, or community of any kind left to return to.

Cut back to paradise, where the lava eruptions stopped a few months ago. I've just returned from the sparkling new black sand beach that the lava created at the edge of the bay where I lived before. Hank and I, and Murphy too, jumped for joy when we saw it. I hooped and hollered, almost drowning out the crashing applause made by the waves as they broke on the pebbly sand of the newest land on earth. (Yes, I found Hank, and Hank had found Murphy. I think that's what Nathan's spirit wanted us to do).

Drenched with sweat after hiking for an hour from the lighthouse over craggy lava rocks, we fearlessly jumped right in the waves to snorkel in the cool water, soon surrounded by my underwater friends once again—colourful tropical fish and green sea turtles. Later, I walked off by myself and sat against a lava-covered tree whose outline curved like my image of Mother Earth. I closed my eyes and waited. After more than a few minutes, I finally heard her voice (which sounded a lot like Sapphy's).

"I wasn't angry, my dear. The fracking caused the quakes and opened the earth's crust. I want the wind and the sun to be the source for your power. My mantle is not meant to be destroyed by unnatural forces. But I did create new beauty as the lava flowed into the sea, did I not?"

Yes, indeed she did.

And calm has returned to the island. I got my insurance money, enough to pay off my mortgage and pay half of the rent in the small off-grid house Hank had found. It's close enough to our old community for me to offer free EFT sessions to others traumatized by the lava eruptions, which is pretty much everyone. They all wore big black rubber masks when the sulphur dioxide fumes got life-threatening, so my simple white cotton and carbon filter mask doesn't put anyone off now. I'm not hiding away any longer but embrace my new monikers—the 'masked crusader' and the 'wounded healer.'

I still see a slight swirl of smoke in the shape of Mother Earth coming out of a fissure. Sometimes, I hear her voice in my head. This morning she said, "Beautiful is a soul who has been through the worst of storms, but finds the courage to pick up their torch and share the light."

# THE BLESSING COOKIES

## LAURIE STEWART

The mid-morning sun slid through the kitchen window, pooling on the counter in a warm puddle. I leaned into it, pretending to be watching the childer run around the yard. I'd been on my feet since dawn, and damned if my hip didn't hurt like blazes, shooting from the flat of my foot to the small of my back. But I couldn't set me down yet, another pie was about ready to come out. I could smell that it was starting to turn brown.

Soon as my daughters and grand-childer arrived, I'd set a spell. I'm the Voice of Lethe, and I need to be able to perform her rites and duties. Especially baking the cookies. They were my burden and mine alone.

Seventy years of rituals, twenty as the Voice. I'd seen more than my share of sacrifice, that's for sure. If depression be an ol' black dog, he wasn't just following me these days, he was humping my leg. The bad one.

It always dogged me this time of year, pardon the pun.

The screen door opened and in blew a scatter of dead leaves, followed by my eldest daughter.

"Bout time you'en showed up, Sissy. My old bones need a break."

"Sorry, Mummy."

I sniffed, half acceptance for her colourless apology and half disgust over it. When would this woman find a backbone? She's over forty! By her age, I was training to be the Voice and raising a dozen childer. But she'd always been like that, a shy, slip of a girl. No wonder she never found a husband, she never talked to a boy in her life.

So, she'd forced me to break tradition and train Tali, my second daughter, for my onerous duties. As if thinking of her brought her to me, the door flew open, banging on the wall.

"I'm here, Mummy! Brought the ham and taters already done." She shoved a lanky boy ahead of her into the kitchen. "Put 'em on the counter, child. No need to stand there holding 'em like a baby sister."

I hid my grin; instead, I grumped a little and told them I'd be resting on the porch. It wasn't a lie, I could barely move my right leg, it kept trying to buckle out from under me. There I was, done for the day before lunch. Except for the cookies, leading the procession out to the far field, and then doing the Blessing ritual.

Harvest Celebration be damned, this would be one miserable day.

I was drifting off when Sissy shook my shoulder to wake me.

"Is this the right rock, Mummy? I found it on the windowsill."

I roused myself to peer into her cupped hand, and my heart stuttered in my chest. It was the green crystal. Lethe's Jewel.

I smacked her hand, and the greasy-looking crystal went clattering off down the porch. She just gawped at me, a little furrow between her brows. Her round face and slanted eyes made her look like a babe at forty.

"Don't be carrying it around! You want Lethe to think y're volunteering?" Her face paled and she started to tear up. I fought back my sympathy. She had to learn.

"Go wash yer hands, right now. And scrub hard." She fled into the house, the door slamming behind her. "Use the lye soap, it's the strongest."

I stood to look for Lethe's Jewel when something in my back twanged, dang near sending me to my knees.

I tried to straighten up, but a shot of pain rocketed to the base of my skull. *Hell and damnation.* I was stuck halfway bent over. What was I gonna do now, today of all days?

There was nobody about strong enough to lift me to try to unlock the joints, but maybe lying on the wood floor would do it. If I didn't end up stuck down there.

But first I needed to find the Blessing Jewel. Some blessing, whoever got the stone in their cookie got to sit at Lethe's right hand for a year, telling her our troubles and victories. Sounds mighty nice until you realize that the invite takes immediate effect.

I'd lost so many to Lethe's blessing over my years of witnessing the ritual. My oldest brother, my twin, my youngest son... Though some hurt more than others.

Oh, the village still prospered and grew, more babes were born a year than those who died, but the growth was slow. Still, Lethe's end of the bargain was held, the poison that killed the rest of the world was ne'er seen here in our valley, and the harvest was always enough to tide us through the winter. Though some years it was just barely enough.

Fact was, it was getting harder every year. Not by much, but noticeable to us old folks who remembered the way it was fifty years ago. Maybe Lethe was forgetting us despite the Blessing.

No matter, I had to find that damned crystal. I shuffled, step by painful step, to t'other end of my porch. I hadn't heard it fall off, it hit something. So, it had to be here.

But what if I didn't find it? What if it disappearing on me was a sign that we'd sacrificed enough? I could stop looking now and go lay down to rest my aches.

Then I saw the glint of dark green near the old stone planter.

My grandson Frankie pushed into the kitchen with a huge roasted turkey. His eyes lit on me, laying on the parlour floor, and he set the platter down. Sissy fussed that it was in the way, and Tali told him to put it on the parlour table, but he jes' ignored them.

He knelt in front of me, a huge man with hands the size of a dinnerplate. His knees cracked as he knelt, and he peered closely at my face.

"Grammaw, you're pale and sweating, hunched like yer back is all hell for pain."

I nodded, he had it right enough.

"You been o'erworking again," he added. "You got tae give more responsibility to the others. Tali's taking over. You let her do stuff that needs doing now."

"Can't, milove. I'm the one Lethe picked, and that's me until I'm dead. Then Tali can do the rituals." I smiled at him. He was a good man. No idea where he got his size; I'm barely nipple-high on the boy. But his heart's as gentle as a lamb, and he does so love his grammaw.

"I put my back out again cleaning up after Sissy. Could ye stretch it for me again?"

"It's time Sissy learned to clean up her own mess."

"Not this one." My tone told him that was the final word on that.

Soon enough, my pain was down so's to do what needed doing, and a pot of valerian tea steeped on the counter beside me. I needed to start the Blessing Cookies—the oven was empty, and the roast potatoes wouldn't go in until closer tae the feast.

I told Tali to watch carefully, as she'd be doing this soon enough. I mixed a plain cookie dough, adding hard little dried currents and squash peel boiled in sugar. They would mask the feel of the crystal.

I showed her how when the batter was ready, to slip the crystal into one side, so it can't be seen and spin the bowl hard. Even a cook should never know where it was.

We then hurried to spoon the soft dough onto tins to slide into the oven. More'n three hundred cookies, one was deadly. Odds were pretty good you'd be safe. I said a short prayer tae the God of the land, the Green One, to protect my family. I sent a quick prayer to Lethe to choose me this year. I had nigh on a century of stories to tell her. Would that be enough to sway her hand?

Through the kitchen window, I could spy Rose breathlessly pushing her fiancé away, her cheeks flushed and dress slightly askew. Her beau stared at her, intense blue eyes drinking in the sight of her slightly swollen lips. He gulped as her tongue reached out to wet those rosebud lips.

It was a joke by the gods that I could see clear what happened far away, and trip over a pair of shoes by the door.

Rose shifted her bodice back into place. They held hands as they set off to the tables being put together in the near field. They was getting married next spring and here it was only the harvest. Be lucky an' there wasn't a quick wedding at Yule, those two.

I was peeling peaches on the porch when the wind carried Rose and her friend's voices to me.

"If I get the stone I'm going to refuse."

Tressa choked, "You can't. It's a sacred duty."

"I can and I will. Just watch."

I sat on the swing, one foot pushing it back and forth, unheeded.

"I'm old, Lethe. My bones hurt and my eyes are getting bad. It's time." There was no response. "My oath is done; 'tis time for a new Priestess. For a new murderer." My voice dropped. "Or none at all. Mayhap we're finished paying for what none of us did."

Like every year, Samhain dinner was strained. Though the whole village gathered, there was no laughter, conversations were whispered. Fear made their voices brittle as they tried to speak to other families without truly acknowledging them.

At the head of the main table sat an empty chair. The finest crystal and china the village had was placed before it. The best cuts of meat and most perfect of the fall fruits were placed gently upon it.

No one so much as glanced in that direction.

After too much of this, I stood up, glaring at the assembled villagers, though my heart wasn't in it.

"That's enough o' that! 'Tis a joyous occasion, one o' us here will be joining the Goddess Lethe in her halls tonight. A great honour to you and your family."

"What if we have plans that don't include dying?" said Rose. "I'm getting married this spring, starting a family." Her voice wound down under my unblinking glare.

"Tha's no way to honour the gods who gave you life, girl. The gods who kept our people alive when the flames burned the rest o' the world to death. An' they choose ye, ye'll go. 'Tis not a matter for you tae choose."

"What will you do if I refuse, Gran? Kill me yourself? With your own bare hands?"

I sat heavily in my seat again.

"Nay need for tha'. The Goddess chooses ye, she takes ye. An' ye no been paying attention these five years ye been at the ritual?"

The plates were emptied now, the sun lowering in the west. Several barrels of apple wine had been drunk, leading to a shrieking, frenetic cheer. A brassy, desperate kind of happiness. I wasn't fooled. The whole village feared what would happen next.

People's laughter was sharp and shrill. Slicing through my head.

The village adults stood in a rough circle in the field. There were well over three hundred adults and hearty youth. Yet the field was silent.

I stood, bundled in an old sweater, in the centre of the circle. My sons stood at the cardinal quarters holding large wooden bowls piled high with the Blessing Cookies.

I gazed at the sky, as had the Eldest before me. My voice, when I began to speak, was deep and far too loud for such a fragile body as mine.

"As it was in the beginning, so it is now. Our Lady Lethe led us out of the firestorm and to this lush valley. We thank her and praise her."

"All thanks and praise to our Lady Lethe," echoed the crowd.

"Lady Lethe is our salvation. She is the source of the fertility and purity of our valley, our food and our people. The Lady led our ancestors here and gave them the fruit trees and the animals to protect and feed us. She gives us clear, sweet water to drink and pure air to breathe."

"All thanks and praise to our Lady Lethe."

"And she asks only one thing in return!"

The crowd shouted the answer back. But not with joy, fear cracked their voices.

"A sacrifice."

I nodded. "A sacrifice of one of us. A healthy adult to tell her of our successes and worries. A friend to sit at her table and keep Her company."

"She must have enough company by now." Rose whispered loudly enough to be heard. The crowd shuffled nervously. Would this sacrilege turn Lethe's favour from them?

"As it was in the beginning and as it will ever be, I have baked the sacred crystal into one of these cookies. As we enjoy the sweetness of the harvest, so we are chosen. The gods alone know which cookie it's in. It is they who do the choosing, and we who be thankful."

"All thanks and praise to our Lady Lethe."

I watched as four young ladies walked to the men holding the Quarters and received their cookie bowls. They were heavy and unwieldy, but there could be only four. Unless I decided to introduce cross-quarters next year. Goddess knew there were enough people to do it.

More than one person looked panicked as they were presented with the bowls. When any cookie could be deadly, they all were.

I touched the lump in my sweater pocket, thinking how I would explain that the Lady had had her fill of death.

I watched as Rose reached for the closest cookie, changed her mind, and reached for the one on top of the pile. She paused, her hand hovering. She finally chose the pale, almost uncooked one near the far edge. There was a good chance that it was made from scraps and put in at the last moment. Smart girl.

I took the cookie from my pocket and held it high. My hand shook a little, but any who noticed would likely think 'twas just age. Everybody was too nervous, watching the bowls come their way tae notice that I had a cookie all along. I had to go through with it now, too late to change my mind.

"Now is the moment of judgment. Now is the moment we fulfill our promise, our word. All hail our goddess of life and death!"

"All hail to our Goddess Lethe!" The words were softer than before, some voices were hoarse whispers. It happened every year, the cookies in hand made the choosing so much more real.

I reached down to pat the lump in my pocket again. This year would be the last. No more death.

The people watched each other for a moment, fear showing in the whites of their eyes. Then they turned to me, alone in the circle's centre.

I held up my cookie, breaking off a piece, placing it deliberately in my mouth. The others mirrored my movements, breaking off small pieces to chew thoroughly before swallowing.

A scream struck me in my in gut—wild, agonized, furious. Rose.

An answering scream sprung up from another part of the circle— Rose's young man standing with his family. People ran toward her, flying to the stricken girl, to give her messages for their gods and loved ones in the few minutes before she died.

But Rose was no meek girl, calmly accepting of her fate. She stared at the shiny green crystal in her hand before throwing it violently across the circle.

"No! I will not die for you!" She screamed into the chill wind that sprang up as the crystal hit the ground and disappeared into the grass. "I am not yours to take. I have a life!"

I stood in shock, then pulled the plain, grey stone from my pocket. A grey stone where I had carefully hidden the crystal.

I moved toward the crowd gathered around the wild-eyed and furious girl. She was dead already, I thought, she just hadn't accepted it yet. Those oafs with their begging eyes and useless questions were jes' making it harder.

A glint of light from the grass drew my gaze. I stared at it for a moment, then crushed it into the soft earth underfoot. Head held high, I moved to my granddaughter's side as quickly as my old hips allowed.

Rose was pale, sweat had started to bead on her waxy face. But her lungs were still working well. She demonstrated by screaming curses at the people begging her for a blessing.

"I will not die!" she repeated. "I'm *not* obeying your rules." But she was weakening. Her knees quivered and gave out, her lover catching her, to bear her softly to the ground.

"My beautiful Rose," he said. "Hush now, and know that I loved you with all my heart." A single tear slid down his cheek.

"No," Rose whispered, "I'm not leaving you, we're to be…" Her voice trailed off, though she still looked at him, her eyes bright with tears and fury.

Then her gaze found mine and the anger burned away her tears.

"You did this. I'll never forgive you." Her voice was soft as the wind, but sharp and deadly as the knife that had cut the lamb for the feast. Rose's gaze thrust her anger like that knife through my heart.

It was the last thing she did. Her eyes seemed to dull as she sagged softly in Litto's arms.

"No, the crystal's gone. Rose threw it an' I canna find it."

The voices stilled for a moment in shock, then picked up even louder and more chaotic.

"Enowt!" I waved my arms, shushing the crowd. "Mayhap, t'was Lethe took the stone from Rose. Like, to have enough friends by now, as Rose said."

"Are we free? Will we lose no more children to that terrible goddess?" a voice asked quietly. He was immediately hushed by a frightened woman.

"What if it's a test? What if you just made the curse worse?"

"It was never meant to be a curse. My Gran told me..." But they weren't listening. I couldn't bear to see their grief and fear, so I moved to the porch to be alone.

I sat on the cold stone step. The man was right, it was a curse. The best of us were taken; the strong, the gifted. My heart broke year after year, but never enough to die, I always lived to see another Blessing Day.

I shoved my hands into my sweater pockets, hiding their shaking. It was anger, not fear or grief. The anger had burned away everything but itself. My fingernails clinked against something in the pocket corner, half-hidden in the loose weave.

I pulled out the small, sharp-edged stone and the light glinted green off of its oiliness. It was the crystal.

But I remembered grinding it underfoot, stamping it into the dirt.

After a long moment, I put it back and slipped away.

The top of the rocky hill by the river was a hard place with jutting rocks and little brush to slow the cold wind. I was breathless, heart hammering, my legs weak, hip screaming in pain. I stared at the water, low and sluggish after a long, hot summer. It would do.

I looked at the sky but had neither energy nor breath to yell.

"It ends here," I whispered. The wind whipped my words away into the silence. "I mean it. No more."

I pulled the crystal from my pocket and frowned at it. So pretty, a bright yellow-green with sharp edges. So deadly. So bright.

I threw the stone as far into the wide river as I could. I watched it disappear in ripples a quarter of the way across. I nodded, that was that.

I could see the start of the badlands. Grey sand with only rocks and scraggly grass. On our side were green fields, orchards, and wild game. On the other, only death.

I didn't wonder why the life ended at the water's far edge, because that was the deal my grandmother had struck with Lethe.

The deal I was breaking.

I wasn't sorry for what I'd done, nor ashamed. Neither was I afraid of what Lethe would do. Next year I would let everyone think one cookie held the stone, and that it was a miracle that they all lived. That Lethe had ended the slaughter.

Yes, that's what I would do. Now to survive another hard winter, so I could do just that next Blessing Day. I slowly headed home.

I picked up the old copper kettle and pumped the tap at the sink to start the water flowing for tea.

A spark of green on the windowsill caught my eye.

# JUNGLE DEMON

## TOM JOHNSON

*The African savanna, Summer 1930*

Lush plains of grass dotted the landscape as far as the eye could see, evidence of recent heavy rainfall. Lion prides appeared well fed, and even the vultures gathered about the remains of freshly-killed prey, as packs of hyenas fought for small bits of leftovers that the great cats had left behind.

An elephant herd was restless as the cows grazed in the African savanna on this dry, hot summer morning. The giant bull, its tusks long and deadly, kept a wary eye on a young male that shifted uneasily among the females. The older bull was the accepted leader of the herd, and he knew the signs that were evident with the youth.

He was experiencing the 'madness' of the mating urge.

Maneuvering closer to the young bull, the big-tusked male kept between it and his cows. The lust in the youth's eyes was like red-hot coals of fire, and he would raise his trunk and trumpet a lustful cry as it tried to get around the bigger guardian.

Young, and out of control, the youthful beast finally went amok and rushed for one of the cows, only to be stopped by the sharp tusks of the heavier male. A deep wound in its side only infuriated the younger bull. He came at the leader full force, to be knocked to its knees when they butted heads with tremendous force.

Trumpeting in defeat, the young bull dashed into the thick jungle, leaving the savanna and the herd behind. His powerful, grey bulk crashing into the growth of trees uprooting the smaller saplings from the earth as it tore through the forest, amok and out of control, scattering a flock of birds in its wake.

Far to the north, another monster of the woods meandered through the dense jungle of tall trees and thick vines, but this one had little shape to prove it was animal. It was not a man. Though at times it might have resembled a man in form, the creature took on the semblance of the forest itself. Depending on the shadows, it could have been green or grey, or even a dark brown. Its body was more like that of a tree trunk, its arms thick as limbs. Perhaps the feet and hands ended in claws, but who could tell with this forest beast?

The monster had been a man in the distant past, but its memory of that time was dim. He had been a fierce warrior of the Maasai until a poisoned arrow from a M'Buto pygmy pierced his heart, cutting him down in the prime of life. His body had lain in the jungle marshes, merging with the vines, roots, and grasses that grew so abundantly in the rich dark soil, until he became a part of the very earth that had received him that fateful day.

He might not have remembered that day, over twenty years in the past, when his hunting party had been ambushed by the pygmy headhunters, for his memory was only partly human now. Somehow the pygmies had overlooked his body, leaving it to rot in the jungle vegetation. But something had been different about this land, something that was magic. For the living plants covered him, becoming a part of him, and wouldn't let his body return to mud and clay, from whence it had come.

Sometime, during the twenty years his body had lain there, the memory of the man guided the things merging with him, attempting to again form the body of a man. The ugly monster did have something of a human shape: two thick legs and arms, and something that resembled a head of sorts. There the resemblance ended. This thing was no man.

It was a jungle demon. The villagers had given it a name; they called it the N'Domo Demon. A monster created by some hellish magic of the land.

Many years had passed now since it had risen from the ground, not knowing who or what it was. Finding food its only purpose in life, the thing roamed the jungle without thought or reason, other than to live. Now the man no longer existed. It had become a creature of huge proportions, standing over nine feet tall. Its girth was equal to its height, if not more so. Its thick legs were like tree trunks, its arms thick and strong as mighty branches, its gait lumbering, but its strength was immense.

A sound rustled the verdant brush ahead of the N'Domo Demon, and the terrible creature stopped and waited as movement disturbed the tranquil surroundings. Suddenly, a sleek body slid through the underbrush, revealing the tawny muscles of a spotted leopard entering the small amphitheatre.

The beast must have smelled the scent of the monster, for it sprang forward, leaping for the ugly thing in its path. Powerful arms caught and crushed the big cat to its massive chest. A hidden mouth ripped the leopard's jugular and drank its blood as the cat clawed and struggled, until it finally became lifeless and still.

Unable to breathe like other creatures, the N'Domo Demon needed the oxygen in the blood of animals, and dined on the beasts of the jungle. When he chanced to come across a jungle village, he would often raid their livestock. Although he found humans distasteful, he had dined on a few men that had tried to kill him in the past.

Once he had consumed the leopard, the huge monster moved on, all traces of the big cat gone. He was well fed now, and his oxygen supply filled sufficiently for today. Like a great snake, he might not need to eat again for a long time.

When night descended on the African jungle, N'Domo Demon stopped to rest his great bulk on the top of a small rise. He was content to remain motionless as the moon rose full above him, and bats flitted to and fro, catching insects that flew beneath the lunar rays. Several times, birds landed on his wide shoulders, thinking him a tree, while small creatures climbed hurriedly over his big feet and scurried off into the dark forest.

Big cats often sauntered by, sniffing the air around him, but this time none detected the thing perched on its haunches in their path. Even poisonous serpents paid him no attention as they slithered over its immobile frame. The N'Domo Demon was merely part of the jungle that night, neither prey nor predator.

The next morning he encountered a tribe of warriors on the hunt for game, their bodies glistening with sweat from the early morning exertion. They wore shorts made of animal skin, their chests bare. A knife was strapped by rope to their waists. Some carried spears, others bow and arrows. Not wishing a confrontation with the humans, N'Domo stood like a great tree among many other saplings and let them pass without bringing attention to itself. However, one of the mastiffs trotting alongside the muscular warriors detoured to sniff at its feet. Just as the monster was about to smash it with a powerful fist, a man whistled for the dog to rejoin the hunting party.

The huge creature of the forest waited for a long time after the men had passed on by before it began its lumbering journey once more. N'Domo Demon was content to be left alone. He was in no hurry, and had no destination. Somewhere in his distant past, he felt there had been purpose to his existence. He vaguely recalled a tribe, a village. There was a small hut, a wife, and a young daughter back then. He didn't remember, but as a warrior he had looked forward to a long happy life, until that fateful ambush, and the M'Buto arrow...

Crossing a small stream after separating from the hunting party, the forest monster felt a long, thick body come out of the water and wrap around him. A large serpentine head hissed as the giant reticulated python began squeezing N'Domo, a final coil encircling his thick neck. The great reptile was in excess of twenty-four feet long, and as big around as a man's chest. It might as well have been trying to crush one of the wide trees of the forest for all the good it was doing.

One powerful hand grasped the neck of the snake and squeezed until the serpent began jerking, trying to escape that vice-like pressure. When the coils came free from its body, the N'Domo slung the snake away from him, the final coil releasing from around his neck. With a loud splash, the python struck the water and swam away, disappearing beneath the surface.

The forest monster would have missed the village if not for the sounds of children playing among the grass huts. At first he didn't see anyone, just heard the strange laughter, as if something was hiding in wait for him to pass. But then two young boys ran from between the grass huts, one chasing the other in play.

N'Domo stood where he was, like a great tree rooted to the ground, watching the bare-footed youths wrestle and roll in the dirt, and a dim memory of other children at play came to him. Of his own childhood, perhaps, or the children of a village long forgotten. And of a time he shouldn't remember at all.

He was momentarily caught off guard when the two boys came running up to him, and one youngster climbed up his thick trunk to sit on one mighty shoulder.

"Where did this funny looking tree come from?" the boy on the ground asked, as he looked up at his little partner on the monster's shoulder.

"N'Keeto, you mongoose without a tail," the other laughed, "this tree has always been here. If you had eyes, you would have seen it!"

"You are a sleeping alligator, N'Gesso," the one called N'Keeto opined, "or you would know this tree was not here before today."

"How can a tree not be here one day, and is now here?" N'Gesso asked, from his perch.

"Climb up, and we'll be able to touch the moon when it rises."

"No, I am afraid, N'Gesso. The tree is juju," little N'Keeto shouted.

Hearing a voice call from one of the grass huts, little N'Gesso dropped from his perch to join N'Keeto on the ground.

"That's mama M'Bomba," little N'Keeto warned. "We'd better hide in the jungle or she'll make us take a nap."

"Someday she'll feed you to an alligator bigger than me," little N'Gesso said with a wink, and then they rushed into the forest to hide just as a young woman in a thin slip came from the nearest hut.

N'Domo watched as the mother of the boys looked for her children in the compound, and then with a shrug of her slender shoulders, she went back inside the hut to escape the noonday heat. The monster recalled more of his fleeting past as he watched the young woman. Didn't he have a daughter named M'Bomba once, and also a beautiful wife? Where was his wife now? Had she pined away at his loss, to die of a broken heart? Or had an alligator lain in ambush at a river stream, and feasted on her lovely body when she came for water? Or perhaps a venomous cobra had crawled into her hut one night and bit her on a toe?

The forest monster remained where he was the rest of the day, watching the activity in the little village. It was a small compound, with just a dozen huts. There were several older humans, and a handful of young girls. Probably the wives of the warriors the N'Domo Demon had encountered that morning. The two boys he had first seen at play were the oldest of the children, though there were a number of babies nursing in the arms of young mothers.

A fierce yell from the jungle late in the evening announced the return of the warriors. The call was evidently a signal to alert the camp that the hunters were returning to the village.

As they entered the camp, the mastiff again detected his scent and barked a couple of times, but didn't venture anywhere near the place of the monster for fear of being eaten. Besides, the hunters had returned with two wild pigs, which the women began cleaning and preparing on spits above a fire. Here was real food, and the dog sensed there'd be a bone in it for him tonight.

By nightfall, while the meat was being cut, the warriors recounted the day's hunt to the children and women around the fire, telling them all that happened while drinking from water pouches the women brought them, in an age-old tradition as primitive as cave dwellers had once performed in similar hunts eons in the past.

Watching from the margin of the forest, N'Domo wondered what the cooked meat might taste like. He thought he had tasted such prepared meat before, but figured the oxygen would have all been burned out of it, thus rendering it useless for his needs.

After the feast, and the village had settled down in their huts for sleep, the monster ambled through the camp and listened to the heavy snoring from within the grass huts. The mastiff had come to accept the creature as part of the camp now, and merely sniffed at the giant's thick legs, following it dutifully. Upon finding a discarded bone from the pig, with strips of cartilage intact, the dog rushed off with the prize.

Finally tiring of the inspection, the monster returned to the margin of the forest and squatted on its haunches to rest for the night. He had no place to go, and was still full from the meal of the leopard. Besides, he found these people to his liking. Tomorrow, he might be hungry again...

The next day, N'Domo watched as the young women hustled

about in the morning sun, preparing leftover meat for the men while they slept. He saw the two young boys come from the hut wiping sleep from their eyes, while their mother, M'Bomba, gave them some jerky to keep them quiet least they wake the warriors.

Several of the young women walked past him, carrying large gourds, and disappeared into the jungle in the direction of the river. N'Domo wondered if the python still lay in ambush, or if it had swum on downriver for easier prey after tangling with him. When all of the women later returned, he knew that the latter was the case.

By now the warriors had awakened and were playfully trying to wrestle with the women, who shooed them away with a smile.

After a brief meal of jerky, the warriors gathered their spears and bows, and departed once more for the daily hunt. Life was simple in the jungle. The warriors hunted daily, or the tribe didn't eat. Food didn't walk into the village; it had to be tracked, and taken by cunning and bravery. Many times, brave young warriors did not return from the hunt. A poisonous reptile, the claws of a lion, or a deadly arrow from a M'Buto pygmy's bow would leave another young widow and fatherless children.

With the sun rising above the little village, the women took the babies inside the huts to feed. The forest monster was preparing to depart for the jungle, when the sound of the two little boys again drew his attention to M'Bomba's hut. They were coming out to play. The N'Domo Demon remained where he was. After all, they might make a good meal today.

Running and playing, the boys were finding it difficult to keep their voices down, and afraid their mother would call them inside again. Reaching the margin of the jungle, they discovered the tree from the previous day, and this time both boys climbed up the thick trunk and sat upon a strong branch.

"It's moved," little N'Gesso stated, matter-of-factly.

"What has moved, you funny-faced mongoose?"

"The tree, you sleeping alligator," N'Gesso grunted. "It was over there yesterday," he pointed to a spot a few feet away.

"The tree has not moved, you mongoose without a tail," N'Keeto scolded his playmate. "Trees do not move. Only the imagination of little boys with funny faces!"

A spectacled cobra crawled over the monster's foot while the two boys were sitting on its broad shoulders, and he kicked it into the brush before it could climb up his body to the little ones. However, its slight movement was detected.

"See!" N'Gesso shouted. "It moves even now!"

His teeth chattering from sudden fear, little N'Keeto shook his head, saying, "Surely, it was just the wind, mongoose."

But now both boys were frightened. Neither could explain the sudden shaking of the tree, and the thought of a terrible juju came to their youthful minds. Stories were often told of demons inhabiting the jungle, especially the kind that ate mischievous little boys. With a sudden loud cry of alarm, they dropped from their perch to race for the safety of the grass huts.

M'Bomba must have heard their cries, for she came running from the hut to check on her children. Rushing to meet the boys, she caught them in her strong arms, just as a loud trumpeting drowned all other sounds within the jungle.

M'Bomba looked up from her kneeling position to see a mad elephant burst into the camp from the tree line. She recognized the look in its eyes, but could do nothing but shove her children behind her, and yell, "Run!"

The boys were also frozen in fear, and could not leave their mother's side, watching in horror as the elephant charged. There was nothing in its path, and death was mere yards from them.

Then the huge tree moved!

A lumbering monstrosity was suddenly between the humans and the charging elephant. The boys, thinking this was another menace, cried out in renewed fear for the double menace. M'Bomba chocked out the name she remembered from childhood tales around the campfires:

"N'Domo Demon!" she cried.

The giant grey hulk of the elephant bore down on the people, its eyes amok with madness. Only the giant bull elephant had been able to turn it aside earlier, and it was back with its herd. It would take a beast of equal strength to stop the slaughter certain to occur within mere seconds.

A tree appeared in its path. A tree that braced itself with one leg forward, the other massive leg stretched out behind it, and two powerful arms opened wide to receive the charging grey hulk. They collided with a terrible thunder, the elephant's trunk and tusks striking the forest monster head foremost. The impact sent the N'Domo backwards several yards, but the grey hulk had been stopped mere inches from the kneeling humans.

The head and trunk of the elephant came up, lifting N'Domo from the ground for a second, but then the monster forced the trunk back down. There, they waged a struggle never before seen by man. A mighty grey beast of the jungle and a monster from the forest were pitting brute strength against each other.

In the interval, M'Bomba grabbed N'Gesso and N'Keeto and carried them to a huge boulder behind the hut, hoping to keep them safe from the two monsters in mortal combat.

Dust churned as the grey hulk of the elephant lifted and shook the forest monster about like a rag doll. It was unbelievable that anything could hold on through its fury. But N'Domo never let go, and finally, the elephant began to tire, and the 'madness' left its eyes.

When there was a short period of calm, N'Domo reached around and grasped the elephant's front legs, lifting them from the ground. Off balance, the elephant crashed to the earth with a great noise and trumpeting, where it lay, exhausted, for several minutes.

The forest monster stood back while the elephant finally regained its feet, and then with another trump, it trotted back into the jungle.

Peeking out from the big boulder, M'Bomba and her two boys saw the huge form of the forest monster as it disappeared into the jungle. This time, the creature did not remain on the margin, but left the village for good.

He would never know why he stepped between the elephant and the woman with her little ones. In fact, he would soon forget the incident. His hunger was still sated. Perhaps he'd find another leopard to feast on tomorrow, should his hunger return.

# THE LIVING AMONG THE DEAD

## TASHA FIERCE

Five million, two hundred fifty-three thousand, one hundred and twenty minutes have passed since I smiled with lips that were not taut, plastic simulacra of human flesh.

Eighty-seven thousand, five hundred and fifty-two hours since my eyes began to sink towards my skull in retreat from the unbearable enthusiasm of the living.

Three thousand, six hundred and forty-eight days since my body responded to a whispered breath tickling the back of my neck with a change in temperature, a smattering of goose pimples on the backs of my calves, an increase in lubrication.

Ten years since I laughed without hearing the skin lining my parched esophagus crackle, without wincing in pain as my throat tears; ten years since I last counted myself amongst those things that can be considered *alive.*

I was twenty-one when I died. My death was considered *tragic*, not only for the reasons of my age and the circumstance, but because of how my mother reacted. She gnashed and wailed over my body in the hospital, insisting they ship my empty brown husk to a facility where it could be maintained for just a while longer, so she could attempt to lure me back from the afterlife.

There were other dead people there, with the same recessed eyes and cast lips being pried open to receive polygonal offerings their families *swore* brought them back to life. I was not fooled. Their eyes seemed a little brighter, sure, but even the baldest suede can be revived with a bit of polish. Being dead myself, I could see their empty skulls through the mask, see that there was no wildfire of consciousness ablaze. I knew with peaceful certainty that these other assemblages of atrophying muscle around me were as alien to the world of the living as I was.

Every morning the owners of the facility left me in the hands of the blood-suckers, the vampires who, with their hollow metal prostheses, drained me of what was left of my life. The undead shuffled through the hallways, their tormented moans punctuating sleepless nights.

I know God is a fiction from my time in these places, where spectres gather while their families pray in vain for them to be filled with the breath of life once more.

I languished in that place for two years before my mother brought me home in her brown four-door hatchback. She sat my body down on the living room couch in front of the TV. She fed me and stroked my hair and spoke to me as if I were still alive. I did not believe her, but after a while her soft sobs late at night wore me down, compelling me to revive. I did not believe her, but one day I began to act as if I were not dead.

In the beginning, when I was new at pretending to be alive, I tried to tell the living about how I *used to* be dead, once I felt close enough to them that I could almost imagine my skin tingling from their breath on my neck. I soon learned to keep the truth of me secret: the living are intensely opposed to relations with the dead, or the passing-as-not-dead. I've found that even so-called necrophiliacs recoil from my liminality, my practiced mastery of living mannerisms. They expect my skin to be cold, but it burns in performative homeostasis. Because I have decided to act alive, my body follows.

Now, my secret safely kept, I derive strength from carnal pleasures, late nights spent with my growing nails carving half-moons in living tissue, pretending at ecstasy I've never known. In sex, too, my body follows, gifting me with an engorged plumpness irresistible to non-deads. Each night I absorb the life-force of a new partner, the ability to make me feel *less dead* their only attractive quality. They call me *exotic*, drunk off the scent of my decomposing musk, the unyielding rigour of my thighs, the inviting vacancy of my concave eyes. They call me *exotic*, and then don't call me at all.

Sometimes, too, I luxuriate in reminding myself exactly who I am. I allow the life to drain from me, through my eyes, my nose, my mouth; I become a tributary to Mother Death, her tidal pull tugging me home. I wonder, *should I stay?*—and cradle the offerings that will deliver me back to her in reverently cupped hands.

Other times, I imagine I were never dead, that I am not actually dead now, that I wished myself into a real live human like Pinocchio, that I redeemed my degraded carapace and reformed myself whole and new. Yet the worst fear of the dead is resurrection, and so I am tormented nightly with the thought that this charade might manifest itself into reality.

And I think—no, I *know*—I can never be remade anew. There is no redemption for the deviant, the discarded, the damned.

After five years of this cadaverous existence, I learn that passing-as-not-dead means I can leave my body behind and exist in between.

One of the living is overly desirous of me, how my sinews smell sweet and ready after too many drinks; how my smile is easy and not at all synthetic before he decides to conquer the underworld, using my naked body as a conduit.

*Dead people can't scream, but—*

Being quite familiar with the process of dying, I realize I can melt into this new death, find solace in its pressing familiarity on my chest, its piercing agony tunnelling up and out the centre of my being. I realize I can fall through the veil if I hold my breath,

and I do,

and I fall *up*.

I dissolve into the space between life and death. I journey to distant and nearby lands, drink with long-dead heroes and unborn villains, dance with makers of history and shapers of futurity, watch and weep at the birth of the cosmos and the death of all the stars that have ever lived, that have ever graced this realm with their light.

When I return to my body, I feel the pressure on my chest and the fullness between my legs replaced with the emptiness of surviving. But there is something else there, too, beginning to fill the emptiness: a sensation wholly absent in my past deaths, a connectedness to a feeling beyond *less dead.*

I know now that I am more than just an imitation of life. I am connected to the ferociously beating heart of it.

These days, I am surrounded by spectres. They float past me as I sit in a dank corner of the occupational therapy building, battling demons on a galactic scale. I evanesce, a ghost myself, into the pool table and the dilapidated sports equipment and the piles of art supplies.

I might have been here for decades, for all I know. It doesn't matter.

While the orderlies are wheeling me back to my room, I'm diving into the centre of the earth and through the other side, conjuring the spirits of mammoths and tyrannosaurs and fish with legs crawling out of the sea. *I have seen more than you can ever know*, I say with my cavernous gaze, and they put their finger on my lips and slide the pills in. *I have seen it all*, I say with my static visage, and they pour water in my mouth and rub my throat before leaving me alone in the sterile room.

They will never know the power I contain, what churns beneath my sallow surface. How full of life the dead can be.

# ALONE

## NATHAN FRECHETTE

The smell of the bed was unfamiliar. Not bed; couch. A strange couch, in a strange place. Max stirred, extended their arm. Their fingers brushed against a rigid edge—A table?—and fumbled until they encountered the familiar shape of their phone. They let out a breath of cautious relief.

7:53 a.m., October 11. Seventeen Twitter notifications, three missed calls, and an insurmountable amount of Snapchat and text messages. They groaned, deleting the notifications. Whatever was happening this early in the morning was definitely not worth dealing with.

They pulled themself to their feet and walked out of the living room. The place grew more familiar with each step they took, and they found their feet had directed them to the kitchen. Diego's kitchen. This was Diego's apartment. Why were they in Diego's apartment?

Their stomach walked them to the refrigerator, and they pulled the door open. There wasn't much of anything inside, but maybe they could find something. As they sifted through the unappealing contents of Diego's fridge, they could feel the others at the back of their mind, restless, aching, their anxiety infectious and raw. Why were they not in their own apartment? And where was—

Jane.

*Flickering artificial light. The overwhelming smell of antiseptic, illness, and just a hint of human feces. Rasping breaths so soft you have to strain to hear them.*

Jane.

*"I don't want to go," she says. "I'm not ready. I don't want to go."*

As the memories flooded their mind, Max found themself unable to breathe, suddenly aware of all of the others' pain, most of them unable to comprehend the sudden loss running through their shared heart. What was the use of being split up into multiple minds if they all had to grieve?

*All alone,* came the unbidden, overwhelming thought. *I'm all alone now.*

Their fingers went numb, their vision started to blur, and they were vaguely aware of the jangle from the contents of the refrigerator door.

"Not to rush you or anything, but if you haven't made up your mind yet, do you mind closing the fridge door at least?"

The faint electric buzz from the aging appliance vibrated in both his ear and his arm, bringing him forward, grounding him first in the hand, then in the ear, until the mouth worked.

"What?"

"You're just standing there with the fridge door wide open. It really isn't meant to refrigerate the whole room, and my electric bill is high enough as it is."

"Oh," said Liam. "Sorry there, big buddy!" He closed the fridge door, turning his trademark all-is-well grin on Diego. How did he get here?

"You okay?" asked Diego.

"I'm fantastic, as always!" said Liam, punching Diego in the upper arm, manoeuvring himself around the larger man and towards the exit. He was always expected to keep up appearances by being sociable and ready for any situation, but no one ever told him anything. Something was obviously wrong. He could feel it, feel the others writhing anxiously just at the back of his mind, but he wouldn't have an opportunity to figure it out while Diego was standing right there, watching him.

"I, uh, gotta get home." He started walking to the front door.

Diego called after him. "Are you sure, Max? I don't think—"

"Bye!" Liam rushed out the door, only realizing he wasn't wearing shoes once he was in the hallway. He could hear Diego on the other side of the door, so he rushed to the stairs, avoiding the elevator so he wouldn't get caught waiting. Fortunately, it was a dry summer day, but not hot enough to make the pavement too hot to walk on.

He searched his pockets as he made his way to the bus stop. He hadn't been in charge in a while, and he was feeling a little rusty. He found his phone, his keys—thank goodness—and a bit of money. He found the bus stop, and waited, ignoring the looks people gave him.

The bus came after a few minutes, and he climbed on, paid his fare, and attempted to walk inside. The driver held out an arm to stop him.

"What do you think you're doing? You're not getting on without shoes."

"Come on, man, I already paid!"

"I don't care. Get off."

"Come on, dude, I'm just going to sit down there. I'm only on for a few stops, I'm not going far."

"Get off my bus, punk!"

Liam blinked, feeling his heartbeat speed up, his jaw fuse shut, and his nostrils flare with the sudden effort to breathe. Somehow, he found it in him to back out of the bus, but he could only just stand there and stare as the bus rolled away.

*I'm not ready. I don't want to go.*

He shook his head, his whole body, like a dog out of water. Whoever had pushed that thought out wasn't doing well. It felt like a lot of them weren't doing well. He had to hurry and get home, where he could lock the door, and no one could see.

"It's okay, guys," he said, as soothingly as he could, not caring about the looks he got for muttering to himself while walking down the streets in his socks. "I got this. Liam'll get you home."

He started to walk.

There was something wet in their ear. Wet and loud, like snorting but at the volume of those high-powered hand driers in public washrooms. Max groaned and reached to push the tongue out of their ear. "It's all right, Mr. Noodlebelly, I'm here, you're a good boy." The Boston terrier shook his entire lower body (he'd never quite mastered the art of just wagging his twisted tail knob) and made three rapid circles on the ground before starting to lick Max's ear again. Max let him for a few moments while they gathered their thoughts. They were sitting on the floor in their living room, and the television was playing. Their back was leaning against the couch, their legs stretched out under the table.

In front of them, on the coffee table, was an empty carton of mint chocolate chip ice cream, a colouring book with crayons, and next to it, the journal, a pen stuck inside to mark where they had last written. They took a deep breath, brushed off Mr. Noodlebelly, and flipped it open, bracing themself for the entries from the last few days.

Sarah's handwriting was both a surprise and a relief. It had been a while since Sarah'd been out there. It had been a while since a lot of them had been out, because Max had been doing pretty well at this whole life thing; they'd been needing the help of their others less and less, and the distress Max and all the others felt had found a way of expressing itself healthily and without blackouts, most of the time.

Until last week. Until...

They breathed through their nose, concentrating on the feeling of the paper between their fingers. Ten seconds to breathe in, ten seconds to breathe out. They could stay in charge.

Sarah had helpfully skipped a few blank pages, leaving out the most recent entries, to start a new fresh page.

*October 11—Sarah*

*I let Linnie have the ice cream because she was feeling restless. It helped.*

"Sure," Max grumbled. "you're not the one that has to live with the stomach ache."

*She already took antacid, so don't take more right now. You should also take a shower.*

*Most of all, remember you are not alone.*

Max stared at that last line for a few moments, then closed the notebook and dragged themself to their feet. They yelped when they tried to stand and fell seated on the couch. Their feet were swollen and felt raw; their knees and legs ached dully and trembled under their weight. They managed to drag themself to the washroom, grunting and moaning along the way, leaning heavily on the walls, Mr. Noodlebelly on their heels.

As they settled down in the warm bath, they reflected that it was almost a good thing about the pain; they'd been too distracted to see the hallway covered in pictures of them and Jane, climbing mountains, marching down streets, holding each other, living the life they no longer had together.

*I'm not ready.*

Max took a deep breath, focusing on the smell of the soap, the warmth of the water, the soft rustle of the bubbles popping, the sting of the water on their injured feet, anything to ground them against the assault of unwanted memories.

*They hold Jane's hand, their grief a bar of solid iron stuck across their throat, unable to speak. "I'm not ready," says Jane, her voice small and brittle. "I don't want to go."*

Max felt the grief locking their throat even now, their eyes stinging, their lungs struggling to draw breath. The grief wasn't entirely theirs right now though. They could feel its power, its shape, and it was definitely Linnie's, big, loud, and equal parts pain, fear, and anger.

*Jane is dead*, shouted Linnie at all of them, her grief more powerful than any other voice, *Jane is dead Jane is dead Jane is dead JANE IS DEAD*

"I'm not ready. I don't want to go."

*Max opens their mouth but isn't able to say anything. They want to tell her to stay, to not leave them, but they know she can't do that. The cancer is everywhere.*

*JANE IS DEAD WHY IS JANE DEAD JANE IS DEAD*

Max blew air through their mouth, letting the tears flow freely down their cheeks. Their left hand pressed down on their sternum, like that would hold in the heart which threatened to beat itself right out of their rib cage. They let out a strangled sob and closed their eyes, trying to concentrate. Maybe if they calmed themself, they could calm Linnie. But how could they do that? How could they do anything, how could life even go on the way it was when Jane was dead?

"I'm not ready. I don't want to go."

*They kiss the back of Jane's hand, trying to find the courage, somehow, somewhere, to reassure her, to tell her that she can let go, but all they can think is that they are terrified of losing her. Jane blinks, crying, even if her dry eyes can't make the tears anymore. Her breath is coming in tiny gasps, which are growing fewer and farther between.*

Don't go. Don't leave me here without you, *they think with all of their heart as tears stream down their face.*

"It's okay, it's okay," they heard themself say, though they were pretty sure they weren't the one speaking. They could still feel the pressure of the hand on their sternum, but the hand didn't feel like theirs anymore. *Of course life goes on,* came a thought from somewhere in their skull; probably Sarah. *Who would take care of Mr. Noodlebelly?*

Max turned their head toward the dog, who was leaning with his two front paws and head resting against the edge of the bath. Mr. Noodlebelly didn't raise his head but simply started shaking his butt again in celebration of Max's attention. Max laughed, wiped away a few tears, and reached out to pet the dog. Somewhere in the back of their mind, they could feel Liam singing gently.

"I'm not alone, Jane," whispered Max, hoping she could hear them.

The knocks came again, and Max sighed as they pulled on their bathrobe. Mr. Noodlebelly danced around them as they made their way to the door. Diego was on the other side, looking slightly frantic.

"Max!" he said as he walked in, looking Max over carefully. They noticed he was holding their shoes in his hands. "I realized you left your shoes, and… are you all right?"

Max shrugged. "I'm getting there. Thanks for bringing the shoes."

Diego put the shoes down, using the gesture to step into the apartment. Max sighed and let him in. He walked to the kitchen, looking around a bit less than casually, Mr. Noodlebelly on his heels, barking at the intruder. Max watched him without a word, hoping their silence would finally discourage Diego from seeking their company. When Diego made to go into the hallway leading to the bedrooms, Max clicked their tongue.

"I'm fine," reiterated Max. "Really."

Diego stopped his inspection, then turned around and looked at Max, his arms folded over his chest. "You didn't seem fine earlier. I can tell when you're acting different. You talk funny."

"Yeah, I was different. It was just what I needed to be to deal with things." Diego had a seat, and Max sighed. "Look, Diego, I told you before. I switch; it's just the way my brain is, it's going to happen sometimes."

"But doesn't that mean that you're not doing well?"

"Well, of course I'm not doing well. Jane is..." Max shook their head, trailing off. The silence stretched for a few seconds, Diego allowing Max to continue. "What I mean is, the switching itself, it's not necessarily a bad thing. It actually helps me most of the time. It helped me today, I just...I needed to be able to sit down and process this."

Max looked up at Diego again, expecting a confrontation, but found him actually...pouting? "I'm supposed to be your big brother," Diego finally said. "I'm supposed to take care of you."

Max found themself smiling this time, and they reached out to squeeze Diego's shoulder. "And you do. Look at you, being here, worrying about me."

Diego frowned at Max, examining their face carefully, then suddenly got up and wrapped them into a hug. "I love you, sib. Come back to my place. I'll make shepherd's pie!"

Max shook their head, still smiling, their eyes misty. "I think I need to have a one-on-one evening with Mr. Noodlebelly. But I'll come by tomorrow, all right?"

Diego sighed. "I just don't think you should stay alone right now."

Max thought of Linnie's grief, and Liam's song, and Sarah's notes.

*Most of all, remember you are not alone.*

They smiled. Life would go on. "Thanks. I'll give you a call later."

# NO ROOM AT THE INN

## EMILY GILLESPIE

The nurses continue their hurried, hushed conversations. You inch out farther into the hall, needing to be closer. Needing to see them. See what's happening. You spot the blonde nurse who talked to you earlier and call out, "Hey can *you* see me?" Urgency punctuates the questions. "Are you there? Can you get me water?" you ask, but she looks past. The cold pressing against your spine continues, like the air conditioner is blowing directly down your back, but the heat is cranked. She can see you, right?

"You need to go back into your room, can't be sitting in the middle of the hall." She doesn't look at your face, barely turns. Need her to look at you, see her face, her eyes. You inch back towards the curtain dragging your weight across the floor. "You need to be totally out of the hall!" the booming voice detached from person echoes. *Wizard of Oz.*

See the doctor, indifferent old fart, talking to one of the nurses, and you pray to V for help to stand, feels like you're floating, and your bad right leg keeps buckling, but you finally make your way over. Breathe in, and out. *You got this Jade.* Beg voice not to betray you.

"When am I getting my sleeping pill and blanket?" The voice sounds funny. You, you forgot to ask about water. Still taste the coffee on your breath.

"The nurses didn't get it for you yet?" He looks at you for a second confirming that yes, he can see you.

The blonde sighs, fixes hair as the doctor tells her what to do.

You go lie down again. Body begs for sleep. Sleep, sleep, need sleep, but the good kind of sleep, not falling further into this blackness. Think about V. Think about when you first met. Silly Jessie, getting off his leash covering you in sand. V running behind, panting her introduction and apologizing, but you let Jessie lick your face and laugh. Responsible V with her morning runs and green smoothies, trying to coach you into some kind of order.

You use your coat as a pillow, build nest, pull old raccoon hat over your ears. Face softens, start to doze thinking of the sun on your skin, sounds of the waves that day you first met Jessie and V by the water. *It's okay Jade. It's okay.* The hospital will take care of you.

The sounds in the background bleed together, becoming a kind of white noise wall that holds you. Breathe in and out, in and out, thinking of Jessie's soft face.

Footsteps getting closer. Someone is there. Clearing throat. Good. It's the blonde again. Blink, trying to get her image into focus, rub eyes. *What time is it?* Can't find a clock on the wall. Not sure where phone went, doesn't matter. How long have you been waiting? At least you still have your coat, raccoon hat.

"I have your pill. If you want to see the psychiatrist you can sleep in one of the reclining chairs." She holds the pill out in a little measuring cup in one hand, paper cup of water in the other. You want to reach for them, can feel the flimsy cup of water in your hand already.

"I, I thought, I thought was sleeping here?" Rocking body slightly with the effort to stay alert.

"No." She almost laughs. "This is an exam room, we need it for other patients. Off to the group room, okay? I'll get you a pillow and blanket."

"Can't be around..." you manage to say, looking around the room as if trying to indicate your unstable mental state with a nod, a can of gasoline left beside an open flame ready to burst. Bad idea—should have read the safety label first.

*What's V going to say if you leave?*

V. V coming to check on you after you hardly left your apartment during Christmas. V helping you sit. Helping you get dressed, bringing you here. She wanted you to stay, figure out what's wrong, owe it to her to try and be okay.

"Well, we need this room, you're going to need to go sleep in the other room, if you're staying." She's already looking away, onto the next thing.

The nurse's words are like a plunge off a dock into a cold lake, and suddenly, I'm too awake. I sigh, breathe in.

"No," I say firmly, the first thing I've been sure of all day. "No!" I repeat roused by the fluorescent lights and their insistent hum. The glare from the over-polished floor reminds me where I am. I can feel my heart thumping through my chest, demanding that I run. Something else stirs in me too, like maybe the caffeine finally kicked in and suddenly this exam room is too small. Any university student will tell you that coffee can blur the line between alert and adrenaline-fueled panic.

I stare at the pill in her hand. The craving for the blue sedative is familiar even though it makes me a zombie. The metallic bite tends to linger in my dry mouth long after the unpleasant dreams dissolve. It makes me sleepy, but not the regular kind of tired, muddled thoughts make it hard to stand. I imagine myself drugged, falling asleep or further into this weird hole, void, in a room, a room filled with strangers. I can't...I yelled at a baby earlier when V was still here. The pit at the bottom of my stomach opened and the cry came out.

I...need...to...stay...awake or else, god only knows what will happen.

Something is really wrong. Scared, scared of myself in this state or whatever, whatever that fog was earlier. Starting to feel like something worse may happen. *To me. By me.* I remember the feeling of the anger rising at the baby earlier, coming from my belly or somewhere deeper. That's why I'm here—I don't know what's happening. This is hard to admit, these pages are starting to feel like some rambling confession, and it's been a very long time since I went to church. Maybe it was better when I didn't know what was going on...

"Is there anywhere else I can sleep?" My voice rises with desperation at the end. They have to help me, put me somewhere safe.

"If you want to stay the night, it has to be in the main sleeping room with the other patients." She says *if* as though I have another place to go. Where else can I go? I feel my breath slip out, shoulders fall forward.

"I can't, I really can't do that. I need to go I guess, unless I'm getting formed?" At this point I don't care if they force me to stay. I don't know what's best, really don't. I need V, she always knows what to do. *Stay*, I'm sure she'd tell me. *Let them help you.*

"You're free to go. The doctor doesn't believe in forming people. He's more in favour of a community approach to mental health."

*But what about tonight?* I want to ask. *What am I supposed to do now? Do you think it's all in my head?* I can't go home, not like this, can't stay. I stumble to my feet from the exam table thinking about the icy dark night waiting for me.

"If you leave now, you forfeit seeing the psychiatrist in the morning as well as the sleeping pill."

I nod as I silently scream, *Help!* My voice threatens to give away to sobs, and she turns her back on me and walks away with the little measuring cup with my pill and the water that I'd waited god only knows how long for. I squat on the floor and push items back into my overflowing bag. My raccoon hat is still safely on my head. I zip my winter coat. It's navy blue with white stains from road salt. I find myself collapsing, buckling again on the floor in the hospital, but this time V isn't here to offer a shoulder to rest my weary head on. I mean, I get why, she starts her new teaching job tomorrow.

Tired, so tired, yet heart's pounding and I still don't know what happened earlier today, or what to expect when I go back to my apartment. I think of the scattered laundry I left in a disarray on the floor, the overflowing garbage, the fridge that's empty aside from old condiments. Dad is waiting for me to return his calls for the last two weeks. "You really need to visit your mother. She isn't well." But I can't just forgive her in a second because she's sick.

*It is okay Jade, it'll be okay.*

I need to pee. I should probably do that, then be on my way, while I can still think. Maybe splash my face with water, get a drink.

Deep breath in, and out. Okay, stand. I hold on to the wall. I got this. I walk past the nurse's desk and I wonder if they still have my pee sample sitting on the table, maybe still holding some clue about what's happening, what's, what's wrong? What's wrong with me? I pass by the room with the other sick people who are waiting to learn what's wrong with them, maybe old doc will be of more help. Ha.

Too many people, I think as I search their faces, each with their own story. Too much, too much, can't even help myself. I close my eyes. It's so loud, like the wave of background noise threatens to take hold of me and carry me elsewhere. *Beep-beep* goes some machine, security is being paged, the lights hum, and a baby cries—maybe no time has passed at all. It's way too loud, and I try to cover my ears with my hands, but it does no good. At least my bag is still in my hand. I want to scream.

I need to open my eyes to see where I'm going. Old doc talking to a new nurse in the hall. Shoulders slumped, dark circles under his eyes, and he looks about ready for bed, too. I wonder why he didn't do more. They all look so overworked and behind. Like they had the time to stop and do paperwork to keep me, and like blondie said, they don't have the fucking room.

No room at the inn. I start laughing. No room at the inn for me. A few months later, I'd see a marketing campaign about mental health still being health. "Get out of the waiting room and in for treatments," it declared. I guess I never found the special password for the secret door, but let me tell you, I tried them all, like jabbing buttons on a broken elevator.

# CHARITY™

## DEREK NEWMAN-STILLE

You know what they say:

"What doesn't hurt you makes you stronger."

"The power of positive thinking is truly amazing."

"Have you thought that maybe a better outlook would help?"

"You would be amazed at what you can accomplish if you put your mind to it."

It was that time of year again.

Fundraiser time.

Charity™ time.

Time for my body to be on display again.

Time for me to grin and bear it with the *Thank yous* and *Oh, I hadn't thought of thats* and *Oh, what a fascinating perspective. I will try harders*. My cheeks hurt almost as much as my leg stump. Both were performing for the amusement of the rich, giving them a chance to treat me as the spectacle they always wanted.

Sometimes I think of these Charity™ events as a continuation of the freak shows of the past…and sometimes I think I may have preferred to be in the freak shows. At least then my performances could have been interesting…and I would be able to choose the character I would play.

Now all I perform are tropes of disability: the self-loathing cripple who can get over anything if he just has a more positive attitude; the poor cripple who could accomplish so much if he only had a cure; the pathos-inspiring suffering body that just tears at the heart (and purse) strings.

I ended up being chosen for these parties because of my background in theatre. It turns out that a theatre cripple was the best person to portray the 'authentic' plight of the disabled to our donors.

I don't know why I am calling them 'our' donors. So much of the money from the charities goes to fund scientific pursuits to find 'cures' instead of giving folks like me the tools we need for basic survival.

People seem to like the idea of giving for a 'cure' so much more. It gets rid of the need to keep contributing, gets rid of those icky aspects of the disabled body, and lets people pretend that they will never be disabled... because, let's face it, they all will, eventually.

Maybe that's why they fund cures. As much as they fear people like me, they are really fearing the (very likely) possibility that they will become like me. Some part of them must know that if they live long enough, they'll all become disabled at some point, and maybe that's what inspires them to give to the charities and fund cure-initiatives because they hope that by the time they encounter disability, they can conquer it with a pill, an injection, or a quick one-day surgery (non-invasive, of course).

They don't want to think about a world without a cure where they might have to live in it with assistance tech, with aug bodies, or with body mods. They want to look as pristine and fleshy as they always do. They don't want prosthetics—they want all-natural bodies... though apparently that doesn't extend to cosmetic surgery. I swear, their faces look more plastic than my leg does.

Not surprisingly, I'm not allowed to wear my leg to the Charity™ ball. They want to see me teetering in front of them. They want to see me move around with my cane. I get it better than most, though. Charlie the Armless Wonder (and yes, that is what they call him) has to sit on his pedestal and drink tea, wrapping his toes around his teapot and gently pouring it into cups, then lifting sugar with a tiny spoon between his toes and adding it to his cup. He even squirts a lemon between his toes when he feels like a bit of a citrusy sting to his tea. "It's all hygienic folks," adds the announcer, "he's wearing latex foot gloves. So, if you want a spot of tea, you can join him for a cuppa by just upgrading your donation status to blue."

Of course, hygiene is their priority. Mustn't have the Normies catching cripple from us. They actually provide latex gloves for people who want to touch my stump... and you would be surprised how many people want to touch it. Of course, a donation upgrade (though they only ask for orange donation status to touch my leg, not blue status like a cup of tea with Charlie would cost) is required for a touch, but so many of them seem to think it's worth it. I'm certain there are at least as many people with a kink who touch me as there are people who are 'satisfying their curiosity.'

I have no question that I am an object of fetishization, and of course, I hate being objectified and treated as some lifeless object... but, is it weird that there is a bit of empowerment in that? I'm not going to give them the power and satisfaction of treating me as something to stare at! I'm going to stare back!!! I might be exploited for my body, but there *is* something empowering about knowing a few of the people here staring at me could not get off without watching me, touching me, and desiring me. If they are going to try to objectify me, I'm going to stare right back at them and think about all of the power I have to control *their* lust. At least that's what I tell myself to get through all of this.

Since everything else about the Charity™ ball is meant to make me feel like I'm subservient, like I should be thankful for the pennies they throw to us to keep us alive for a little longer, I get a bit of a kick out of at least being in charge of the bodies of some of the kinky folks. I love to ignore them as they gaze at me, giving them just a glimpse of stump—but not enough for them to complete their fantasy—enough that they have to paint in the pictures as they fuck their able-bodied partners, the Normies that they have to imagine legless.

When the announcers tell them I used to be an artist before my 'tragic accident,' I cringe. I am still an artist. In fact, outside of this Charity™ show, I sell art to some of these spectators. They only ever want art about crippled bodies though; it helps them to show to their friends how charitable they are by supporting a disabled person, and apparently a sunset or a forest doesn't have as much power to make people acknowledge their charity as one of my legless images. Well, that, and there are some art patrons who want paintings of the stump for their 'personal collections' (another reason why I only give little glimpses of my stump).

The announcers don't like to mention I'm an artist because it gets away from their message that I can't contribute anything to our society, that none of us can give anything back, so we need every penny possible from the generous people who support the charities. They also don't want to tell them that the pennies that go toward basic living expenses aren't enough and wouldn't allow us to survive without our side hustles.

"It's so tragic, dear," she says, as her latexed fingers flex around my stump.

"What's that?"

"Oh, that you used to be something incredible, then all this happened."

"They didn't mention this, but I am still—"

"I bet you did so much. I bet you loved to walk in the woods to get inspiration."

"I can still—"

"I am really just amazed with all that you can put up with. I would just die if I had to go through this." She turns to one of her friends, who is just touching her pay sensor to the booth to upgrade to orange status, and says, "Wouldn't you just die?"

"I can't even imagine. And he looks so young to have to give up so much."

The docent at my booth passes her a latex glove, so she could have the next touch.

"Sometimes I paint with my stump," I say, trying to push boundaries a bit to get their attention. Both look up at me with a mixture of excitement and revulsion. "Yeah, I like to get paint all over it. Cool and wet and sticky, just like the blood when they had to saw my leg off. It's so visceral. Sometimes I get a bit of leg hair into my paint, but I keep going."

Both women shake their heads in disgust. It's apparently enough to have the second woman pull off her latex glove and change her Charity™ status back to red.

I have to smile as they walk away, casting backward glances at my stump imagining it slathered in paint, and likely picturing it dripping in blood as it was cut. I know that I'll get sanctioned for this. The government Charity™ advisors keep cameras on us at all times, and we are penalized whenever we break their carefully-crafted illusion. But they know that my stats are generally high, and

I tend to get a lot of donations for 'The Cause' by playing their role, so I'm not worried about losing much.

Some of the people on display at the Charity™ balls barely scrape by, getting minimum allowances because they can't garter as many supporters. Some of them didn't develop the skills that I did. Some of them were disabled before The Department of Charities was introduced, and the pitiful government allowances for people with disabilities dried up in favour of a 100% Charity™ model. Tax payers decided that disabled people weren't thankful enough for what we were given, that we were asking too much by demanding accessible spaces and access to services. We received the clear message that this was an able-bodied person's world and that 'disabled meant unable' to contribute to society. I'd like to say this was a radical change from the era of disability living allowances, but some of the older people in our community tell me that these attitudes were always there—they had Normie friends and neighbours who would complain when they got a wheelchair parking space that was a couple of centimetres closer to the door to a store. People would see them working and *still* call them lazy, say they were "sucking from the government's tit," and "taking money from hard-working taxpayers."

Normies seem to like it more when they are considered generous for giving money to us. They want to look us in the eye when they give us our charity and see us accept their money with gratitude. So, we have to perform. We have to paste on our thankful faces, tell people how generous they are, then shuffle back to our institutions or apartments in the ghettos until we are trotted out for another show.

I talk about these Charity™ shows as being like freakshows, but the real wonders of the freakshow happen after our time on the government stage. We have created our little poor communities where we can be different, where our real bodies can show, and where we can get our freak on. Not everyone likes to really Crip it up. So many people like to hide their differences under Normie clothes, but the East End is a place where we can play the freak.

I am so happy to let my Normie Performie smile slip and put my piercings back in around my mouth, glad I am done the act for the day. I drop the boring teak cane they make me use when performing and tuck it into my locker. I pick up the nicer glass one with the lion heads carved into it and the elephant standing where their manes meet, his trunk forming the handle. I love it. It's both so much about the natural world and yet also so delightfully crystalline and unnatural. It is so me, a combination of natural and artificial.

I find myself disgusted by the prosthetics that the charities give me. They put so much money into making the prosthetics look *natural*, wanting to make them so hidden that they make us look like Normies, but then they remind us constantly that we aren't Normies and never can be. I modified my prosthesis. I wanted it to be art that said, "Fucking look at me. Don't look away. Don't pretend I am not there until it is time for me to be on stage. See ME. See my leg and remember that people like me exist and are part of society and can't be ignored."

My current leg is a glass spiral in purple and green that twirls around the post at its centre to turn my leg into a vortex of colour and shape. It took me ages to perfect a shatter-proof glass that wouldn't break into shards every time I took a step. I finally found something that can take a few kicks and a lot of abuse and keep on moving.

I wear pretty short shorts to show it off as much as possible, though the glass gets cold pretty easily, and damn it hurts once it

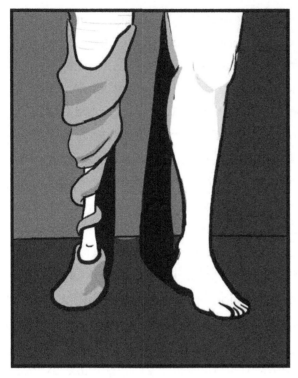

gets chilly.

As I affix my leg, the docent approaches. "That was some stunt you pulled."

"Oh, which one?"

"Don't even"—he collects himself—"The stump-painting. How did you think that would go?"

"I thought it would tell them that I am an artist. They seemed worried that I couldn't do art anymore."

"You know damned well they wanted you to be the tragic *former* artist. Is it really that hard to play the part for a bit?"

"You know what? Yes. Yes, it is hard."

I could hear conversations stop, feel the weight of eyes on us.

"Don't all of you think it's hard? And I don't mean that it's hard to be disabled like they keep saying as they introduce us to our patrons. I don't mean that it's hard to live like this, and we need help. I mean that they fucking *make it* hard. They make it hard to live in their world because they want us to play a role...all...the... fucking...time. We pretend that when we leave these Charity™ events, we can be ourselves, but we're always performing, always asked to play our parts as dutiful cripples waiting for Charity™. I don't know about you, but I'm fucking tired of it. I'm tired of performing, tired of acting in the scripts that society gives us. I want to stick my stump into government business and ask them how they are going to make space for it."

In films, this is the point where there is a rallying cry from all of the other people who are tired of oppression, where we realize our commonalities and come together to make society better. This is when our oppressors decide they are going to defend us and are ashamed at what they have done. The problem is that our oppressors don't know they are oppressors, and their oppression is so complete, we can't see a place for ourselves outside of it.

We've forgotten how not to be oppressed.

We believe that this is the best we can ask for.

There is silence.

"I hope it was worth it. It's all recorded, of course. We let you people go without recordings out there in the East End, but not in here. It's all on film, and it's not going to play well for the Reps. They aren't going to let this go. You're out of here, and you're not coming back. This isn't the image we want to portray to our sponsors. You are damaging the chances of all of these people getting support. How dare you put others in jeopardy because you want a soapbox to stand on?"

Even I was silent.

I walk out without even the sound of whispered gossip.

Sam had been a pretty good Charity™ Rep for me. He didn't have the big money that some of the higher-ups got. He was working for basic living income, and they really made him work for it.

I might not agree with the message he had to support, but I respected all of the work he'd done, trying to help us to the best of his ability. Was he a government stooge playing the role he was given by the government to keep us oppressed? Yes, in a way... but he actually accepted those messages and believed he was doing the right thing. He works overtime to make sure we got our cheques on time, which most reps didn't. He gives us tips about how to work the system (yes, there are still stopgaps in the system).

I guess I was both surprised and not surprised when he showed up at my door even though I'd been cut off.

"Hey."

"Hey. Thanks for coming. I know you aren't supposed to." I couldn't make eye contact with him.

"I know. I heard everything, but I guess... I guess I wanted to make sure you were okay."

"I'm really not..."

"I know." He looked down at his shoes in shame. They had seen better days. They were breaking a bit at the seams and needed a good polish.

"I'm sorry I put you in this awkward spot. I just... I couldn't do it anymore. I couldn't be the performer."

"You used to act."

"Yeah, and I haven't really been able to stage act since I started doing the Charity™ shows. Even in the weird *avant-garde* stuff we do in the East End theatre, I feel like I'm still playing self-loathing-cripple for Normies—" I caught myself. "Sorry, for able-bodied people. I have to funnel all of my artsiness into paintings because I can't play any part other than the one I'm asked to play again and again... and it never ends, you know?"

"I know. It's why I used to ask you to give acting lessons to the other disabled people to help them get some support."

"Come on, you've been with us enough that you can call us Crips.

Come on, 'one of us, one of us.'"

"I can be one of you, one of you, but if I call you Crips, I'd be fired faster than you can run—"

"Have you seen how slowly I move?"

"Okay, then, It'd be faster than *I* can run to Normieville."

I laugh, loving that he's at least willing to call the able-bodied parts of the city 'Normieville'.

"So, I know you aren't here to bring me a cheque this time. What can I do for you? You're not going to ask me to give acting lessons to the new Crips, are you?"

"No, no. I—" He pauses, tapping his foot. He keeps fumbling with something in his pocket. He's not as good at hiding what he's doing as we are. He hasn't had to perform himself before. "I have something that might... that might help out. It's something new from the government. It's sort of a last-ditch thing before we... before we have to leave you to your own devices.

"You mean, before you have to cut me off."

"Yes... That."

He pulls a small prescription bottle from his pocket.

"It's called Inspiration™."

"You are fucking kidding me."

"Look, I—lots of people in the Charity™ industry have started taking it, and before you say it, no, not just the disabled people. I'm talking about most of the docents, most of the Reps... Okay, even me."

"You want me to drug myself into accepting things."

"You know that it's that or the streets."

"I'd rather the streets."

"You really wouldn't. Trust me. Also, Inspiration™ doesn't do much to you. You'd still be you. You'd just be more... more thankful,

I guess, more able to look at your life and like it. You wouldn't have to put on the performed smile at Charity™ shows…you would actually be smiling. You would actually *like* the people who come up to you and want to hear about your experiences. You would still be an artist; you would be a story-teller, sharing your tales with them."

My skepticism is as loud as my silence is quiet.

"Look, I know that you're worried about losing your artistic skills—"

"I'm worried about losing myself."

"Have I lost myself?"

"I really can't say. I've only really known you as the person you are now."

"That's not important. Do you like the person I am now?"

"Yes. I think you mean well, but now I am wondering how much of you is you and how much of you is Inspiration™."

"Does it matter?"

"Yes."

"Okay, look, I don't want you to be on the streets. I want you to be safe. I want you to be secure. I want you to have all of the things I have."

"Then maybe you need to fight the Normie government to make that happen."

"What do you think a Crip government could do?"

"First, I knew I could get you to use that word. Second, I think we could do a lot. Look at what we've done with the East End. We welcome all different bodies."

"Do you? How about Ms. Andersen?"

I pause. Ms. Andersen is different. She has dementia. She doesn't even know where she is.

He gives me a knowing look.

Was I being just as ableist? Am I drawing artificial lines between bodies?

"Okay. I guess some people aren't as welcoming as I would like, but we can work to change that."

"How?"

"Government support. Taxes. Like it used to be."

"And how are you going to convince people to pay taxes to support you? That already failed once people decided that you could live off of Charity™. The people who don't financially support Charity™ aren't going to want to start giving you money, and the people who support Charity™ already believe they are giving you enough. How do you convince them to change things?"

"Art."

"Sure. How long will that take? How long does it take to convince people to change things? And how many artists will it take to convey a message that is stronger than the one people are getting from telethons?"

"I thought you said you were taking Inspiration™. It sounds like you are pretty pessimistic."

"I'm on a low dose, okay?" he insists. "Also, I have thought through all of this. It's why I started taking Inspiration™. I used to think I could change things, but people don't want to change. I can fix things within the system. I can make your lives better working from the inside than trying to take it down."

"Are you sure?"

"Yes. That's why I take Inspiration™, to remind myself that I am sure. To remind myself that I have tried everything, and this is what works. I need it to get over my weekly dose of *Pessimism*."

"Weekly?"

"My visits with you," he says, chuckling. "You are the drug

conflict for Inspiration™. They could stuff you in a pill bottle and call you Pessimism™ if people wanted that."

I want to laugh along. I know he's being playful in calling me Pessimism™, but I can't take it lightly just now.

"Maybe people need a dose of Pessimism™. Maybe it makes them work harder to change things instead of being optimistic that things will get better on their own."

His expression sobers. "I'm sorry, I didn't mean to suggest you were harmful."

"No, I know. But I stand by what I said. Maybe pessimism is generative? Maybe it gets people to ask questions. Maybe it shakes things up. No, it isn't nice. No, it doesn't help us get through our day, but it can change things."

"Isn't that sort of an optimistic perspective on pessimism? Aren't you saying that pessimism is where we can have the hope of a changed future?"

"I, I hadn't thought about that. Can pessimism be hopeful?"

I tap at my glass leg, enjoying the little vibrations it sent. I always tapped when I was thinking and Sam knew this, so he didn't interrupt, but that tapping seemed more significant now. Those little vibrations that I had to work so hard to ensure wouldn't crack the overall structure. I used to be pessimistic about the possibility of my glass leg being able to hold up, so I experimented with different glass to keep it from cracking. The possibility of fragmenting kept me experimenting, kept me changing and finding new methods.

"I think my pessimism can be generative," I say. "I think it makes me experiment more. I think it makes me unsatisfied with something that could break, could fragment, could crack, and it makes me want to keep trying something until it works."

"What are you—"

"Look at my leg. It's made of glass! It is almost defined by its ability to shatter, but I crafted it into something that works. I swirled together different chemical compositions until I got something that could hold up, that could keep getting tested with every step and still stand up. Maybe if we had a more pessimistic society, we could make something stronger, something that swirled things together into something strong?"

"But wouldn't all of those people be depressed?"

"You know as well as I do that depression isn't that simple. Depression and pessimism aren't the same thing, and Inspiration™, at least the way you've described it, isn't an antidepressant. It's a suppressant. It suppresses possibilities by making us content with the way things are. So, yeah, I guess I am optimistic about pessimism. And, no, I won't be taking Inspiration™. I think you're right about me—I do see hope in pessimism. I guess I'm an optimistic pessimist who's *inspired* by pessimism. I see the glass half empty, but I want to fill it up."

My hand taps twice more upon my leg as I add:

"And I will do anything I can to fill it up."

# AUTHOR AND EDITOR BIOS

Learn more about the folks of *Nothing Without Us*! If you enjoyed their stories, please consider following them on social media and/or finding out more about their other works.

## ~ EDITORS IN CHIEF ~

**Cait Gordon** is the creator of the Spoonie Authors Network and author of *Life in the 'Cosm* and *The Stealth Lovers* (Renaissance). Her short stories have appeared in *Alice Unbound Beyond Wonderland* (Exile Editions), *We Shall Be Monsters* (Renaissance), and the upcoming *Space Opera Libretti* (McNett and Rossman). She teamed up with Talia C. Johnson to co-edit *Nothing Without Us* as part of their plan to take over the world. Narf. Cait currently lives in the Narnia region of suburban Ottawa, but you can find her at spoonieauthorsnetwork.blog, caitgordon.com, or on Twitter (@CaitGAuthor).

**Talia C. Johnson** is a multi-faceted woman who is transgender, autistic, Jewish, queer, and more than the sum of her parts. She is an ordained Kohenet priestess, and her work centres on bridging faith and queer communities, educating, counselling, and mentoring. She has worked doing freelance sensitivity editing for queer and trans representation and is Chair of the Board of Heartspark Press, which is run by and publishes works by trans women and CAMAB non-binary people. Talia joined Cait Gordon to co-edit *Nothing Without Us* and is 'The Brain' of NWU's dynamic duo. You can find Talia at taliacjohnson.ca and on Twitter (@TaliaCJohnson).

## ~ AUTHORS ~

**Myriad Augustine** is a non-binary trans queer, a mixed-race person of colour, a chronically-ill mad writer, and ten thousand other things that don't fit neatly into a paragraph. As someone who exists at numerous intersections, they are obsessed with writing about liminal identities - the crossroads, the collisions, and the questioning. They've crafted lattés and interview profiles, gone door to door selling knives and politicians, and generally wandered the professional landscape accumulating stories in place of savings. More of their work and other writing can be found at: www.myriadworks.ca or on Twitter @MyriadAugust.

**Shannon Barnsley** is a writer, poet, and folklore devotee from New Hampshire, currently living in Brooklyn. She holds a degree in Creative Writing/Mythology & Religion from Hampshire College. Since graduating, she has been found giving tours at a haunted 18th century Shaker village, translating British English into American English for an independent publishing company, managing multiple chronic illnesses, and wandering in the woods. Her first book, *Beneath Blair Mountain*, was published by 1888 in Fall 2015. You can find Shannon on Twitter (@ShanBarnsley), Instagram

(@frejafolkvangar), Facebook (BardOfFolkvangar), and at frejafolkvangar.wordpress.com.

**Carolyn Charron** is a speculative fiction writer with stories in three Flame Tree Publishing anthologies (*Supernatural Horror, Dystopia & Utopia*, and *Murder & Mayhem*) and online in *The Saturday Evening Post*. She also reads slush for Apex and Lightspeed magazines and has been a juror for Speculative Literature Foundation grants. Carolyn lives in Toronto with her family and is currently working on a Canadian historical trilogy combining a lesbian blacksmith, magical clockworks, and a menopausal pirate. You can find Carolyn on Facebook (Carolyn-Charron-709050372504031), at carolyncharron.blogspot.com, and on Twitter (@CarolynCharron).

**Elliott Dunstan** is a queer, disabled writer and poet living in Ottawa. Previously published by Queen of Swords Press, Battleaxe Press, and Bywords Poetry, he also self-publishes an urban fantasy serial on his website and is finishing up a degree in Ancient Greek and Roman History at Carleton University. You can find out more about Elliott at elliottdunstan.com.

**Tasha Fierce** is a god in chains, but is also a queer, disabled non-binary fat femme, a Black feminist, a writer, a gardener, an anarchist, a witch, a lover of shadow, and an intermittent ray of light currently residing in the occupied Tongva territory known as Los Angeles. Their essays have appeared in *White Riot: Punk Rock and the Politics of Race* and *Hot & Heavy: Fierce Fat Girls on Life, Love, and Fashion* as well as *Bitch Magazine, EBONY.com, Bitch Planet* and other publications. More of their fiction can be found at tashafierce.com, and they tweet as @tashajfierce.

**Nathan Fréchette** is a queer, transgender sequential artist, illustrator, designer, publisher, and author. He has published over a dozen graphic and prose short stories in anthologies and magazines in Canada and Europe, as well as five novels, three graphic novels, two works of nonfiction, and the online comic *Some Assembly Required*. He taught creative writing for over a decade, and has degrees in Film Studies and Sequential Art. Nathan is also the co-founder and Overseer of All the Things at Presses Renaissance Press. You can find him at nathancarofrechette.ca  or on Twitter (@NCFrechette).

**Emily Gillespie** is a Toronto based author, disability activist and professional daydreamer. Her work explores the themes of memory, identity, and disability. Emily has a BA in English, and an MA in Critical Disability Studies. *Dancing with Ghosts* (Leaping Lion Books, 2017) is her first novel. In 2018, she won a contest for her short-story *D is for Despair*, sponsored by the Ontario Book Publishers Organization. She currently teaches at Workman Arts in Toronto. She is working on a second novel and experimenting with zines and poetry.

You can find Emily on Facebook (Gillespie.Em), Twitter (@emilygillespiem), or on her website at emilygillespieblog .wordpress.com.

**J. Ivanel Johnson:** Having lived and taught in four different countries, from remote mountain areas to cliffs above the sea, J. Ivanel has always had scenic vistas and varied characters to inspire her writing. She published her first poem when she was 11 and has rarely stopped in the forty-five years since. She now writes a regular blog (bluebellmountainblog.wordpress.com) on living self-sufficiently on the land she, her husband, and mother farm in New Brunswick's beautiful Appalachians—detailing some of the hilarious happenings that occur there. You can also find J. Ivanel on Facebook (JIvanelJohnson) and Twitter (@JIvanelJohnson).

**Tom Johnson** was a voracious reader from childhood, beginning with Golden Age comic books to classic literature. Exciting adventure stories entertained him until he discovered science fiction and hardboiled detective mysteries. By his early twenties, he found The Shadow and Doc Savage pulp reprints, was hooked on the fast-paced action novel, and became interested in writing. Tom and his wife Ginger have received numerous awards for their work with keeping the old stories in the spotlight for new readers seeking escape in a thrilling adventure novel.

You can find Tom on Facebook (tomginger.johnson) and at his website (jur1.brinkster.net/index.html).

**Diane Koerner** has been writer and teller of tall tales all her life. After a chemical injury at work, she moved to Hawaii to heal in paradise and changed her profession from medical advertising to holistic health and environmental journalism, and documentary filmmaking. And now—fiction. You can follow Diane on Facebook (diane.koerner.9).

**Tonya Liburd** shares a birthday with Simeon Daniel and Ray Bradbury, which might tell you a little something about her. She has been nominated for the 2017 and 2018 Rhysling Awards, and been longlisted in the 2015 Carter V. Cooper(Vanderbilt)/Exile Short Fiction Competition. Her work is used in Nisi Shawl's workshops and Tananarive Due's UCLA Horror course. She is also the Senior Editor

262 of Abyss & Apex Magazine. You can find her blogging at spiderlilly.com or on Twitter (@somesillywowzer).

**Raymond Luczak** lost much of his hearing at the age of eight months due to a bout of double pneumonia and fever. He grew up in a hearing family of nine children in Michigan's Upper Peninsula. He is the author and editor of 22 books, including *The Last Deaf Club in America* (Handtype Press), *QDA: A Queer Disability Anthology* (Squares & Rebels), and *Flannelwood: A Novel* (Red Hen Press). He lives in Minneapolis, Minnesota. You can find Raymond at raymondluczak.com and on Twitter (@deafwoof).

**Joanna Marsh** is a mentally ill writer of trans experience born and raised in Nova Scotia. She graduated from Halifax's University of King's College in 2013 and has been doing a variety of different things (mostly her best) ever since. In 2016, she was announced as one of the writing runner-ups for the Top Cow Talent Hunt and wrote *Immortal Longings* in *Aphrodite IX: Ares.* She can be found being angry about the patriarchy on Twitter (@thriftbirds).

**Derek Newman-Stille** is a Disabled, Queer, Nonbinary writer, editor, academic, activist, and artist living in Peterborough, Ontario. They teach at Trent University, where they are completing their PhD at the Frost Centre for Canadian Studies, examining the representation of disability in Canadian Speculative Fiction. Derek is the eight-time Prix Aurora Award-winning creator of the digital humanities hub *Speculating Canada* (speculatingcanada.ca) and the associated radio show. They are the editor of the recently published collections *We Shall Be Monsters* (Renaissance) and *Over the*

*Rainbow: Folk and Fairy Tales From the Margins* (Exile Editions). You can find Derek on Twitter (@DNewmanStille).

**Dorothy Ellen Palmer** is a disabled senior writer, accessibility advocate, retired high school Drama teacher, improv coach, and OSSTF union activist. Her work appears in *Refuse: CanLit in Ruins*, *Wordgathering*, *Broadview Magazine*, *Alt-Minds*, *All Lit Up*, *Don't Talk to Me About Love*, *Herizons*, *Little Fiction Big Truths*, *49th Shelf*, and *Open Book*. Her first novel, *When Fenelon Falls*, (Coach House, 2010), features a disabled teen protagonist in the Woodstock-Moonwalk summer of 1969. Her disability memoir, *Falling for Myself*, appears with Wolsak and Wynn in Fall 2019. You can always find her tweeting @depalm.

**Jennifer Lee Rossman** is an autistic and physically disabled sci-fi writer and editor who hates eye contact and spent her childhood giving people nicknames. She co-edited *Love & Bubbles*, a queer anthology of underwater romance. Her debut novel, *Jack Jetstark's Intergalactic Freakshow*, was published by World Weaver Press in 2018. You can find Jennifer at jenniferleerossman.blogspot.com and on Twitter (@JenLRossman).

**Madona Skaff:** With a degree in biology, Madona somehow ended up in mining research. Her scientific background has always managed to inspire her SF stories and frequently sneaks into her mysteries. Among her short stories is the Arthur Ellis Award finalist, *First Impressions* (*The Whole She-Bang 2*). She is the author of *Journey of a Thousand Steps* (Renaissance), a novel about a marathon runner disabled by MS who turns sleuth to find her missing friend. You can find Madona at madonaskaff.com or 'friend' her on Facebook.

**Maverick Smith** is a Hard of Hearing, queer, Trans, disabled, nonbinary settler-Canadian who tackles themes of equity and social justice in their writing. Maverick is honoured to be included in this anthology. In addition to having had their work published in several different anthologies, Maverick has also been a featured author at Naked Heart: An LGBTQ Festival of Words which is presented by Glad Day Bookshop. You can follow Maverick on Goodreads (goodreads.com/author/show/16189396.Maverick_ Smith) or 'friend' them on Facebook (maverick.smith.543)

**Laurie Stewart** is a homesteader, a zombie apocalypse expert, and a writer. She has published short stories in several genres including horror, steampunk and fantasy. Laurie is currently working on her first cozy mystery. She is also a proud Spoonie and CBD advocate. You can follow Laurie on Twitter (@LStewartTheBard), Facebook (Laurie-Stewart-Writer-Filmmaker-Painter-9009853090), and at lauriestewart-author.com.

**Jamieson Wolf** is an award-winning, number-one bestselling author of over sixty works and writer of *Two Steps at a Time* (two-steps.org), a blog about having multiple sclerosis and cerebral palsy. In the spring of 2019, he released his memoir, *Little Yellow Magnet* (Wolf Flow Press), to share his journey of learning to navigate life after an MS diagnosis. Jamieson is also an accomplished artist who works in mixed media, charcoal, pastels, and oil paints. He currently lives in Ottawa, Ontario with his husband Michael. You can find Jamieson at jamiesonwolf.com, on Facebook (jamieson.wolf), and on Twitter (@jamiesonwolf).

**George Zancola** has published short stories and poetry in the *Hearing Voices Cafe* newspaper, as well as the *Friendly Voice* newspaper, which is affiliated with the Secret Handshake in Toronto. He was also published in the *Open Minds Quarterly,* and the *Unexpected Sky,* an anthology of writers from the Inkwell Writing Group. He was born and raised in Toronto, Ontario, where he currently resides. George considers himself a 'mad' writer, as he writes almost exclusively about the psychiatric experience, of which he is a survivor. You can find George on Twitter (@GZancola).

**Nicole Zelniker** is an editorial researcher at The Conversation US and a graduate of the Columbia Journalism School. She has published several pieces of poetry, multiple short stories, and a nonfiction book about race and mixed-race families titled *Mixed.* You can find Nicole at nicolezelniker.wordpress.com or follow her on Twitter and Instagram (both are @nicolezelniker).

# ACKNOWLEDGEMENTS

This anthology wouldn't exist without our planet, Sol III (also known as Earth), oxygen, food, water, and of course, human sentience. It maybe also wouldn't exist without our brilliant authors or our publisher, Renaissance, whose mandate is to elevate diverse voices.

The stories of our brilliant authors have made this anthology more than the sum of its parts, so we thank Myriad Augustine, Carolyn Charron, Joanna Marsh, Elliott Dunstan, Jennifer Lee Rossman, Raymond Luczak, Nicole Zelniker, Dorothy Ellen Palmer, Jamieson Wolf, J. Ivanel Johnson, Tom Johnson, Tonya Liburd, Shannon Barnsley, Madona Skaff, Maverick Smith, George Zancola, Diane Koerner, Laurie Stewart, Tasha Fierce, Nathan Caro Fréchette, Emily Gillespie, and Derek Newman-Stille (who also wrote the foreword).

Big thanks go to the copy editors and proofreaders at Renaissance, and the cultural sensitivity editors, who helped make these stories shine.

We'd especially like to give a shout out to Nathan Fréchette for realizing our vision for the cover design, drawing his brilliant story images, narrating the audiobook, and leading our Kickstarter.

We're so appreciative of author Claudie Arsenault, who shared our Kickstarter updates every day and boosted us on Twitter, and Carolyn Charron, who donated her time to craft a beautiful Spoonie sweater as a reward item.

To all of our Kickstarter donors, we are beyond grateful that you cared enough to financially back this project. We thank our anonymous backers as well as the following folks:

James Andrewartha

J.A. Angelo

Wil Bastion

Tara and Aeva Chisholm

Robin Elizabeth

Finbarr Farragher

Danielle Gudbranson

Lorraine Harding

Happy Hands Toys

Elizabeth Hosang

Marilyn Kay

Irene and Bernard Kinney

Andie Larson

Diane Matheson-Jimenez

Caitlin M

Dani Pacey

Kelly A. Osterberg

Kyla R.

Genesee Rickel

Markie Rustad

Della Sewell

The Storybrook System

Jamieson Wolf

Finally, we editors-in-chief are glad we had each other throughout this process. We shared in the highs and the lows, and we might have coped through any pressure by spewing our particular brand of wacky humour—that pretty much nobody understands but us.

# Renaissance.
## Diverse Canadian Voices

Renaissance was founded in May 2013 by a group of friends who wanted to publish and market those stories which don't always fit neatly in a genre, or a niche, or a demographic.

This is still the type of story we are drawn to; however, we've also noticed another interesting trend in what we tend to publish. It turns out that we are naturally drawn to the voices of those who are members of a marginalized group (especially people with disabilities and LGBTQIAPP2+ people), and these are the voices we want to continue to uplift. Our team is the same; we seem to naturally surround ourselves with people who are, like us, people with marginalized identities.

To us, Renaissance isn't just a business; it's a found family. Being authors and artists ourselves, we care as much about our authors enjoying the publishing process as we do about our readers enjoying a great story and seeing a new perspective.

pressesrenaissancepress.ca
pressesrenaissancepress@gmail.com

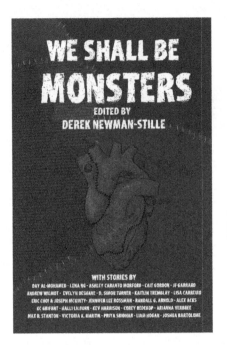

"It is true, we shall be monsters, cut off from all the world; but on that account we shall be more attached to one another." Mary Shelley, Frankenstein

Mary Shelley's genre-changing book Frankenstein; or, the Modern Prometheus helped to shape the genres of science fiction and horror, and helped to articulate new forms for women's writing. It also helped us to think about the figure of the outsider, to question medical power, to question ideas of "normal," and to think about what we mean by the word "monster."

Derek Newman-Stille has teamed up with Renaissance Press to celebrate Frankenstein's 200th birthday by creating a book that explores Frankenstein stories from new and exciting angles and perspectives. We Shall Be Monsters: Mary Shelley's Frankenstein Two Centuries On features a broad range of fiction stories by authors from around the world, ranging from direct interactions with Shelley's texts to explorations of the stitched, assembled body and narrative experiments in monstrous creations. We Shall Be Monsters collects explorations of disability, queer and trans identity, and ideas of race and colonialism.

With stories by Day Al-Mohamed, Lena Ng, Ashley Caranto Morford Cait Gordon, JF Garrard, Andrew Wilmot, Evelyn Deshane, D. Simon Turner, Kaitlin Tremblay, Lisa Carreiro Eric Choi & Joseph McGinty, Jennifer Lee Rossman, Randall G. Arnold, Alex Acks, KC Grifant, Halli Lilburn, Kev Harrison, Corey Redekop, Arianna Verbree, Max D. Stanton, Victoria K. Martin, Priya Sridhar, Liam Hogan, Joshua Bartolome

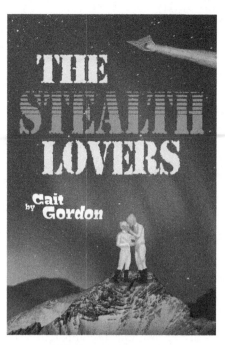

LGBT/Science-Fiction

## *MANY YEARS BEFORE THEY LANDED ON CINNEH, TWO YOUNG MEN STARTED BASIC TRAINING, ALSO KNOWN AS "VACAY IN HAY."*

Xaxall Dwyer Knightly might only be a private, but his sergeant is fascinated by him. During a combat exercise, Private Knightly wins the distinction of being the first-ever trainee to throw an opponent through a supporting wall. The teen has the strength of five Draga put together.

Vivoxx Nathan Tirowen, son of General Tirowen, stands tall with a naturally commanding presence. A young man of a royal clan, the private has an uncanny talent with weaponry. The sarge is convinced that Private Tirowen could "trim the pits of a rodent without nicking the skin."

When the two recruits meet, Vivoxx smiles warmly and Xaxall speaks in backwards phonetics. Little do they know the bond they immediately feel for each other will morph into a military pairing no one in Dragal history has ever seen.

## THIS IS THE STORY OF THE STEALTH— LEGENDARY, FORMIDABLE, AND FABULOUS.

# Did you enjoy this book?

Independent authors and publishers rely mostly on word of mouth publicity.

Please consider helping others discover this title by posting a review of it online, on Amazon, Goodreads, a blog or social media.

Made in the USA
Las Vegas, NV
27 August 2021